NEVER

ENDING

Also by Martyn Bedford

Flip

NEVER

ENDING

MARTYN BEDFORD

WENDY LAMB BOOKS

Text copyright © 2014 by Martyn Bedford
Jacket art copyright © 2014 by Colin Anderson/Getty Images

All rights reserved. Published in the United States by Wendy Lamb Books, an imprint of Random House Children's Books, a division of Random House LLC, a Penguin Random House Company, New York.
Published simultaneously in Great Britain by Walker.
Wendy Lamb Books and the colophon are trademarks of Random House LLC.

Visit us on the Web! randomhouse.com/teens
Educators and librarians, for a variety of teaching tools, visit us at RHTeachersLibrarians.com

Library of Congress Cataloging-in-Publication Data
Bedford, Martyn.
Never ending / by Martyn Bedford. — First edition.
pages cm
Summary: Traumatized by grief and guilt after her younger brother dies during a family vacation, fifteen-year-old Shiv is sent away to an exclusive clinic that claims to "cure" people like her.
ISBN 978-0-385-73991-7 (trade) — ISBN 978-0-385-90809-2 (lib. bdg.) — ISBN 978-0-375-89856-3 (ebook) — ISBN 978-0-375-86553-4 (pbk.)
[1. Grief—Fiction. 2. Guilt—Fiction. 3. Family problems—Fiction. 4. Psychotherapy—Fiction.]

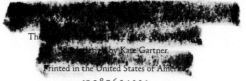

Th

by Kate Gartner.
Printed in the United States of America

10 9 8 7 6 5 4 3 2 1
First Edition

For Pat Croxall,
and for my nieces and nephew:
Aimee Croxall;
Beth, Jed and Tasha Devey;
&
Meghan and Rosie Hodgson;
Catie McMahon

BEFORE KYRITOS

Waking in the dark chill before dawn, she imagined her first glimpse of the swimming pool, shimmering at their journey's end. The sun soaking honey-coated heat into her skin as she stands at the water's edge.

Liquid light unfurling before her. Blue and white and silver and gold.

She imagined diving in.

The unearthly night, the wearying hours that would carry her from it, dissolve in a swirl of water and light and bubbling air. Down and down she plunges, then rises again—laughing, *bursting* to the surface of a new, scintillating morning.

The first of many magical days.

ONE

The start of something else.

They drive for hours to a remote part of the country Siobhan has never been to, or heard of. She listens to music, gazes out at the passing countryside, the relentless unspooling of the road—pick-pick-picking away at the edge of her seat until the seam rips and she can work her fingers inside to excavate the foam padding bit by bit.

After a while, she catches herself at it. Makes herself stop.

Beside her, Dad keeps his eyes dead ahead, gripping the steering wheel like he expects someone to try to take it from him at any moment.

From time to time, he points things out: a lone deer at the edge of some woods, a hang glider, an exit sign for a city where he lived before he met Mum.

Handfuls of words separated by long stretches of silence.

The sight of the shredded foam piled up in the well beside her seat makes her feel sick; not nauseous, but sick with self-disgust. Like someone on a diet confronted with the empty wrappers of all the chocolate she'd vowed not to eat. The tips of her middle fingers are rubbed raw and she has broken a nail.

"Dad . . . ," she begins, and a conversation of sorts starts up.

If you smile when you speak you say nicer things.

Granny O'Driscoll told her that. The one whose name she inherited, Siobhan. Shiv, she calls herself, though Granny O had refused to shorten it—making her point by always addressing Shiv as Shi-*vawn*. As in, *Shi-vawn, will you put a smile on your face before your mouth drops off altogether.* Now, Shiv tries hard to smile, to be pleasant company. To be normal. Dad doesn't deserve to have her shut herself away inside her head. He loves her. That's why they're doing this.

She almost tells her father she loves *him,* but the words stall in her throat.

"How're you feeling about it?" he asks. "It" is their destination.

Shiv shrugs.

His eyes stay fixed on the road. "You don't want to back out?"

Back out. Not "change your mind," which would amount to the same thing but also something quite different. "No," she says, "I don't want to *back out.*"

There. Nasty again. She managed about ten minutes of nice.

Dad lets it drop. They've been over this too many times. *Backing out* would mean going home, to that house. It would mean continuing to live with Mum, the way she is; with Mum and Dad the way they are. Without Dad, much of the time. Without Declan, of course. Above all, it would mean having to live with the person she has become, the long weeks of the summer holiday laid out before her like a maze with no center and no exit.

Even so, her "no" sounds more certain than she feels inside.

3

What she's leaving behind isn't the problem, it's what she's heading toward. After weeks of anticipation—looking forward to this, willing it to come sooner—the day has finally arrived, and her determination will dissolve if she lets it.

What if it doesn't make her well again?

It has to. Nothing else has worked. This is her last shot.

"I don't want to be like I am anymore," she says.

Dad lowers a hand from the wheel to hold hers. He goes to speak but has to start again, his voice husky. "Two months really isn't so long, Shivvers."

Shivvers. He hasn't called her that since she was in primary school.

After a moment, Dad tries to release her hand but she holds on, squeezing his fingers, and he has to drive one-handed for a bit longer.

Before leaving the motorway, they stop for lunch. Shiv isn't hungry but her father makes her choose a sandwich, and they take their food over to a window table.

She inspects her fingertips; they sting like crazy.

He didn't seem to notice her damaging the seat; what would he have said if he had? Nothing. Before Kyritos, Dad would've flipped over something like that. Not anymore. Not with her.

"You okay?" he asks.

"Uh-huh."

His gaze flicks to her fingers, then away. "Another hour from here," he says. "Give or take."

Traveling with him, just the two of them, reminds her of a trip to London a year or so ago, during her "budding artist" phase. Dad decided to whisk her away for the weekend to an exhibition. They went by train and stayed in a smart hotel. It had been wonderful, having Dad to herself. In the gift shop at Tate Modern, he bought her a pad of cartridge paper and a charcoal set in a sleek black folder which she carried around for weeks afterward, until it was filled with sketches.

Dad took two for the wall at his office. As far as she knows, they're still there.

She looks at him, opposite her, stirring sugar into his tea. His shirt is creased from the drive, and he looks tired. Dad's been in Kyritos again the past few days; not that you'd guess it from his pale complexion. Yet another link in the long chain of *due legal process*. He only flew home late last night, and she suspects he would still be out there now if it weren't for *her*. And if Mum weren't such a mess.

As though sensing her watching him, Dad looks and up and smiles; she smiles back. Her smile feels ill-fitting, like a false mustache, or like she has forgotten how her face works and is having to learn all over again. Dad's smile looks much the same.

It's too warm in the café. Shiv removes her hoodie and drapes it over the back of her chair. She catches Dad registering the T-shirt.

"What?" Her tone's hard.

"Nothing."

"I wear his stuff a lot. If you didn't spend so much time at work, or in Greece, you'd know that."

In the hush that follows, a waitress appears at a nearby table, clearing the clutter. Her gaze lingers, and Shiv wonders if the waitress recognizes her from the papers or the TV news. No; there's nothing odd in her expression.

"Sorry, Dad," Shiv says.

He waves her apology away.

Dad has finished his sandwich already; Shiv sips her hot chocolate. "Eat up," he says, indicating her plate, his mouth half full.

She leaves her food where it is. An Adele track is playing; the one Shiv, Laura and Katy sang (appallingly, hysterically) at the school Christmas karaoke. Just seven months ago. It hardly seems possible she could have been so unconditionally happy.

"She's no better, is she?" Dad says.

Mum, he means. That dig about him not spending enough time at home must've been turning over in his mind. "She talks to him," Shiv says. "Most of the day, she lies on his bed."

"You wear his T-shirt."

How easy it would be to send Dad's drink into his lap. But she puts the anger in a box and puts the box in another box, like she's been taught to. Dad keeps his eyes on the table, his food, the window, anywhere but her face.

"We're not very good at this, are we?" she says, softening her tone.

"No." Dad shakes his head. Laughs, sort of.

"I have to pee," she says after a moment.

In the loos, Shiv imagines breaking something—a hand dryer, a soap dispenser. It'd be over before either of the women in here could stop her. She shuts herself in a stall. The urge to destroy hasn't been this strong for days. It's as though the "bad" part of her brain knows where she's being taken and is reminding her that— wherever she goes, whatever she does—it won't give in without a fight.

Afterward, at one of the basins, she catches sight of herself in the mirror.

Tell me how to stop this.

Then, under her breath, "Tell me. Help me, please." The mouth in the mirror opens and closes, as though it's the reflected Shiv asking for help, not the real one. Staring at that face, she can't say for sure which is which.

Back at the table, Dad is consulting the directions.

"All set?" he says, offering a smile of reassurance. Shiv knows she looks terrible but can see him trying to hide his concern.

Keep her spirits up, that's his strategy. *Be positive at all times.* She can only imagine how much effort that must take, what with all he's had to deal with.

Soon they'll say goodbye, Dad will hand her over to strangers, and they won't see one another again for two months.

They have played out this kind of scene so often: the troubled (in trouble) daughter, the protective father trying to do his best for her. With the police, with consular officials, the press, social workers, solicitors, with her form tutor, her head teacher, with magistrates, counselors, doctors, therapists.

"Siobhan, I don't know who you are anymore," he said

7

a month or so ago, after she'd piled all her schoolbooks in the back garden, doused them with paraffin from the shed and set them alight.

"Me neither."

The final leg of the journey takes them through rolling farmland. *Undulating,* Dad calls it. Shiv likes that word. GPS is no use here, so Shiv has to navigate. It's a pretty route—black-and-white cows grazing beside a twisty river, sunlight glazing the wooded hills that huddle above the valley. Blue sky and fluffy clouds. If you asked a young child to paint a picture of the countryside, it would look like this.

At a T-junction, Dad asks, "Left or right?"

"Straight over," she says automatically.

It's the sort of joke her brother would've made, and they both laugh—naturally, at first, then self-consciously. Amusement trails an echo of loss, Declan's sense of humor tuning in and out like a wayward radio signal.

"Left," she says.

Dad puts the car in gear and makes the turn.

He switches off the air-con and lowers the windows to let in the breeze and the scents of the hedgerows and the sounds of birdsong. The lingering traces of the noisy, too-warm, too-bright, food-stinking motorway café are swept away, along with some of the tension between them.

"Hello," Dad says, "I'd like to buy a goldfish."

"Certainly, sir," she replies. "How about an aquarium?"

"I don't care what star sign it is, I just want a gold-fish."

Another of Dec's *many* terrible jokes. They do the funny-but-sad laugh again. Take turns to tell a few more. When they eventually lapse back into silence, the grin stays fixed on Shiv's face until they reach the next turn and Dad has to jog her out of her reverie to tell him which way to go.

"Oh, er . . . right, I think." She looks at the map, points. "Yeah, turn right."

They are close. Silence falls.

The entrance lies at the end of a lane only wide enough for one vehicle at a time. Not that there are any others. They haven't encountered another motorist—or cyclist, or anyone on foot for that matter—for so long the country might be under curfew. They're confronted by tall wrought-iron gates mounted on stone pillars. A CCTV camera on top of one pillar is aimed at their car. To either side, a perimeter wall, at least five meters high, runs in both directions as far as the eye can see. EDEN HALL is etched into the right-hand gatepost, the letters worn and blotchy with lichen. There is no more-recent nameplate, nothing to identify what goes on here.

Reaching through the open window, Dad presses the button on an intercom panel set into a metal post. Staticky crackle. A disembodied voice asks for "the resident's name." "Siobhan Faverdale," Dad says, and reads out the reference number from the acceptance letter.

After a pause, the huge gates swing open to let them through.

Parallel lines of poplars tower over the drive, flanking

it like soldiers forming a guard of honor. Then, as the drive curves, the land rises and the trees give way to banks of rhododendron, a sweeping, vibrantly green lawn, a backdrop of woodland—and she catches sight of the buildings.

"Oh, *wow*."

The weeks of waiting, today's long journey, all the hopes and fears she has assembled around her stay. Shiv can scarcely believe she's finally here.

The main house could be the setting for a TV costume drama. It's built of sand-colored stone, transformed into glistening honeycomb—so gorgeous in the lemony sunlight you might break off a chunk of wall and eat it. Just two stories high, but wide, with a terra-cotta-tiled roof and a domed clock tower. Smaller buildings—old stable blocks, a coach house, a gardener's cottage—cluster around a courtyard, where a sign directs them to visitor parking.

Just then, a break in the rhododendron to their left brings a surprisingly large lake into view in the lower part of the grounds, a flash of sun silvering its breeze-chipped surface before it disappears again behind a conifer hedge.

The sight of the water is so fleeting she can almost believe she imagined it.

It's a lake, she tells herself. That's all. Nothing to be afraid of.

Even so, by the time Dad slows the car to a halt in the courtyard, her breathing is only just beginning to return to normal.

He kills the engine and they sit quietly for a moment.

If he spotted the lake as well, he doesn't say so; but her reaction can't have escaped him. He's busying himself with paperwork from the folder in the glove compartment, although there can't be a document in there he hasn't checked five times today. A couple of cars are parked here already, and Shiv wonders if they belong to the parents of some of the other new arrivals and, if so, when she'll get to meet them. And what they'll be like. And why they're here.

Shiv swallows. Dries her palms on the legs of her cutoffs.

They're both still wearing their seat belts, she realizes. Like they're ready for a quick getaway if either of them changes their mind.

"You'd think someone would come out to greet us," Dad says.

As though his words caused it to happen, a door opens in one of the buildings across the yard and a woman emerges—no more than a silhouette, in the glare—her footsteps clicking on the brick cobbles as she approaches the car.

Behind her, fixed to the wall, is a sign, neat blue text on a gray background: WELCOME TO THE KORSAKOFF CLINIC.

The formalities of Shiv's admission fill the rest of the afternoon. Dad is with her, initially—signing papers and so on—but too soon it's time for him to leave.

They say their goodbyes in the parking area, her suitcase propped beside them like an obedient dog. Dad draws Shiv into a hug, crushing her, kissing the side of her face. He smells of tuna mayo and sugary tea.

"Bye," she manages to say.

"Bye, love." He whispers the words in her ear. "Take care of yourself, eh?"

She wants him to call her *Shivvers* again, but he doesn't. When they break apart she sees that one of her hairs has come away, snagged in the bristles Dad missed with his razor. It looks as though someone has written the letter C on his jaw in thin black pencil. His eyes are pink, moist.

"You can *do* this," Dad says.

She can't tell whether he's trying to reassure her or himself. From his tone, he might almost be pleading with her.

Back in the clinic's reception suite Shiv composes herself, dries her face, tries to concentrate on the next stage. They show her a list of "forbidden items" she must hand in for safekeeping: cigarettes, lighter, matches, scissors, razors, drugs (recreational), drugs (medicinal), alcohol— that sort of thing. Along with just about every kind of electronic device. No iPod, while she's here, then; no phone (although there's no signal round here in any case, she's told). Money is on the list too—cash and cards (debit), cards (credit)—and she has to give up her young person's travel pass.

No distractions. No self-harm. No running off.

The fact that she doesn't have any prescription drugs raises an eyebrow. She was on sedatives for a few weeks right after it happened, she admits . . . but, no, she's not taking anything now. Her counselor, her GP, think she should be. But she isn't.

They check her case to make sure she hasn't tried to sneak anything through.

Next, a medical. A young nurse in a blue tunic—*Zena,* the name tag says—escorts her into an examination room that smells of antiseptic and is so clean and shiny Shiv feels grubby just setting foot inside. The slender, fair-skinned nurse, with wispy blond hair and ice-blue eyes, barely looks out of her teens.

"You get to examine me?" Shiv asks.

"Don't worry, I wear surgical gloves for the really intimate stuff."

Her tone, her smile, make it clear this is a joke, meant to ease the tension. Shiv fixes her a look. Nurse Zena reminds her of a water nymph in a picture book she had as a child. "There's nothing *wrong* with me," Shiv tells her. "Physically, I mean."

She hands Shiv a gown and indicates a changing area behind a screen. "Blood pressure, temperature, heartbeat, weight, blood sample—that's all it is. Oh, and you pee into a bottle." Zena pauses, smiling again. Friendly. "You do that bit in private."

After the medical, Shiv is escorted to the main building, to her room on the second floor. She has an en suite bathroom to herself. She's one of six residents, she's told: four female, two male, aged thirteen to seventeen.

That word again. *Residents.* Not patients.

Shiv will get to meet them all at dinner, her escort says.

Alone in her room, she heaves her suitcase onto the bed, opens it and begins stowing her clothes in the wardrobe and the drawers underneath. She's always done this whenever she goes anywhere. First job: unpack.

Her brother *never* unpacked, content to pull clothes from his case as and when he needed them.

The suitcase is the one she took to Kyritos. Of course; it's her only one. She must've known it while she was packing to come here, but the realization has only just struck her. The flight labels have long been removed, but the red ribbon she fastened to the handle for easy identification on the baggage carousel is still attached.

Shiv considers untying it, throwing it away. In the end, she decides to leave it.

The room is okay in a functional kind of way. Besides the wardrobe and narrow bed, there's a not-quite-comfy-looking brown armchair—IKEA, at a guess—and a small chest of drawers. The furniture is pine-effect, the walls and ceiling plain white, while the curtains and carpet are patterned in yellow-and-brown swirls, to match the duvet and pillowcase. It puts her in mind of chocolate sponge and custard. A print of lollipop-shaped trees hangs on one wall.

It's like a room in a cheap hotel.

Her determination to be optimistic, to go into this

with the right attitude, shudders as the "other" Siobhan, the girl who wants to smash things, rears her head again. It's an effort to ignore her, but Shiv manages. Centers herself. Focuses on the bedroom, on the window, which is ajar, a breeze pushing halfheartedly at the curtains. From some way off comes the plaintive, lonely cry of a pheasant.

She wants to speak to Dad.

The loss of her phone, the lack of a signal even if she still had it, only sharpens the urge to call him. Not that she knows what she'd say.

The phone was switched off the whole way here and she hasn't checked for messages since breakfast. As usual, there weren't any. She's had it a week, since that journalist somehow got hold of the number for the old one, and she has only let a few people have the new number. Dad, Mum, the counselor. Laura and Katy. Neither of her friends has made contact. Okay, so they're out of the country—Laura, kayaking in Colorado; Katy, touring Italy with her folks in that huge camper van. But how much do texts cost? Too busy having the time of their lives to type: *hey shiv how u doin*? Those end-of-term hugs and tears and miss-yous; the promises to keep in touch. Yet when school broke up, Shiv got the impression Laura and Katy were secretly relieved not to have to see her for the summer. Or speak to her.

But then, she hasn't contacted them, either. They don't even know she's here. Her "best" friends have no idea how she's doing. All the talking they've done, or not done, since she returned from Greece has only made Shiv see how far apart they've been driven by what happened.

Shiv goes to the window. It's after six, but the day is still full of light. Her room overlooks a vegetable plot to the rear of Eden Hall and, beyond that, an apple orchard, then rough pasture that rises to meet the wooded hill she saw from the drive.

No view of the lake, then. That's something to be glad about.

A droning noise snags her attention. She spots the plane, high overhead, the sound seeming to come from somewhere else altogether. Shiv wonders where it's headed. Not Kyritos, she supposes. She pictures the passengers, watching a movie, eating a meal, peering down at a miniaturized landscape—oblivious to her, thousands of meters below.

It seems a lifetime ago, that flight. Or something that happened in another life, to someone else. A pretty stewardess, handing out boiled sweets to people to ease the discomfort in their ears during takeoff; her brother asking for two, one for each ear. The stewardess laughing, like it was the first time she'd heard that joke.

The tears come. So often they come, these days. Great gulping sobs that escape from her throat faster than she can breathe.

At last, the tears stop. She stands there, braced against the windowsill.

"Jee-*zuss,* what is this *carpet* all about?"

Startled, Shiv twists round to see an older girl in the doorway, her scarlet minidress a shocking gash of color.

"Yellow and brown? *Really?*" the girl continues. "Is the decor sponsored by the Brownies or something?" She gestures at the window. "No wonder you were going to *jump*. Although, hmm, second floor—is that gonna be high enough, d'you think?"

Shiv laughs despite herself. Wipes her cheeks with the cuff of her hoodie. She's cried in front of too many strangers to care about adding another to the list.

"I'm Caron. With a *C*." The girl points at the wall with the lollipop-trees picture. "I'm next door. We can tap messages in code to each other in the night." She smiles in the pause that follows. "Okay, this is where you say *your* name."

"Oh . . . Shiv."

The older girl frowns. "That's not a name, that's a *syllable*."

Another laugh escapes Shiv. "It's short for Siobhan." She does the it's-Irish-but-I'm-not explanation.

"Well, hi, Shiv-short-for-Siobhan."

Caron steps farther into the room and performs a pirouette in the center of the swirly carpet. She has jet-black hair down to her bare shoulders and a fringe cut on the diagonal. Shiv watches her slip off her shoes—high-heeled, scarlet, to match the dress. Her lipstick is the same vibrant color and so are her earrings.

"These are *killing* me." She flicks the shoes away with her toes. "But if I pack them in the case they crush." Then, indicating the bed, "D'you mind?" She flops down.

Shiv ought to feel invaded. She's not usually keen on people with what Mum calls "big personalities," but she can't help liking this girl. After a few minutes with Caron, she feels a hundred times better than when she was sobbing at the window.

"Seven bloody *hours*," Caron groans. She's lying on her

back, legs dangling off the end of the bed, arms raised, performing Tai Chi–type movements, as though painting the ceiling with an invisible brush. "Where've you traveled from, Shiv?"

Shiv sits in the armchair. Names the town where she lives.

Caron stops mid-brushstroke and eases up onto her elbows. "Siobhan who?" She stares at Shiv. Serious all of a sudden.

Shiv could make something up but decides not to. "Siobhan Faverdale."

Caron sits up properly, eyes still fixed on Shiv's face. Almost in a whisper, she says, "My *God,* you're the sister of that boy."

It's Caron's idea to take a stroll in the grounds before dinner. After a day on the road, a walk and some fresh air will do them both good. Shiv suspects the real reason is to jolt them out of the somber mood that's taken hold.

Caron heads back to her own room and reappears in a pair of crimson sandals.

"D'you only wear red?" Shiv asks.

"Nooo, because that would be weird. Don't you think?"

Outside, they wander aimlessly along the gravel paths of a rose garden. It's a mild evening, the day's warmth leaching from the ground, the air fragrant with roses and woodsmoke and cut grass. The distress that overwhelmed her at the window is spent; in its place, calm has settled on Shiv, so total she can't quite believe how upset she became. It's always like this afterward. After her violent outbursts too.

"You nervous about all this?" Caron asks.

"Yeah," Shiv says. "Me and therapy don't really get on."

"Jee-zuss, *tell* me about it."

Shiv wants to ask why Caron's here but isn't sure how she'd take it. She doesn't know what to make of her. The clothes, the brash self-confidence, it's not how she'd expect someone to be, checking into any psychiatric clinic, let alone this one.

As soon as they're out of sight of the main building, Caron hoicks up her dress and shoves a hand in her knickers. "'Scuse me," she says, producing a lighter and two cigarettes. "*Some* things they can confiscate, some they *can't*."

She lights one of the cigarettes and offers the second to Shiv.

Shiv gapes at her. "Okay, one, I don't smoke; and, two . . ." She gestures at where the cigarette came from.

"Oh, right. Fair point."

They continue out of the rose garden, passing through an arch in a hedge and up some stone steps, to find themselves in a kind of grotto around an ornamental pond.

"This place is meant to be different, though," Shiv says, picking up the thread of their earlier conversation. "It's supposed to *work*."

"So they *say*." Caron draws on the cigarette; exhales, directing the smoke away from Shiv. She nods at a weathered wooden bench. "Shall we sit down for a bit?"

"I thought you wanted to walk?" Shiv says.

"We *have* walked."

"We've only come about two hundred meters."

"Shiv, *zuss*, what are you—some kind of *fitness* freak?"

"No, I just—"

"A triathlete or something. I mean, how *old* are you, anyway?"

"Fifteen," Shiv says. "You?"

"Seventeen. So that puts me in charge, and I say we do the sit-down thing."

"Walking, sitting—what's the third part of the triathlon? Smoking?"

Caron lets out a snort of laughter and smoke. "That's actually quite funny."

They sit down. They fall quiet, the tranquility of the surroundings seeming to cast a trance over them. It's a companionable silence, as though they are old friends rather than two people who've only just met.

"Why were you crying?" Caron asks, breaking the spell at last. Then, "Actually, scrub that. Why *wouldn't* you be crying? Why wouldn't any of us?" She draws on her cigarette, her lips making a kissing sound. "So, what *else* did you do to get sent here? Apart from the obvious."

"I smash stuff," Shiv says. "Windows, doors. A load of wine bottles in Tesco. Car windscreen wipers—I went right along our street one night, ripping them off. Some of the wing mirrors too. Anything, really."

"Yeah?"

Shiv tells her about setting fire to her schoolbooks.

"Actually in one of the *classrooms*?"

"No, at home—in the garden."

Caron seems disappointed.

"One time," Shiv goes on, "I lost it so badly with the

educational psychologist, she had to buzz for backup." She shrugs. "It's funny, when I went back to school— you know, after Greece—I worked harder than I'd ever done in my life. Class swot." She shudders with the chill as the evening starts to close in. "*Outside* school I was doing all sorts of shit but . . . I guess it was the one thing I hung on to."

"A life raft," Caron suggests.

"Exactly. Then, one day, I thought, Why bother? Why not just let rip?" Another shrug. "If it weren't for my 'extenuating circumstances,' I'd have been kicked out long before the summer holiday saved them the trouble."

"And, what, you're the coolest kid in school now?" Caron says, teasing.

"No, I'm the weirdo. The one nobody looks at or talks to."

"Yeah, well, better that than *sympathy*." The older girl makes a gagging sound.

Shiv gives her a sidelong look. Caron's face is pale in the gloom of the grotto. Sympathy is right. It's good to meet someone as sick of it as she is. Who understands.

"What about your friends?"

Shiv thinks of Laura and Katy. "They hug me a lot," she says. "But it's like I've been diagnosed with something—so even while they're hugging me, I get the feeling they'd rather not touch me in case they catch it too."

Caron nods. "What they want is for you to be the way you were before. But you *can't*, can you? None of us can ever be that."

Just as the dinner gong sounds and they get up from the bench to head back inside, Shiv spots him.

A glimpse of white among the rhododendrons down by the drive. He stops, as though aware of being observed, and half turns their way. Then the figure continues, disappearing, swallowed up by the bushes. The briefest of sightings . . . but she could swear it was Declan.

Shiv realizes she has been holding her breath. She releases it.

Usually, she sees him in the street, or in a busy supermarket, or in the school playground—crowded places, where some boy has Dec's haircut, or build, or his way of walking, or a top the same color and style as one he used to wear. This is the first time she's seen him on his own.

"You okay?" Caron looks where Shiv was looking.

"I'm fine. It's nothing."

As the rental car crunched to a halt on the dazzlingly white stone chippings of the villa's parking bay, Shiv released her grip on the door handle and sank back into her seat. She gave an exaggerated sigh. Beside her in the back, Declan—who had both hands over his face—tentatively parted his fingers.

"Are we . . . are are are we . . . still *alive*?" he said, through fake sobs.

"Blimey," Dad said, laughing with relief. "I thought the drivers in *Italy* were crazy."

"Is that *you*, Daddy," Declan said, with childlike wonder, "or am I in *heaven*?"

Shiv turned her face to the window, her shoulders shaking. There was a stone wall overflowing with a brightly flowered climbing plant of some kind; if she focused on those flowers, on the bees gathering pollen, she might not wet herself laughing.

"You handled it *very well*, love." This was Mum, her teasing voice. "Foreign roads, an unfamiliar car, several hundred kamikaze Greek drivers—and you only swore seventeen times."

"One of those was the C-word," Shiv said. "Doesn't that count treble?"

"Look." Dad let go of the wheel and splayed his fingers. "I'm shaking."

"Mum," Dec said, "I think you'll find kamikaze is Japanese, not Greek."

Their father exhaled, tipping his head back against the headrest. As he did so, his foot must have slipped off the clutch and the car, its engine still running, stalled with one last lurch.

Declan covered his eyes. "No, nooo, we're *moving* again!"

They burst out laughing.

Dad lowered the windows, letting in flowery, resinous smells so familiar to Shiv from previous holidays. The blast of heat was delicious. Ahead, a small olive grove separated their villa from the next, each grizzled tree standing in the scrawl of its own shadow.

They were here! The early start, the long trip . . . all of it fell away like a shrugged-off coat.

"D'you think we can go the whole two weeks without using the car?" Dad said.

While Dad unloaded the cases, Shiv followed her mum and brother round the side of the villa, spring sunshine soaking into her skin. It'd been pouring rain when they left home, the weather's gift to England for the holiday. They'd viewed the property from every conceivable angle in the photo gallery on the website—even so, as they entered the garden, the sight of the real thing stopped them in their tracks.

"Oh, my goodness!" Mum said.

They were on a flagstone terrace, patterned in marshmallow pink and white, overlooking a glittering swimming pool. Beyond that, the land descended to a bay—a swathe of blue-green sea so still it might have been painted there. Just the other side of the garden's low stone wall, a solitary goat grazed in the shade of an olive tree. Their appearance on the terrace caused the goat to lift its head with a jerk and cast an inscrutable stare in their direction.

"Hey, look—springboard," her brother said, nodding at the pool.

Dec had found a tennis ball and was bouncing it on the flagstones. Bounce-catch, bounce-catch. With his dark hair and olive skin, he could almost pass for Greek.

"This is *so*—"

"*Beautiful,*" Shiv said, finishing Mum's sentence.

"It's very foreign, isn't it?" Declan said.

"Funny, that." Shiv gave him a friendly shove and the tennis ball popped out of his hand, bounced down the steps and into the pool with barely a splash.

"You know," Mum said, "I think this is even better than that place in Sardinia."

Shiv gave a mock gasp. "But that was 'the villa to end all villas.'"

"That goat isn't happy," Declan said. "Look, he's at the end of his tether."

Mum and Shiv groaned. Shiv felt a bubble of joy well up; the first day of a holiday could sometimes be fraught—the traveling, the tiredness—but not this one.

She continued down the steps, skirted the pool to the bottom of the garden and stood on the wall to take a look at the bay. From there, she could see the zigzag path through the dunes that led to the beach they'd read about on the website—*a gentle stroll brings you to a quaint fishing village with its welcoming tavernas, and just beyond the harbor, an unspoiled sandy beach ideal for swimming.* She spread her arms, closed her eyes and tilted her face to the sun.

Which was when the wet tennis ball smacked her in the back of the head.

"First strike of the holiday to the boy Declan. Oh, *yesssss.*"

By the time she'd caught Dec and brought him sprawling to the grass, they were weak with laughter. They untangled and flopped onto their backs, side by side, gasping for breath.

"You fight like a girl," she said.

"So do you, as it happens."

Sisters weren't meant to like their kid brothers, especially when the brother was too smart for his own good. Her friends *hated* theirs. Declan, though, had always made Shiv laugh, right from when he started to talk. He was her mate. Often, they didn't need to speak to know what the other one was thinking, or to set themselves off laughing over some private, unfathomable joke.

In cahoots, Mum called it. *You two are always in cahoots over something.* Dad reckoned they were twins who happened to have been born two and a half years apart.

She even liked his clothes. *Borrowed* them sometimes. Like he was an older sister rather than a younger brother. That baggy T-shirt he was wearing now, for instance—a birthday present he'd barely taken off since he got it— that was pretty cool, with its quotation from *The Catcher in the Rye:*

Don't ever tell anybody anything. If you do, you start missing everybody.

Not that Shiv was altogether sure what it meant.

26

One time, Aunt Rosh had asked him what he wanted to be when he grew up and, without a moment's hesitation, he'd said: "Holden Caulfield."

Now Mum joined them on the lawn, sitting on one of the wicker sun-loungers. She'd got the camera out already and was firing off the first of what would no doubt be several hundred holiday snaps. She might've been posing for a glamour photo herself—yellow summer dress dazzling in the glare, the villa reflected in duplicate in the lenses of her sunglasses. Like a 1960s film star.

"It looks bigger in the flesh," she said.

"The villa is made of *flesh*?" Declan said.

Shiv took her first proper look at the building. It was in the Greek style, with white walls, blue window frames and shutters, pantiled roof and a pergola draped with vines that shaded a dining area on the lower terrace. A balcony overlooked the poolside—an ideal place to watch the sun set over the bay. That was where Mum and Dad would share a bottle of red, last thing, their voices drifting to her room. She still associated family holidays with falling asleep to her parents' murmured conversation somewhere outside at the end of long, warm day.

"There's a welcome hamper!" Dad called from inside the villa.

"Wine?" Mum called back.

In reply, Dad made a whining noise.

"It's a form of mental cruelty," Dec said. "*Dad Jokes.* Banned in forty-seven countries around the world."

"Forty-six," Shiv said. "North Korea refused to sign the treaty."

"Ah, yes, you're *right,* Shivoloppoulos. Can't believe I forgot."

Declan got up and perched on the edge of Mum's sun-lounger. Shiv sat on the other side of Mum, who put an arm round each of them, massaging their backs.

"So, Child A and Child B—do we like it here?"

"Hm," Shiv said, "I suppose it'll do until we reach the holiday villa."

At that moment, Dad appeared at the poolside, wearing his tartan swimming shorts and goggles, his nose gleaming white with sunblock. "Right," he said, "who's coming for a dip?"

After dinner, the residents are shown into a small, windowless room, done out in shades of blue and furnished with six chairs in a single row facing a plain oval desk with a further four chairs lined up behind it. The residents fill up the row of six, as instructed. Shiv sits between Caron and a girl called Lucy: a plump, moon-faced chatterbox, the same age as Shiv—friendly, if overeager—who dominated the conversation (and the food) at Shiv's end of the table during dinner. Next to Lucy is a girl whose name Shiv can't recall, then one of the boys—the younger one. Mikey? Yes, Mikey. He must be thirteen or he wouldn't be here, but he could pass for ten. Short and slight, twitchy with nervous energy, continually roughing his fingers through his shortish dark blond hair or fiercely chewing his nails.

"OCD," Caron whispered to her, at dinner, nodding in his direction.

At the end of the line is Docherty, who insists on being called by his surname. He looks seventeen going on twenty, with a U.S. Army–style buzz cut and a spider's-web tattoo on his right elbow. Good-looking in a hard, getting-into-fights kind of way. He barely spoke at dinner. It was a strange meal all round, the conversation stilted, cramped by self-consciousness. They all seemed to heave a sigh of relief when it was over and the orderly who'd supervised them ushered everyone out of the dining room.

"Shame to break up the party," Caron muttered to Shiv on their way out.

Shiv tried hard to keep a straight face.

Now, as they settle into their seats in the Blue Room, a second door opens and four staff file in. Two men and a woman are in blue-and-gray uniforms, a cross between a tracksuit and something a paramedic might wear. At the rear is an older woman in a sharp gray business suit, carrying a stack of buff-colored cardboard folders.

The uniforms sit facing the patients across the oval desk but the suit remains standing, taking up position at one end of the desk. She sets the folders down.

"Good evening, everyone," she says. "And welcome to the Korsakoff Clinic."

She beams, arms spread, the illumination from the spotlights in the ceiling reflecting off her glasses and giving her mannishly short salt-and-pepper hair a silver sheen. Fifty? Sixty? Those glasses look expensively stylish; the twinkly eyes behind the lenses are the same shade of green as Mum's.

"I am Dr. Pollard," she tells them, "the director of the clinic. My colleagues," she points in turn, "are Assistants Webb, Hensher and Sumner."

Shiv tags them: Webb is the cool black guy; Hensher is the awkward ginger guy; Sumner is the too-smiley, fake-tanned blonde. None looks older than thirty.

"There are other staff here, of course," Dr. Pollard continues. "Gardeners, cooks, cleaners, security, a maintenance chap, a nurse—Zena, whom you will have met—

and a couple of orderlies . . . but the four of us"—she gestures at herself and her colleagues behind the desk—"will be the ones who supervise your treatment." She pauses. "We will be the ones who help to make you well."

A snort of laughter farther along the row. Mikey.

The director's gaze settles on him, lingering for a moment, as though she's debating whether to challenge his reaction or ignore it. She ignores it.

The look establishes her authority better than any words.

"Okay, *so*," Dr. Pollard says, returning her attention to the group, "what is this strange place in which you find yourselves? What *is* the Korsakoff Clinic?"

Her gaze trawls the queue of residents, like she's waiting for a hand to go up—or, worse, is about to pick one of them to answer.

The director presses on. "Those of you who've read the literature we sent to your parents and guardians will have an idea of who we are and what we do. No doubt some of you will have *Googled* us as well." She says the word as though holding it between tweezers like a captured cockroach.

Shiv has read the literature. Shiv has Googled.

As soon as she'd been recommended for referral, she tried to find out as much as she could. Not that there's much *to* be found—not about what goes on here, anyway. The Korsakoff Clinic's methods appear to be cloaked in mystery, rumor and misinformation. Even its own information booklet gives only a vague outline of the treatment program. Most of the text describes the place's history. So Shiv knows the clinic was founded by the Korsakoff Institute, a psychotherapeutic research body established a decade ago thanks to the bequest of an anonymous, and *very* wealthy, American donor. It is named after a neuropsychiatrist whose theory is at the root of the clinic's "therapeutic strategy." Shiv made little sense of it (at least, Wikipedia's definition). But by all accounts, it has created a buzz in international psychiatric circles, with three clinics opening around the world—in the United States, Canada and Germany—and now a fourth, in the UK. The British clinic is partially funded by the government after winning a contract to test its innovative methods in small groups. Since it opened a year ago, three sets of adults have been treated here.

Shiv and the others are the first teenagers.

"What I want to get straight," Dr. Pollard continues, "is why you've been sent to us in the first place." That beaming smile, which disappeared with Mikey's interruption, resurfaces. The gap between her front teeth is almost wide enough to fit another tooth. "Of all those referred to us, why have we chosen to accept you? What makes the six of you so special?"

"Cos we're the *craziest* of the cray-zeeez." This is Caron.

One or two of the others laugh; even Assistant Webb cracks a grin.

"It's Caron, isn't it?" Dr. Pollard asks. When Caron nods, the woman presses her palms together and says, "Sorry to disappoint you"—that gap-toothed beam again—"but, no, you're not the craziest young people in the country. You are, however, just the type of crazies we happen to like."

Should they find this funny? No one seems quite sure.

"Your specific individual circumstances are different, of course." Dr. Pollard is serious again. "But you're all here for the same three reasons." She counts them off on her fingers. "One, you've each suffered a traumatic bereavement. Two, this trauma has resulted in psychological delusion, making you a danger to yourself or to others. And, three, conventional therapies have failed to help you."

A hand goes up.

"Yes, Mikey," the director says. She doesn't need to ask *his* name, then.

"What's that?" He leans right forward in his chair, leans abruptly back again; starts gnawing at a thumbnail like he's trying to rip it clean off.

"What's what, Mikey?"

"What you said." He shoves a hand through his hair. "Psycho-thingy."

"Psychological delusion. Is that what you mean?" The boy nods, irritated; *of course* that's what he meant, his expression says. Dr. Pollard adjusts her glasses. Then, like it's any kind of an explanation, "Well, Mikey, *that's* what we're all here to find out over the next two months."

Shiv swaps glances with Caron, lip-reads the older girl's mouthed "WTF?"

The director, meanwhile, has taken the top folder off the stack she set down on the desk. "Now, before I hand over to Assistant Webb," she says, "I'd like to make one other thing absolutely clear: Whatever your experience of treatment has been so far—whatever form of counseling or therapy or, heaven help us, *medication* you've received—you will start with a clean slate here at the Korsakoff Clinic."

She raises the folder, gives it a little flourish, like a conjuror about to perform a trick. Shiv can see that it is thick with papers.

"This is one of the files we request from those under whose care you have been until now," the woman says. "Your case notes." Then, glancing at the cover, "Which one of you is Lucy?" The plump girl next to Shiv raises a hand. Addressing her directly, Dr. Pollard says, "I have read your notes, Lucy, of course I have. I have read all of your notes," she adds, taking in all six residents with a sweep of her free hand.

She pauses.

"And this is how much bearing they will have on your treatment here."

Dr. Pollard goes to a corner and drops Lucy's folder with a *whumph* into a large bin. She picks up the next file and does the same. Then the next and the next.

Assistant Webb's presentation is more orthodox.

He explains the *rules and regs* of the clinic, the dos and don'ts. This is a psychiatric institution, he stresses; as such, certain restrictions apply. By day, they are largely free to move around inside the building and most areas of the grounds—when they're not in scheduled therapy sessions, that is. But by night—from Lights-Out at ten-thirty p.m. to Wake-Up at seven a.m.—they will remain in their bedrooms. For fire-safety reasons, their doors will not be locked at night, but they *are* alarmed—so if anyone tries to leave his or her room between these hours it will trigger the alarm and bring the late-duty security guy running. Same goes for any attempt to leave the building during *Shut Down,* as Webb refers to it.

"You have an intercom panel in your room for use in an emergency." He stresses the last word. "The intercom will also sound the Wake-Up buzzer and enable us to broadcast any announcements to you all at the start of each day."

There are CCTV cameras inside the building and at various points around the gardens and grounds, he adds, before emphasizing that these and the other security measures are to ensure the residents' safety.

"This is not a prison. You are not prisoners."

He hands out copies of the timetable—the schedule for the first month of their stay. It's the same every day, six days a week. Sunday is a rest day; also laundry day.

As he outlines the daily activities, Shiv wonders if the others are as distracted as she is. By the papers and folders, still protruding from the waste bin in the corner. Or by Dr. Pollard, who has taken her seat and is watching them intently, gaze shifting from resident to resident. She has removed her glasses and set them down on the desk, the lenses aimed at the six of them like a second pair of eyes. Her dramatic finale has left an almost audible aftershock humming beneath everything Assistant Webb says.

"Any questions?" the director asked, when the last folder had been binned.

No one put their hand up.

If the residents were startled into silence, the staff

seemed unsurprised by what their boss did. Maybe they'd seen it before, with the adults who'd been here. Her party piece. From their neutral expressions, Shiv couldn't say what they made of it.

Shiv was impressed enough.

Her counselor these past months had been so straight, so *earnest,* the trashing of the case notes was a blast of fresh air. Maybe this place really is different. Maybe its treatment really does work.

Assistant Webb is still talking. Shiv makes herself study the schedule, "key therapeutic activities" highlighted:

Morning	Afternoon	Evening
7:00—Wake-Up	1:00—lunch	6:00—Buddy Time
8:00—breakfast	2:00—Talk	7:30—dinner
9:00—Walk	3:30—Break	8:30—Recreation
10:30—Break	4:00—Write	10:30—Lights-Out &
11:00—Make		Shut Down

"Really, the activities are self-explanatory." With the faintest smirk, Webb says, "At Walk, you walk; at Make, you make stuff; at Talk, you talk; at Write, you write."

"What about Buddy Time?" Caron asks.

"You have been divided into pairs, three sets of buddies. You're meant to befriend your buddy, get to know them, spend time with them, look out for them," he says. "When you're feeling crap, your buddy is there to get you through it."

"What if your buddy is feeling crap too?" Caron, again.

Mikey cuts in. Agitated, talking to himself. "I ain't having no buddy."

"Hate to break it to you, Mikey, but you're on my buddy list, same as everyone else." Assistant Webb turns to another sheet on his clipboard. "Yep, your name's right here: Mikey and . . ." He looks up. "Which one of you is Siobhan?"

"*So,* you drew the short straw," Caron tells Shiv during recreation.

"I think he's quite sweet."

"*Sweet?* Mikey?"

They're sitting on beanbags in the rec room. Before dismissing them all, Assistant Webb suggested this evening's recreation period was an ideal chance for buddies to introduce themselves. Not one pair of buddies is here, though. The girl whose name Shiv forgot (Helen, it turns out) is playing pool by herself. She is fourteen, she says, but so short her feet leave the floor whenever she leans across the table to reach the cue ball. She's buddied with Docherty, who has gone for a run. Helen seems not to mind in the least. With her plaits, her Asiatic eyes and calm aura, she reminds Shiv of a Native American shaman.

Caron's buddy, Lucy, disappeared to the loo with a promise to join them afterward. That was half an hour ago. And Mikey was first out of the Blue Room, without a word to anyone.

"You and me should ask to be buddies," Caron says.

Caron is in a grump—craving nicotine, on account of

having to ration her secret stash, and disappointed by the rec room. *(No TV, no DVD player, nothing to play music on . . . just pool, Ping-Pong and board games. That's B-O-R-E-D.)*

"We need to play something," Shiv says. "Take your mind off cigarettes, yeah?" She scans the shelves of games. "How about Scrabble?"

Caron shakes her head. "You can't smoke those plastic tiles. They just melt."

Eventually, they settle on Buckaroo. It's a total hoot. They play for ages—persuading Helen to join in—and are surprised when an orderly comes to remind them it's nearly time for Lights-Out and Shut Down.

"It's going to be okay here," she says as she and Caron pause outside their rooms to say goodnight. Her face feels stretchy from all the laughter downstairs.

"I thought you and therapy didn't get on."

"I like Dr. Pollard. She seems . . . different." Even as she speaks, Shiv isn't sure whether she's just glad to be here at last. Committed to giving it a go because the alternative—well, there is no alternative. She pictures those files thumping one after another into the bin. "Caron, this place—it's where I belong."

Caron is quiet for a moment. "Zuss, girl," she says, finally, giving Shiv's arm a rub, "you say that often enough, you might even start to believe it's true."

Sometime during the night Shiv has the sense of a light shining in her bedroom. Too faint to be the main bulb; in any case, that snapped off automatically at ten-thirty. Sitting up in bed, she sees that the light is on the far side of the room—a rectangle of illumination on the wall. An image of some kind.

Shiv slips out from under the covers and goes over to investigate but, as she approaches, the light vanishes. In her just-woken state, it takes her a moment to realize she must have stepped in front of the projection beam. She turns and, sure enough, there's a thin shaft of light issuing from a fixture in the ceiling—what she mistook for a sprinkler or smoke detector. It's illuminating her T-shirt.

Stepping aside, she allows the image to re-form on the wall, careful to stay out of the beam this time as she leans in for a closer look. The picture is faint and grainy from being enlarged.

Declan.

In snorkel, flippers and bright red swimming shorts, captured in midair as he leaps off the side of a boat.

FOUR

At breakfast, Shiv discovers that *everyone* was woken in the night by the projection of an image of their lost loved one onto their bedroom wall.

It's all anyone is talking about.

Or not talking about. Some of the residents—Lucy, especially—are too upset to discuss it. Caron looks dreadful as well: no makeup, her hair unbrushed, her eyes puffy. No one had much sleep, it seems. Docherty is angry, wanting to know how the clinic could pull a stunt like that without warning. Wanting to know how they got hold of the pictures in the first place.

Shiv knows where the image of Dec came from. It's one of countless photos her mother took in Kyritos; which means Mum herself—or, more likely, Dad—must have given it to the clinic. Not that they necessarily knew what it would be used for.

The picture stayed on Shiv's wall for maybe an hour before the beam shut off. All the time, she didn't take her eyes off it—shifting the armchair and settling herself in front of the photo as though watching a DVD. Even after the room snapped to black again, she went on sitting for a while before fumbling her way back to bed. Sleep was a long time coming. So, like the others, she's exhausted.

But is she upset? Is she angry?

Shiv isn't sure how she feels. What she does know is

that when her wall went blank she desperately wished the image of her brother would come back again.

Assistants Webb and Hensher breeze into the dining room just before nine a.m. to muster the residents for the first activity: Walk.

They won't discuss last night's picture shows.

"Everything we do is part of your treatment" is all Webb says as people crowd round him, firing off questions.

Amid much grumbling, he and his colleague usher everyone out of the room and along to a corridor at the back of the building. It leads to the door where Shiv and Caron exited Eden Hall for their stroll in the rose garden yesterday evening. Already that seems a long time ago.

Ranged along one side of the passageway is a set of shelves lined with neatly folded yellow jumpsuits and pairs of Wellington boots in various colors and sizes.

"Girls, can you change in there, please," Webb says, indicating a door marked Laundry Room. "Mikey and Docherty, you can use the utility room." He nods toward another door on the opposite side of the corridor. "All the gear is labeled with your names and should be the appropriate size."

"Jumpsuits," Caron says to no one in particular. "In *yellow*?"

Once they're all changed, Webb and Hensher lead the six of them outside, the residents filing out in their lurid jumpsuits like terrorist suspects entering the exercise yard at a detention center.

This time it's the white guy, Hensher, who addresses

them. Less self-assured than Webb. His voice is nasal, a little high-pitched, and as he talks, a mottled flush spreads across his throat. "Hundreds of years ago, Eden Hall was a monastery," he says, as though reciting, "and our activity this morning is inspired by a walking meditation practice used by the order of monks who lived here at that time."

Assistant Hensher smoothes the palm of one hand over his scalp, shedding flakes of dandruff from his ginger stubble. "So"—he clears his throat—"we will walk in the grounds for an hour and a half—"

"An *hour and a half*?" Caron blurts out. "The walking I've done in my *entire life* doesn't add up to an hour and a half."

One or two of the others snigger. Shiv does too, glad to see Caron getting back to something like her sparky, snarky self.

"An hour and a half." Hensher, flustered, tries to stay on script. "We walk in single file, with Assistant Webb leading. Keep to his pace, please—no quicker, no slower—and leave a gap of about two meters between you and the person in front." He pauses. "We will walk . . . In. Complete. Silence."

"'S that it?" Mikey pipes up. "We're going for a *walk*?"

Webb cuts in to correct him. "Walking *meditation*. You walk . . . and think."

"What about?" Mikey still sounds cross. Truculent.

"You could think about your sister, Mikey," Assistant Webb says matter-of-factly. "Same for all of you. Walk is an opportunity to reflect on the person you lost."

Dawn was hours ago, but it feels like daybreak as they set off; a weak light leaks over the land and the air is chilly, the grass soaked with dew. Their route traces a figure eight around the gardens and grounds and tree-clad slopes of Eden Hall. It passes quite near to the lake at one point, though Shiv is relieved to see that a chain-link fence prevents them from going too close. DANGER: DEEP WATER a sign on the fence says.

Shiv takes care to keep her eyes on the ground along that stretch of path.

At first, Walk barely warms her, so gentle is the pace. Her limbs feel heavy, her joints stiff, and she can't strike any kind of rhythm. None of them can. It might be down to embarrassment at the weirdness of what they're doing, or just that it's harder than it looks to walk very slowly, in a line, in sync with seven other people.

She's supposed to focus on Declan but all she can think about is Mikey's face when Webb said what he did. His dead sister.

So, Shiv and her Buddy have both lost a sibling.

Mikey is three places ahead. He might be improvising a mime on "anger"; arms flailing, legs scissoring away as though kicking the heads off imaginary flowers. He repeatedly veers out of line or strays too close to the person in front (the "shaman" girl, Helen), like a driver in slow-moving traffic—frustrated, desperate to overtake.

It's not until the second circuit that Shiv begins to close down the distraction. The simple, hypnotic repetition of setting one foot in front of the other takes effect. A litheness seeps into her limbs. Her mind stills. Not a meditative trance or anything like that; it might just be

43

that the lack of sleep is finally catching up, reducing her to a state of semi-stunned autopilot.

Whatever, it's pleasant. Strangely calming and invigorating all at once.

In some ways Walk reminds her of the hikes Aunt Rosh took them on when they visited her in the school holidays. Only without the constant chatter, the pauses for tree-climbing (Shiv and Dec) or bird-watching (Aunt Rosh).

On the third circuit, Webb calls them to a halt, and Shiv can't quite believe an hour and a half has passed when it barely seems ten minutes since they set off.

Walk has finished in a grassy clearing in the woods.

Caron flops on the ground with an exaggerated groan, as though they'd been made to run the whole way. "Where are the foil blankets? The high-energy drinks?"

There *are* drinks. Webb and Hensher produce bottles of water from their rucksacks and pass them round, along with granola bars. Shiv sits down beside Caron. The others sit too—or, in Lucy's case, lie flat out as though sunbathing. Mikey remains standing, at the far side of the clearing, scuffing around among the undergrowth. Mumbling to himself. Docherty sets himself apart too, sitting with his back to them on a fallen tree at the edge of the bark-chip trail.

"Thirty minutes," Assistant Webb announces.

Caron unwraps her granola bar. "Jee-zuss, what exactly *is* this? It looks like hamster food stuck together with glue."

"Not glue," Shiv says. "Snot."

"Oh, nice." She lets out a laugh. "*Thank* you for that, Shiv."

"Don't mention it."

They're quiet for a moment, side by side on the grass, elbows touching. A cabbage-white butterfly performs an air dance from one side of the glade to the other. Shiv bites into her snack bar. It tastes better than it looks and she finishes it in three mouthfuls, washing it down with a long swig of water, conscious of Caron watching her. She expects the older girl to make some jokey comment. But she doesn't.

Voice lowered, Caron says, "I hardly ate anything afterward."

Shiv holds her gaze. "Me neither," she says, just as quietly.

"I lost about ten kilos."

Shiv nods. "My counselor called it a 'manifestation of guilt.' *My brother can't eat anymore, so why should I?*" She scrunches the granola wrapper, then flattens it out again. "But I just didn't see the point of anything anymore. Including food."

"Maybe you were trying to join him?" Caron says.

"Join him?"

"Starve yourself to death."

"Oh, right." Shiv looks around but none of the others seem to have overheard.

"Has it ever crossed your mind to . . . *do* something, Shiv?"

She stares off into the trees. "I've never actually tried to, no."

"I have. Antidepressants." Caron places a hand on Shiv's back and gives it a rub, as though Shiv was the one who'd just confessed to taking an overdose. "Want my advice?" the older girl says. "Don't *ever* imagine that getting your stomach pumped is a fun way to spend an evening."

In another part of the woods someone is chopping logs, the *thwock-thwock* of the ax echoing in the trees. It's hard to tell which direction the sound is coming from. Shiv saw one of the gardeners from her window this morning, tending the vegetable plot. An old guy who reminded her of Panos, on the boat in Kyritos; most likely, there was no resemblance but the idea had come to mind because of the picture in the night.

Beside her, Caron has lapsed back into silence. She is breaking her granola bar into pieces and letting them fall into the grass between her feet.

"Caron . . . ," Shiv begins, then trails off.

"Hm?"

Shiv hasn't found the right moment, or the nerve, to ask this question before. She asks it now, so softly she's almost whispering. "Who did you lose?"

Caron doesn't reply, doesn't even look up from what she's doing.

"D'you mind me asking?" Shiv says.

"My best friend. Melanie." Caron dusts the last of the crumbs off her fingers; keeps her head lowered, eyes fixed on the ground. "We were at a party and there were some pills going around and I . . ." She stops, takes a breath. Starts again, nodding to herself. "I took one and talked Mel into taking one as well. She'd never done E or anything like that."

Shiv doesn't ask anything else. The girl looks wrung out. The feisty Caron is the screen she puts up in front of this one.

"Her first time," Caron repeats. "How *unfair* is that?"

Shiv might take her hand, or put an arm round her—rub her back, as Caron did for her just now; but Shiv is two years younger and, somehow, it doesn't seem right. Instead, she just lets their elbows come into contact again.

Hensher is moving among the group, collecting wrappers and empty bottles.

Webb is the first to react. Then Hensher, scattering the litter everywhere.

On the far side of the clearing, Mikey is standing at the base of a tree, repeatedly drawing his head back and smashing it against the trunk as hard as he can.

By the third day, Dad was relaxed enough to *sing* as they drove away from the villa that morning. For once, no one begged him to plug in the iPod instead. With the car windows open and the fragrance of spring flowers mingling with the chlorine-scent of their hair, damp from a pre-breakfast swim, the collective good mood washed over Shiv like a warm breeze.

She inspected her forearms to see how her tan was progressing. "So what's the story with these turtles?" she said.

"I had a flyer here somewhere," Mum said.

"I've got it." Declan brandished the leaflet.

The trip had been his idea, each of them proposing a what-I'd-like-to-do-tomorrow plan before all four options were put to a ballot. "A democratic process, here in the birthplace of democracy," as Dad put it. And so there they were, heading for a half-day cruise with lunch, turtle-watching and snorkeling included.

Declan read aloud: "'Why not let Poseidon Adventures take you on a—'"

"It's *not* called that," Shiv said.

He showed her the leaflet. Sure enough, *Poseidon Adventures*.

Shiv laughed. "So, what, we get hit by a tidal wave and the boat capsizes—"

"Ah, no," Dad said. "That's on the *full*-day cruise—we're on the *half*-day."

"That was such a sad film," Mum said. "The scene where she drowned—what was her name? You know, the big woman with the curly hair."

"Shelley Winters," Dad said. Mum always forgot actors' names and Dad always knew who she meant. "And she didn't drown, she had a heart attack after swimming underwater for too long."

"Anyway," Declan said, with a wave of the leaflet. He cleared his throat and resumed reading, adopting an actorly tone. "'Why not let Poseidon Adventures take you on an unforgettable tour of the . . .' blah-de-blah . . . Oh, here we go: 'Our glass-bottomed boat permits you'— *permits* you?—'a close-up encounter with the famous turtles for which this island is re-known.' That would be *renowned,* then."

"Can we have the *unedited* version?" Shiv said.

Her brother looked at her over his sunglasses. "Shivoloppoulos, I am in the zone here." Then back to the leaflet, "'These magical prehistoric creatures have *frequent* our shores since the dawn of time. They live for up to a thousand years and—'"

"Thousand years my arse." Dad snorted.

"'—and can grow as big as ten meters in diameter.'"

"Ten—"

"'*If* you are lucky,'" Declan continued, "'you might see one attack a dolphin foolish enough to stray into the turtle's territory. When these marine beasts are evenly matched, the fights can last for hours, leaving the waters awash with blood, while local fishing crews gather to watch the spectacle and place bets on the outcome.'"

"Read it properly," Dad said, amused.

They were winding their way down the precipitous

49

cliff-top route to a harbor a few kilometers along the coast from the villa. The sunlight made a golden haze of the dust the tires kicked up from the roadside verge. Shiv tried not to look over the barrier at the sheer drop to the sea far below.

"'According to Greek mythology,'" Declan went on, "'the very first turtle was created by the great god Poseidon when he cast one of his sons adrift at sea, nailed hand and foot to an upturned shield, as a punishment for having sex with an otter.'"

"Oh, Declan, *nooo*," Mum said, trying not to laugh. "That's disgusting."

At the wooden jetty, the boat was bobbing at its moorings and a queue of holiday makers—mostly Germans and British, by the sound of it—had formed, ready to board. Shiv, Mum, Dad and Declan tagged onto the end.

"'*Poseidon Four*,'" Dad said, reading the name on the far-from-gleaming white hull. "I don't like to ask what happened to the *first* three."

The Brits in the group laughed.

The smell of salt, seaweed and fish was pungent but not unpleasant. A breeze would've been good, though. Even through rubber flip-flops, Shiv felt the heat of the boards boring into her feet. Gulls shrieked and the mooring posts creaked as *Poseidon IV* shifted on the swell. At the back of the boat, an oldish bloke (a sea dog cliché, with wrinkled nut-brown skin, shaggy dark hair and beard) was doing things with ropes. Toward the front, facing away from the waiting tourists, a much younger guy sorted masks and flippers into two large plastic tubs. He was tall and broad, the thin yellow cotton of his polo shirt drawn taut across his shoulders as he arranged the snorkeling kit with easy efficiency. Shiv caught herself staring at his calves, the muscles flexed beneath bronzed skin as he braced himself against the roll and pitch of the deck.

"Welcome, welcome!" This was the beardy one, who'd finished with the ropes and was doing the smiley, meet-and-greet thing. "You folk ready to see some turtles?"

He pronounced it with a "d" in the middle.

"Turdles?" Declan whispered, raising an eyebrow at Shiv.

"Baby turds," she whispered back. "They're surprisingly cute."

The boatman received a self-conscious chorus of yeses. *"Okay."* He offered a hand to the first of the passengers. "Please, sir. Be careful when you step, yeah?"

Shiv had stopped paying attention because the young guy was making his way to the rear of the boat to join in helping people aboard. The curly black hair, the brown eyes, the slim hips, the sinuous grace of his movements. He looked eighteen or nineteen, she reckoned, but . . . *wow!*

As the queue shuffled forward, she was tempted to position herself so he'd be the one to take her hand as she stepped off the jetty, and they'd lock gazes . . . but no. They were going to be on the boat together for the next three hours, so there was no need to be too obvious. Not so soon, anyway. She got in line for Old Beardy. Smiled and said thank you as he helped her aboard. Sat down with the others. Posed for the first of the photos Mum would take during the trip. And the whole time, Shiv didn't catch the young guy's eye or even glance in his direction.

Old Beardy was Panos; the younger one was Nikos. Father and son. Panos skippered the boat out to sea while Nikos looked after the front-of-house stuff: taking the money, health-and-safety announcements, the sight-seeing spiel. His English was very good. For his age, he had bags of confidence and charm. The nice kind. Not the flirty, sleazy self-assurance of a guy too aware of how attractive he is. Male or female, young or old, each passenger received the same open smile, the same warm tone. To the children he was a fun-loving entertainer, while with the pensioner couple from Kent (*we're here for turtles, not snorkeling*), Nikos was solicitous and respectful.

The only awkward moment came when he remarked on Declan's T-shirt (the Salinger one again) and asked him to display the quotation to the other passengers.

"Any friend of J.D.'s is a friend of mine," Nikos said, offering a handshake. But Dec just flushed several shades of red and, for once, was lost for words.

As for Shiv, Nikos paid her no more or less attention than anyone else.

For a while, during the turtle-watching, she almost forgot about him. Along with everyone else, Shiv was transfixed by the strangely beautiful creatures—whether she was scanning the sea for a glimpse of a reptilian head breaking the surface or gazing into the shimmering depths as a turtle glided beneath the boat's glass bottom.

After lunch, *Poseidon IV* sailed farther up the coast with the son at the wheel while the father sat at the prow, smoking. One way and another, Shiv wasn't getting to see as much of Nikos as she'd hoped. The ache in the pit of her stomach had nagged at her since she'd first set eyes on him, and if the boat trip hadn't been so wonderful, she might easily have made herself miserable. But the turtles, the light sparkling on the water, the lulling rhythm of the boat, the spectacular cliffs, the tingle of the sun on her bare skin—on a day like this, she couldn't fail to be blissfully happy.

The boat slowed, describing a long curve into a cove where a finger of land provided a natural shelter and the sea calmed to pondlike stillness. Nikos brought the vessel to a halt and shut off the engine while his father dropped anchor.

"You've got your hair caught in the buckle."

Shiv stammered a thank-you as Nikos cupped the back of her head with one hand while he gently freed the trapped strands of hair.

To be standing so close to him in her bikini . . . *Jesus.*

She'd meant to put on her one-piece bathing suit beneath her clothes for the boat trip but had worn it without thinking for the pre-breakfast dip in the pool, and it was still damp when they'd set off. The two-piece was *brief,* meant for sunbathing more than swimming. Shiv was the last of the snorkelers to kit themselves out; the others were in the water already, or lining up to go in. But Shiv had managed to make a hash of the headgear.

"There you go," Nikos said, adjusting her mask and repositioning the snorkel for her. "So, you been snorkeling before?"

"A couple of times, yeah."

"Okay, enjoy."

She made a sad face, as far as that was possible in a mask. "Er, sorry, I can't."

He looked puzzled. "How come?"

Shiv pointed at the floor. "You're standing on my flippers."

Nikos laughed and took a deliberate step back, arms spread in apology.

That was their first conversation. The second took place after the snorkeling, as the boat headed for home.

Panos was at the wheel again while Nikos gave his final spiel. He was talking about turtles' egg-laying habits and had produced the dried-out remains of a hatchling which hadn't made it from the nest to the sea. The tiny corpse, like something made out of leather, was handed from passenger to passenger with a mixture of revulsion and fascination. Shiv thought it was the saddest, most exquisite thing she'd ever seen.

After the talk Nikos set to work, repositioning the rubber fenders along one side of the boat, ready for docking. Shiv watched him covertly.

Too soon the trip would be over. The thought sank a weight in her chest.

She noticed the baby turtle then, lying on a seat where

one of the passengers had set it down. Shiv checked to see if she would be noticed. No. Mum and Dad were engrossed in conversation with the old English couple and Declan was leaning over the side rail, one arm outstretched to catch the spray from the vessel's wash.

"You forgot this," Shiv said, the desiccated creature in the flat of her palm.

Nikos stopped what he was doing and straightened up. Thanked her.

As he took the baby turtle from her she felt the graze of his fingernail. She kept her voice steady. "I never knew something dead could be so beautiful."

He smiled but didn't say anything.

"There's a museum in Oxford," Shiv went on, "where they've got these tiny heads—I mean, actual human heads that have been shrunk to about the size of an apple and, I don't know, *preserved*." She was losing her way with this, waffling on. She shrugged. "Anyway, that baby turtle kind of reminds me of them."

"Some folk think it's fake," Nikos said, slipping it back into its plastic case.

"It isn't, though, is it?"

"No." He put the case in his shorts pocket. Then, "You enjoy the snorkeling?"

Shiv nodded. Her throat was so tight she could barely talk. She had put her T-shirt back on and wore a beach towel as a sarong. Her top was translucent with damp and she was aware that her hair must be a mess, sticking up and claggy with seawater.

She managed to say: "My name's Shiv, by the way. Short for Siobhan."

"Irish?"

"The name is, yeah. Not me. I'm English." She scratched around for something else to say, to keep the conversation going.

As it happened, he beat her to it. "So, are you staying this side of the island?"

"Yeah, just a few k up the coast." She pointed, naming the village.

"Oh, I know that place. My grandmother lives near there."

Nikos had resumed work as they spoke, loosening one of the fender ropes and letting out some extra length before refastening it. He had a livid crescent-shaped scar at the base of his right thumb, she noticed. The black hairs on his wrist were curled tight by moisture, the skin sparkling with encrusted salt.

Hardly able to believe what she was doing, Shiv told him the name of the villa.

Nikos paused, half turning to look at her over his shoulder. "D'you mind me asking, Shiv, but how old are you?"

"Seventeen," she said, without the slightest hesitation.

FIVE

The Make session goes ahead without Mikey. Or Webb, who escorted him back to Eden Hall after the assistants had stopped him from dashing his brains out. It took them a while to calm him down and persuade him that he needed medical attention. His forehead was caked in blood, dirt and bits of bark, one eyebrow split right open.

Shiv couldn't believe he hadn't knocked himself unconscious.

As Assistant Hensher led the rest of the group from the clearing and along a trail to the Make area, a shocked hush descended. It was as though Mikey had dazed them more than he'd dazed himself.

And so, now, in silence, they emerge into what looks like a picnic site, laid out with wooden tables; they enter a camouflage-green Portakabin to collect cartridge paper, pencils and drawing boards; they go back outside to take their places at one of the tables. In silence, they listen to the instructions.

Their task is to draw the face of the person they lost.

"It doesn't matter if you can't draw very well," Hensher tells them. "It doesn't matter how close a likeness it is. What matters is that you create an impression of that face in your mind and try your best to put it down on paper."

He stresses that, as in Walk, talking is not permitted during Make.

"Any questions?"

Lucy raises a hand. "Do we draw their living face? Or their dead face?"

After the session, Lucy falls into step with Shiv and Caron as they all troop back through the woods. She apologizes for failing to turn up in the rec room last night. *Tummy bug,* she says. Caron doesn't make an issue of it, although Shiv can tell she doesn't believe the girl. There's just room for the three of them to walk side by side, Shiv and Caron slowing to Lucy's pace on an uphill section. Her panting provides a backing track to their conversation. Even though they've spent two hours absorbed in Make, the talk quickly turns to what happened before that.

"D'you think Mikey's all right?" Lucy asks. "He looked a mess."

"It's the *inside* of his head that's the problem," Caron says.

"Same here." Shiv's tone is sharper than she intended. "Same for all of us."

"You'd think I'd have more empathy, wouldn't you?" Caron says. Not nastily, though. "Sorry if this sounds selfish, but I'm here to sort out *my* life. Not his."

"Psychiatric patients are shipwreck survivors, but they do not share the same lifeboat," Shiv says. "Each is in a lifeboat of their own, adrift on the same sea."

The other two girls widen their eyes at her.

"Something I read on the Internet," Shiv says with a shrug.

"You *Google* that stuff?" Caron says. "Zuss, no wonder you're screwed up."

They all burst out laughing, drawing curious looks from some of the others filing along the bark-chip trail in the direction of Eden Hall, and lunch. The path has begun its descent, the sun dropping coins of light all about them through the branches.

They continue discussing Mikey, exorcising the shock of what they witnessed, it seems to Shiv—or at least try-ing to make sense of it. No amount of talking it over can rid her of the image of his smashed-up face. It might be this, or a delayed reaction to the incident—or just that she's tired and hungry—but Shiv has begun to feel nau-seous, trembly, a little light-headed.

"I thought he was trying to kill himself," Lucy says.

"No chance." *This is my territory,* Caron's tone suggests; Shiv recalls her admission, at Break, about having taken an overdose. "If you're serious about suicide," the older girl says, "you don't head-butt a tree with two care as-sistants standing twenty meters away."

The trail narrows just here, forcing them into single file; Shiv lags behind, shutting out what the other two are saying about Mikey.

Shutting out that face.

It was there in Make, too: trying to draw Dec as flashes of Mikey's bloodied features superimposed them-selves. She never saw Declan's face at the end. So even if she wanted to (why *would* you?), she couldn't have drawn his dead face, as Lucy had put it. But she was unable to draw his living face either.

Shiv wasn't alone in finding Make tough. Caron, sitting opposite her at one of the tables—spare pencil between her lips as a surrogate cigarette—had little to show for the two hours. A few scrawls on the sheet she handed in to Assistant Hensher and several balls of crumpled paper littering the ground where they sat. By the end, she looked as frustrated, as upset, as Shiv felt.

If Walk had stilled their minds, Make had stirred them up again.

The trees are thinning, big blots of brightness forming up ahead—*approaching* them, it seems, as though rather than Shiv, Caron, Lucy and the rest walking out into the daylight, the gloom of the woodland is being slowly erased to release them. The other two let her catch up, Lucy in full flow now. Only half listening, Shiv gathers that the girl is well into a monologue about studying marine biology at university, when the time comes. *If* the time comes, she adds.

Shiv knows she must rest or pass out altogether.

"Hold up a sec," she says, spotting a tree stump at the edge of the path. She sits down a little unsteadily. Holds her side. "Stitch," she tells them as they pause.

Caron gives her a questioning look. Concerned. Not buying the "stitch" excuse.

Lucy just picks up where she left off. "I've already been off school for seven months, yeah, and I really don't know if I'll be well enough to go back this side of Christmas. And what with my GCSEs next year . . ." She trails off. Puffs out her cheeks. "Sorry," she says. "Dad calls me Mimi when I get like this—as in *me, me, me*. He goes, 'Oh, Mimi's here again.' I mean, he used to. Before."

Before what? Shiv wonders.

The girl's cheeks are pink but Shiv isn't sure if that's

60

from walking or because she's upset. Shiv dips her head. The wooziness has eased but the nausea is still there, and her skin is cold and clammy. She wonders if she's about to have one of her turns; she doesn't think so, but it's hard to tell when one is sneaking up on her.

Caron rests a hand on Shiv's shoulder. "All right, girl?"

"Just a bit tired."

When she's recovered, they set off again—the last of the group, now. Lucy is talking about marine biology again. Shiv's always imagined herself doing English when she goes to uni, or maybe history—nothing science-y, anyway. Right now, she can't imagine going to university at all. Or getting a job, or what that job might be. Or marriage or kids or where she'd be living. Anything. Even her own GCSEs—next summer, same as Lucy's— seem pointless, fantastical. Since Declan died it's like all of her own possible futures have closed down, become as unattainable for Shiv as her brother's never-to-be-lived life is for him. Just to be thinking about what she might be doing a year from now, five years, or ten, or fifty, seems wrong. Grotesque. Offensive.

How can she contemplate growing older when Dec never can?

Then there are the times when she wishes she could wake up one morning and two or three years will have passed overnight and she won't feel like shit anymore. But that would mean not missing him, not wishing he was still alive, not remembering how he died. Not hating herself.

She can't conceive of waking up to a morning like that if she lives to be a hundred.

When they reach the orchard behind Eden Hall, Assistant Hensher is still waiting for them; a sheepdog rounding up the last of the flock. Shiv tells Caron and Lucy to go on ahead—she'll come and find them in the dining hall.

"I'd like to see Mikey," she says to Hensher, once the others are out of earshot.

"Mikey?" Hensher can't be much older than Nikos, yet the contrast between them is about as stark as it gets. She shuts down the thought of Nikos. "I'll have to check where he is," the care assistant says, unclipping a radio from his belt.

"I just want to make sure he's okay," Shiv says.

Hensher manages to meet her gaze. "D'you mind me asking why?"

"Because he's my buddy."

Mikey is in the sick bay, resting, so Nurse Zena can keep an eye on him for signs of concussion. When Shiv goes in, the young nurse is sitting at a desk in an adjoining office area, writing notes on a white card. Hensher must've messaged her, because she smiles, gestures Shiv to go on through.

"How's he doing?" Shiv whispers.

Zena whispers back. "Worse than the tree, is my guess."

Mikey is on an adjustable bed, the back raised, his head propped up by pillows. For once, he doesn't look agitated or keen to be anywhere except right where he is. Shiv changed out of her jumpsuit before coming here, but the boy is still in his, the yellow fabric spattered in places with dried blood. His fringe is encrusted too, like he's tried to highlight his short dark blond hair with ketchup.

"Hey," Shiv says.

He doesn't reply, just looks at her through half-shuttered eyes. A dressing covers most of his forehead, his right eyebrow is zippered with soluble stitches and the skin around his eyes is several shades of purple. The rest of his face is deathly pale.

Shiv pulls up a chair and sits beside the bed. "Most people walk *round* a tree," she says, putting on a cheery grin. "Not straight through it."

Mikey points at her T-shirt. "What's that mean?"

She doesn't look down at the slogan; she doesn't need to. "It means if you make friends with someone it's going to hurt when you stop being friends with each other. Or if they go away."

He looks unimpressed. Actually, it's difficult to know what he's thinking.

"It's from a book," Shiv says. *"The Catcher in the Rye."*

"Yeah?" It's not a curious "yeah?", more of a so-what "yeah."

"It was my brother's." Shiv plucks at the front of the T-shirt. "My dad thinks it's a bit morbid, me wearing his stuff."

Mikey just sniffs. Touches the gauze patch on his forehead, as though to check whether any blood has seeped through. It has. He wipes his fingers on the bed-sheet.

"Your head must hurt," Shiv says.

"She gave me something so it wouldn't." A glance

toward the open doorway to the nurse's office. "I told her I didn't want nothing, but she jabbed me anyway."

She wonders why he asked not to have pain relief. Why he bashed his head against a tree in the first place. She doesn't ask. Whenever she kicks off, she hates people asking why. *Why? Why? Why?* She suspects Mikey's the same.

"Got yourself out of Make, anyway," Shiv says. She starts to tell him about the session but the boy cuts across her.

"Why are you here?" he asks.

Shiv hesitates. "I don't know, I guess I just—"

"Feel sorry for me."

"No, I . . . it *upset* me. Seeing you do that to yourself."

"You seen the freak show; now you've come to see the freak."

Shiv can't help laughing. "Are you always this obnoxious?"

He goes sulky on her, trying to stare her down. The boy who doesn't want a Buddy. "No one asked you to come," he says.

She keeps her voice soft. "How old was your sister, Mikey?"

He looks at her, fiery-eyed. Says nothing.

"Younger than you?" Shiv says.

His eyes are an amazing color—hazel, but flecked with yellow. He breaks eye contact. Takes a bite out of one of his thumbnails. "Nine," he says, aiming his words somewhere over the far side of the room. "Feebs was nine."

"Feebs?"

"Phoebe. I always called her Feebs. Or Feeble, some-times—to wind her up."

"Phoebe? Seriously?"

"Yeah, why?" He sounds cross.

"Nothing, it's just—" She touches the front of her T-shirt. The slogan. "That was the name of Holden Caulfield's sister."

From Mikey's expression, he has no idea what she's talking about.

Shiv changes tack. "Were you *friends,* you and Feebs?" He doesn't answer. "Cos I was, with my brother. Declan. Dec. He was a year younger than you, but he . . ." She won't cry. She absolutely won't cry. "He was my best mate."

"He was on the TV," Mikey says. "You both was."

Shiv nods. "Yeah. Yeah, we were."

The others have been more subtle about it—Shiv's "celebrity" status—but it's been buzzing beneath the sur-face in the way some of them look at her, or the sudden halt in conversation when she enters a room. She can't tell if it's resentment (*Why did your story make the head-lines when ours didn't?*) or curiosity—the thrill of meeting someone, for real, whose face you've seen on the news. Like she's a singer or actress.

A hush envelops them. Just the ticking of a clock and the *scritch-scritch* of Nurse Zena's pen in the adjoining room. Food smells drift in from elsewhere in the build-ing, and Shiv realizes how hungry she is.

"Two more minutes," the nurse calls out. "I need to do a couple of tests."

On Mikey, she must mean. Shiv shifts in her chair,

starts to say her goodbyes. But the boy stalls her with a question.

"What did you do?"

He's looking at her hands, the tips of the fingers she rubbed raw digging away at the seat in Dad's car yesterday. They'd scabbed over but opened up again in the shower this morning and have been weeping on and off ever since. Shiv looks at them. Tells Mikey how they got to be like that.

"I damage things," she says. Then, gesturing at his face, "You damage yourself, I damage other stuff. We're the wrong way round, you and me."

"How d'you mean?"

"Girls usually turn the hurt in on themselves; boys usually hit out."

"I don't believe all that shit," Mikey says, shaking his head. "All *this* shit," he adds, with a gesture that Shiv supposes to mean this place, the clinic.

I do, Shiv stops herself from saying. *We have to, or what else is there?*

"See you later," she says instead, rising from her seat. Halfway to the door, she pauses, turns back toward him. "Mikey, how did Feebs die?"

He looks at her for so long she wonders if he's going to answer. Finally, he does. "She drowned." His voice is hard, heavy with self-disgust. "I tried to save her, but I didn't. And she drowned."

Nikos didn't show up at the villa that evening, after the turtle trip, or the following day. Shiv was caught between breathless expectation that he might appear at any moment and the appalling certainty that she'd never see him again.

What had she been thinking, telling him where she was staying?

There probably wasn't a single day on the boat when one of the tourists didn't come on to him. He could take his pick: Italians, Americans, Swedes, French—sexy, confident girls. No way would he bother with an English schoolgirl who'd still been wearing a dental brace two months ago. Most likely, he'd be having a laugh with his mates about the skinny kid who had lied about her age.

Shiv couldn't decide who she hated the most: Nikos, for not coming; or herself for being stupid enough to believe he would.

She'd gone over and over the moment when she told him the name of the villa. The way he spoke to her, the way he looked at her, the way he smiled, the way he stood so close. He *liked* her. Shiv was sure of it. Just as strongly, she'd never been less sure of anything.

Another day, forty-one hours since she'd last seen Nikos.

They were packing for a trip to the local beach. Shiv didn't want to go. She wanted to stay around the villa; but she'd persuaded them to do that the previous day, complaining of a stomach upset. Mum and Dad—especially Dad—wouldn't agree to *frittering away* another day just lazing by the pool. In any case, Nikos would be out on the boat again till late afternoon.

"You feeling up to this?" Mum said, rolling up towels to go in the beach bags.

"Yeah, I guess."

Dad came by, looking for his sun hat. "D'you think it was something you ate?" he asked. "That lunch on the boat, I wouldn't be surprised."

Shiv glared at him. "What, they're *foreign,* so the food's *bound* to be dodgy?"

She'd been like this for the past two days, veering between bickering snipes and sullen silence. Meanwhile, Declan kept on about the *brilliant* turtle trip and how he wanted to emigrate to Greece one day and run boat cruises for tourists.

They chose the end farthest from the windsurfers and Jet Skiers, pitching camp beneath two thatched parasols in a line that ran the length of the beach like so many giant straw hats. Snack kiosks, tavernas and a minimart fronted onto the strand and, behind them, the hills of the interior rose sharply above the resort, gleaming pink-and-green. Positioning her lounger directly in the sun, Shiv stretched out, stripped to her bikini and lightly coated with Ambre Solaire. Mum sat in the shade with a book of Sudoku puzzles. Dad and Declan went into the sea to swim.

She must've fallen asleep because the next thing she knew, Mum was tickling the sole of her foot and saying, "Wakey-wakey."

She jerked her foot away. "Hm?"

"We're going for some lunch," Mum said.

"I'm not really hungry."

"I'll eat yours, then." This was Dad, his sun hat too bright in the glare for her to look at him. He grinned, rubbed his belly. "I love it when you're off your food."

They sat at a table on the terrace of a taverna over-looking the spot where they'd spent the morning. Shiv saw that Dec had written his name in huge letters in the wet sand near the water's edge.

The waiter took their order. When he'd gone, Mum asked Shiv if it might be a good idea to put a T-shirt on.

"So the waiter can't gawp at my boobs, you mean?"

"Yes, exactly."

"Those are *boobs*?" her brother said, helping himself to three chunks of bread. "Wow, they don't look anything *like* the ones on the Internet."

"Declan, please."

"You're the one talking about boobs, Mum."

"You think it's my responsibility to cover up, then?" Shiv said, addressing her mother. "A guy is perfectly en-titled to stare at a girl if she's wearing a bikini, yeah?"

"You're *twelve*," Mum said to Declan. "You shouldn't be looking at porn."

"Yeah, right. And make sure to warn those bears about shitting in the woods."

Mum turned to Dad. "I thought you'd set a filter on his PC?"

"*Mum,*" Declan said, "it was *me* who showed Dad how to set it."

"Dec, that bread is for all of us," Dad said. "And don't swear at your mother."

"Am I allowed to swear at *you,* then?"

"I'd be surprised and disappointed if you didn't."

Shiv pulled on a T-shirt. Her brother snaffled the phrase book from Mum and began reciting random words in Greek in the solemn tones of a TV newsreader. He was still at it when the food arrived. Mum had dolmades, Dad had a plate piled with small grilled fish—complete with heads, eyes, tails—which crunched like nachos as he ate them. Shiv and Declan both had cheese-and-tomato pizza.

"You could eat that at home," Dad pointed out.

"Ah, but we are not 'at home,' Father," Declan said, his mouth half full. "So if we are to attain our weekly recommended pizza quotient—RPQ, as nutritionists call it—we have no option but to eat some while we are here."

For the first time in nearly two days, Shiv smiled.

Back on the beach, Shiv and Dec knocked a ball back and forth with a pair of plastic bats. But he became too competitive, so Shiv decided to go for a swim, then sunbathe some more.

She'd been toasting her back for a while when Declan squatted beside her sun-lounger and asked if she fancied wandering along to the far end of the beach.

"To do what?"

"I dunno. Watch the Jet Skis, or scramble on the rocks or something."

Shiv half opened one eye to look at him. She was about to say no but stopped herself. Scrambling on rocks with her kid brother (in Cornwall, in Pembrokeshire, in Brittany), collecting shells and cuttlefish bones and odd-shaped bits of driftwood—these were among Shiv's earliest, fondest memories of family holidays.

"Yeah, okay."

They walked along the water's edge, the occasional bigger wave sluicing past their ankles. Shiv's shoulders tingled with sunburn, so she pulled on her T-shirt again; beside her, Declan looked more Mediterranean than ever after five days in the sun.

If Laura or Katy had been there, Shiv could have discussed Nikos with them. She ached to talk to *someone* about him. But it wasn't going to be her brother.

"Sorry for being a bitch just lately," Shiv said, after they'd walked for a bit.

"Define 'just lately.'"

"Today. Yesterday."

"Oh, right," Declan said, "only I thought you meant, like, since you were ten."

She gave him a shove. "Ha, ha, you're so *funny*."

"I like to think so."

"And don't think I've forgotten what you said about my boobs."

"Don't worry, Shivoloppoulos—small is the new big, apparently."

The next shove caught her brother off balance, landing him on his bum in the shallows. "Oh, *yessss,*"

71

Shiv said, laughing, "the Boy Declan, beaten up by a *girl*."

He chased her, kick-splashing her a few times before a truce declared itself. They fell back into step, reminiscing about previous holiday "skirmishes." Declan's favorite was the one a couple of years earlier, at a restaurant in Corsica, where he dropped a live beetle into her lap and Shiv's leap out of her seat sent Dad's red wine all over his brand-new chinos.

After their laughter subsided, her brother said, "I wish we'd got snorkels."

Shiv glanced at the sea. It did look inviting. She tried not to think about Nikos, adjusting her mask that time. Snorkeling wasn't her thing, really, but her brother had loved it—he was the first into the water and the last out, only returning to the boat when Nikos bellowed good-naturedly that he would set off without him. Then, as Declan was clambering back on board, Nikos had grabbed him under the armpits and swung him onto the deck in one easy movement, declaring, "Hey, I caught me a fresh turtle!" Which made everyone laugh, apart from Dec, who looked mortified.

Farther along the beach, Shiv saw there was only one Jet Ski still out on the water and all of the windsurfers had come in, their sails spread above the high-water mark like huge butterflies basking in the sun. Had the breeze dropped, or was it siesta time? The answer revealed itself with a roar of male voices from one of the tavernas, where a TV was showing a football match.

"What did you think of that guy on the boat?" Declan asked suddenly.

Shiv shot him a look. Had he seen them talking? "Which guy?"

"You know, Nikos. The snorkeling guy."

"Oh, right." Shiv shrugged. "Okay, I guess. Why?"

"Nothing," her brother said.

His expression gave nothing away and, as they continued to the end of the beach, he showed no interest in pursuing the topic. Shiv was glad to let it drop too. In any case, they'd reached the clutter of rocks beneath the promontory separating that bay from the next.

The whole time they were scrambling, Shiv and Declan barely spoke, each absorbed in their own thoughts. A gap had opened between them. They were too old for this. *She* was, anyway. It only struck her, now they'd got there, that she'd grown out of playing with her kid brother among the rock pools.

Back at the sun-loungers, Mum gave Declan some money and sent him off to buy ice-creams. Shiv sat in the shade of one of the parasols and took out her phone. Katy had sent a text since the last time she'd checked (*3!!! ate too much chocolate! am fat n sick but mostly fat xx*) but there was nothing new from Laura. Shiv started a reply to Katy.

Mum was working sun lotion into her shoulders and the back of her neck. "Can you do my back please, Shiv?"

"I'm texting."

"Over to you, then, love."

Dad sat behind Mum on the lounger, spraying lotion on his palms. "When my sensual touch gets you all flustered, try to remember we're in a public place."

"Dad, *please*," Shiv said. "That's just too—"

"Hey, guys." This was Declan. "Look who I just bumped into in the shop."

Shiv glanced up. Dec held four ice-creams, leaking over his bunched fists. Beside him, in a blue-and-white basketball top and blue swimming shorts, was Nikos.

"Hi, everyone," Assistant Sumner says with the forced enthusiasm of a children's TV presenter. "Welcome to your very first Talk."

Room S-10, second floor.

Sumner is the one who smiled too much at Dr. Pollard's introductory briefing last night. She wore her frizzy blond hair down that time; this afternoon it's fastened in a ponytail. The tan is as fake as ever. She can't be much older than twenty-five.

The chairs are arranged in a circle. Clockwise around the room are Assistant Sumner, Lucy, Caron, Shiv, Helen and Docherty. No Mikey.

She tries not to think about his sister. Phoebe. Feebs.

S-10 is garish, the light from the window behind Sumner accentuating the orangey-red carpet and buttercup-yellow walls. It's the decor of a kindergarten, only without the childish pictures and scattered toys. The chairs are purple, comfortable, in a school common-room kind of way. In the center, a low table is set out with a plastic jug of iced water and six plastic glasses.

Sumner asks about Walk and Make and earns a few noncommittal responses.

She nods, as though they were words of profound wisdom. "Okay, I know what you're all thinking." She leans forward, her gaze touring the circle. "You're thinking"—she puts on an anxious face and makes her voice go wobbly—"'Ooer, I don't know what happens at Talk.'"

"Can we have three guesses?" Caron says.

Sumner continues to smile. She hasn't stopped since they came in and it has become unnerving. "How it works," she says, ignoring or possibly not registering the sarcasm, "is we sit in silence until someone feels moved to speak. Once they finish, others may respond. Then we wait for the next Speaking. And so on and so fifth."

So fifth. It's the sort of jokey thing Dad would say.

"Speak about what?" This time it's Lucy.

"Whatever *grabs* you." Sumner mimes grabbing. She smiles. "So long as it's related to your reason for being here."

"Group therapy, then." Caron doesn't bother to hide her disdain.

Shiv knows where Caron is coming from. She was placed in a therapy group herself back in the early days. First session, the participants tossed a beanbag, the thrower saying their name, then asking the person they threw the bag to *What's your name?* The first time the bag was tossed to Shiv, she let it hit her chest and fall to the floor.

She lasted three sessions before she was withdrawn from group work.

It was too soon, she tells herself. She wasn't ready to be helped.

Sumner is laying down ground rules, talking about mutual respect. Shiv sits straighter in her seat, tries to focus, to give this a fair go.

A little brass bell signals the start of Talk.

Assistant Sumner asks them to close their eyes. At first Shiv keeps hers open, embarrassed by the idea of sitting with them shut in front of relative strangers. But the others all close their eyes—even Caron—and watching everyone else when they are oblivious to it makes Shiv feel like a spy. She closes her eyes too.

Gradually, everyone settles and a hushed stillness envelops the room. Shiv has never been to a meditation class, but this is what she imagines it's like.

As in Walk, it's Declan she's supposed to be thinking about.

She can't. Her mind is too buzzy with waiting for someone to speak: who will it be and what will they say? Other distractions too. Thoughts of Mikey and their conversation in the sick bay.

How did Phoebe drown? Shiv wanted to ask, before Nurse Zena appeared in the doorway, needing to tend to her patient. *Why couldn't you save her?*

"I heard a noise from the bedroom, but I didn't go to see if she was all right."

Lucy. The first Speaker. After such a long silence, Shiv was starting to wonder if anyone would break it. Lucy explains that she is talking about her niece, Milly, who died while Lucy was babysitting. It's like she's giving evidence about an incident she witnessed but which didn't directly involve her. Shiv knows *that* voice. She has used it herself, recounting Declan's death for the umpteenth time. People give you a weird look; they don't see that it might be the only way to get the words out.

A response. Helen, the shaman, who played solo pool in the rec room last night before Caron and Shiv coaxed her into Buckaroo.

"Why didn't you go to her?" she asks. More curious than accusatory.

"Because I was on Facebook." Lucy uses the same neutral tone as before. "And when I logged off I'd forgotten about the noise in the bedroom. Forgotten all about Milly. I just sat there and ate a whole pack of biscuits in front of my sister's TV. Then I fell asleep on the sofa."

After a pause, she says, "When they came home I still had crumbs on my top."

It's all too easy to imagine the scene: the click of the key in the lock, the front door easing open, the sister's whispered (not to wake baby) "Hi, we're home." Lucy, jerking awake, a sleepy, biscuity taste in her mouth, standing up, hurriedly brushing crumbs off, the brother-in-law entering the lounge, drunk, saying something funny, the clip-clip of the sister's shoes along the hall as she goes to check on their little girl.

The anxiety in her voice—from concern, to panic, to terror.

Shiv shuts the scene down. She doesn't want to picture the sister's face as she bends over the crib; she might see her own face instead, peering at Declan.

Helen responds again. "How did Milly die?"

"She choked," Lucy manages to say. "She was sick and

she choked. I was stuffing my fat face with biscuits while my little niece choked to death."

No one says a word for the longest time after that. A vast chasm of silence.

Then, deadpan, Caron asks, "What type of biscuits were they?"

The timing is perfect. In the microsecond before her question registers with the group—in the shocked disbelief when Caron's words *do* sink in—it's as though all the air has been sucked from the room. When Lucy, of all people, lets out the first snort of laughter, it sets off a chain reaction right round the circle, all the tension of the tale of her niece's death released in one mighty blast of relief.

Shiv is doubled up in her chair, gasping for breath. Almost wetting herself. They all are, by the looks of it—even Assistant Sumner. Everyone's eyes are open, weeping tears of mirth, the patients exchanging glances with one another to make sure it's okay for them to find something so appalling so funny.

Then Lucy, barely able to speak for laughing, says, "Chocolate Hobnobs." And sets them all off again.

The real tears soon follow; the collective shame. Lucy, sobbing her heart out, clasped in Caron's hug; Caron crying every bit as hard, whispering *I'msorryI'msorryI'msorry*. Shiv and the rest sit, heads bowed, not watching them.

When the bell brings Talk to a close, Sumner says they're free to take a break before returning to S-10 at four p.m.

for the final session of the day: Write. In ones and twos, they leave the room, till Shiv and the care assistant are the only ones remaining.

"Need some head space?" Sumner asks. Smiling. She's sorting out materials for Write, taking a storage tub from a shelf and distributing its contents around the table: a school-style exercise book and ballpoint pen placed in front of each seat.

"Something like that."

"It's tough, isn't it, Talk?" When Shiv doesn't reply, the young woman gestures at the chair where Lucy was sitting and says, "Shiv, it's okay to laugh."

"Yeah, I know." Her counselor told her something similar. *Your brother wouldn't want you to be miserable for the rest of your life.*

"Comfort break," Sumner says, excusing herself. Maybe she's just giving Shiv that *head space.* "Promise not to scrawl any rude words in the Write books."

"I don't know any rude words," Shiv says. Sumner laughs.

Alone, Shiv picks up her exercise book. Blue, her name already printed on the front on a sticky label. The *b* and the *h* in *Siobhan* are the wrong way round. She sets the book back down.

It's too warm in here. Too stuffy.

She goes to the window and jiggles it open to let in a wash of fresh air. Looking *out* the window is a mistake. The lake. She should've anticipated that.

A figure near the lake snags her attention. A boy. Declan?

But she registers the yellow jumpsuit, the white

dressing on his forehead. Mikey. He is standing by the fence, staring in the direction of the water, gripping the chain-link mesh as though trying to uproot the fence altogether.

They are in their circle again. Write is like Talk, only written down, and not to be shared with the others. Just with Sumner, when she collects their books at the end.

As Sumner explains all this, Shiv's attention drifts. The most disconcerting aspect of this room isn't its oranges-and-lemons decor but the faint echo of the young woman's voice. Even now that she's stopped talking and people have begun to write, the background murmur continues. It's as though Sumner's remarks have been taped, then immediately played back at low volume.

Shiv shuts her eyes. Listens. Listens really hard.

"Shiv?"

"Sorry?" She opens her eyes.

"Are you all right?"

Assistant Sumner is standing up. Then Shiv realizes she is as well. The plastic water jug is in her hand; some of the contents have slopped onto the floor by her feet.

"Put the jug down, please."

No, she won't. Shiv swings her arm back, then forward, flinging the jug at the window as hard as she can and sending an arc of water across the room. The jug narrowly misses Sumner and crashes against the windowsill before ricocheting into a corner. Water streaks down the glass, dripping off the sill and onto the carpet in a dozen miniature waterfalls.

Silence. Everyone is staring at Shiv.

Sumner smiles her regular smile. One shoulder of her uniform is soaked. She flinched as the jug flew past but looks calm and collected again. Her eyes don't leave Shiv's. Her expression is one Shiv has observed before—in her counselor, and other people; like they're making notes about you without actually writing anything down.

"D'you need a time-out?" She makes a T sign.

Shiv frowns. Her gaze settles on the jug, and for a moment, she can't figure out how it came to be where it is. She starts to say something about the echoey voice but finds herself talking about Mikey instead. The lake. The fence.

Her words trail off. Sumner gives her time.

"I'm okay," Shiv says eventually. She sits down, as though to prove it. She picks up her pen, her blue exercise book. Turns to the first page. Writes.

"There you go," Shiv says, sliding the book across the table to Sumner.

"Really, I'd like you to write a bit more th—"

"It's all there. Go on, read it."

Assistant Sumner looks at her for a moment, then turns back the cover. Shiv has written:

I killed my brother.

Nikos collected them in a battered blue Toyota pickup, two windsurfing boards in the back. Late, but nothing happened on time here. Mum and Dad were loading the car ahead of a kids-free trip to the island's main town; Declan was repeatedly throwing the yellow tennis ball against the front wall of the villa. Shiv sat on the steps eating cornflakes. They heard the noise of the engine before the Toyota swung into view. Shiv set the cereal bowl down, suddenly unable to eat.

Nikos pulled up and killed the engine. "Hi."

"*Kalimera*," Dad said.

Declan caught Shiv's glance and rolled his eyes.

It had been Dad's idea for Nikos to take Shiv and Declan windsurfing. At least, Nikos had made it seem like Dad's idea. Just as she suspected, he had made it seem like he'd happened to bump into her brother in the minimart, en route to visit his grandmother. When Dec brought him down to the beach, Nikos stayed and chatted for a bit, addressing Mum or Dad and barely acknowledging Shiv.

Somehow, it had cropped up in conversation that he was going windsurfing the next day. "You could all come too, if you like. Free lessons."

He'd made it sound like some crazy whim that he didn't expect to be taken seriously. But Declan had jumped on it. *Can we? Please?* So Dad gestured at Shiv and Dec and suggested the "younger and more athletic half of the family" should go.

"If you're sure you don't mind, Nikos?"

Nikos didn't mind at all. As he said his goodbyes, Shiv could've sworn he gave her the most fleeting of winks.

Nikos got out of the pickup. Shook Dad's hand. Mum fussed over them—did they have their rucksacks? (yes); snacks and drinks? (yes); and did Shiv have her phone and was it fully charged and topped up with credit? (yes, yes and yes)—and Dad failed to get Nikos to accept thirty euros toward their lessons.

"I always go windsurfing on my day off," Nikos said. "It's no big deal."

Dad peeled off one of the tens and gave it to Shiv instead. "For ice-creams."

"Nikos, can you have them back by five?" Mum said. "Is that okay?"

It was okay by Nikos. And by Shiv. *Seven hours.* It was all she could do to keep a grin off her face as they slung their gear in the pickup.

"Can I ride in the back?" Declan said.

Dad glared at him. "No, you bloody can't."

They'd unloaded the two boards and carried them down to the beach.

"Have either of you been surfing before?" Nikos said. "Actual surfing."

They both said no.

"How about skateboarding or snowboarding?"

Declan said he'd done a bit of skateboarding; Shiv had tried snowboarding last year, at a dry-ski center. On a Year 9 trip, she just stopped herself from saying.

Nikos was wearing a basketball jersey again—green and gold stripes this time—and Shiv had to keep her gaze from straying to his bare arms and shoulders. "Okay, forget everything you learnt," he said. "Surfing, skateboarding, snowboarding, it's all about you and the board—about what you do with that board to control it, yeah?"

Shiv nodded, like this was exactly her experience of snowboarding; in fact, she'd had no control and spent most of her time falling.

"This is different," Nikos continued. "On one of these"—he gestured at the two sailboards lying beside them on the sand—"you're not surfing, or boarding, you are *sailing*." He looked at them in turn. "The wind moves the sail and the sail steers the board. Windsurfing isn't about you and the board, it's about you and the sail."

"Don't expect me to be any good," Shiv said.

Nikos grinned, holding eye contact. "You'll be fine."

"Oh no, she won't," Declan said. "She's rubbish at anything like this."

"Hey, show your sister some respect."

"Actually, she's not my real sister—Mum and Dad adopted her from a care home for kids who've been abandoned by their natural parents *because they're so humiliatingly crap at sport*."

"Is he always this funny?" Nikos asked, laughing.

Dec looked pleased and embarrassed all at once.

Shiv had been worried that Dec would cramp things,

but she was more relaxed for him being there, more able to be herself. It was nowhere near as intense as it would've been with just Nikos and her. If it wasn't a date, she didn't have to act like it was.

Nikos had brought them to a small bay at the top of the island, which he said was calmer and more sheltered than those on their stretch of coast—enough breeze to sail the boards, but not too tricky for a pair of beginners.

It seemed tricky enough to Shiv. But Nikos was patient and encouraging. To and fro he went between Shiv and Declan, wading or swimming to whichever of them needed help, or standing waist-deep in the sea, watching their efforts and calling out advice.

"Neutral position," he kept reminding them each time they had to remount.

"This is exhausting," Shiv said as Nikos helped her back on the board for the fifth time in as many minutes. She'd long since lost all embarrassment at flapping around like a drunken seal while he manhandled her, or the sail, or both out of the water.

Her brother, of course, was a natural. The only times he got dumped in the sea were when he tried to show off to Nikos.

After a bit, Shiv retreated to the beach for a breather. She'd hoped Nikos might take the hint and join her, but he stayed out on the water with Declan, mounting the other board and shadowing her brother in case he got into difficulty. Shiv watched them. They both looked so happy, so engrossed, she caught herself smiling too.

Nikos made windsurfing look easy.

He was the first to come in, hauling his sailboard clear of the waterline and flopping down beside Shiv on the beach mats. Water trickled from his skin in tiny rivulets as he lay on his back, hands behind his head, and made a show of regaining his breath. He was wearing swimming shorts and nothing else. Shiv tried not to stare at the dark hairs in his armpits and the line of hair below his navel.

"That's it, now," Nikos said. "Your brother will sail all the way to Turkey."

Shiv laughed. "I just *knew* he'd be better than me."

He squinted up at her, raising a hand to shield his eyes from the sun. "With windsurfing you're really competing with yourself, not anyone else."

"That's very philosophical," Shiv said, teasing.

"I'm Greek," Nikos said. "We *invented* philosophy."

Shiv scattered a handful of sand across his belly, then immediately regretted something so immature, so obvious; but Nikos didn't seem to mind.

"How come your English is so good?" she asked, to cover her awkwardness.

He'd grown up helping out with the boat trips, he explained, and picked up a lot of English from talking to the tourists. It was his best subject at school. "Now it's my degree at uni," he said. "In Thessaloniki."

"What year are you?"

"Second."

That made him at least nineteen. Jesus.

"Usually, I don't come home at Easter, but my big brother is getting married next week. So, really, you are incredibly lucky to have met me."

"What did you say you're studying? Advanced Arrogance?"

Nikos liked that. He sat up, brushed the sand from his

stomach. "Okay, you got me." He made a mock-serious face. "I apologize for being arrogant."

"You're not arrogant. You were lovely to everyone on the boat."

"But I'm not being lovely now?"

"Stop it," she said, laughing. She raked her fingertips through the sand. "Maybe you're just nervous today." Shiv shrugged. "I think we both are, a bit."

She amazed herself, coming out with a line like that. She'd only had two boyfriends—both her own age, neither relationship lasting long. She was out of her league here. He simply nodded, though; said she was probably right. And just like that, they were talking about all sorts of things. Stuff she never knew she knew about. Nikos listened, asked questions. He paid her attention. Shiv's breath burned in her chest and her mouth was dry, but she was being witty, bright—being the sort of girl, the sort of *young woman,* she needed to be if she was going to hold the interest of a guy four years older than her.

She was keeping her balance a lot better than she'd done just now in the sea.

"How's he doing?" Nikos said, shielding his eyes again to look for Dec.

"There." Shiv pointed.

They watched Declan. It was impressive the way he stuck at it, even if he messed up. Falling off seemed like part of the fun for him. Her brother looked so slight out there, holding on to that boom, the sail straining against the breeze and dragging the board across the water at quite a clip.

"He's such a great kid," Nikos said.

"Yeah. Yeah, he is." Shiv smiled. "I hope you don't mind being idolized."

"That's nice of you, Shiv. I think your brother quite likes me too."

She let out a snort. "You really *are* arrogant, aren't you?"

Somehow they were sitting a little closer. With her chin on her knees and arms clasped round her legs, Shiv's elbows were within nudging distance of his. She was glad she'd worn her one-piece, with its shorts-style bottom half and T-shirt-style top. She felt less exposed than she had on the boat, in her bikini.

She turned toward him. "You know when you bumped into Dec at the shop yesterday?" she said. "Did you sort of do that . . . deliberately?"

He smiled. "I called by your villa first. No one was in, but the car was outside, so I figured I'd head down to the local beach on the off chance you'd be there."

"Seriously?"

"I'd come to the villa the day before as well, actually—in the evening." He shrugged. "But I chickened out."

Shiv tried to keep her voice steady. "Am I so scary, then?"

"Not you, your mother and father. I didn't think they'd be so keen on some local guy hanging round their daughter. You know? And if I knock on the door there's going to be the whole 'How did you know where we were staying?' thing, and I—"

"You didn't want my parents to find out I was the type of girl who gave her address to some guy she'd only known for a few hours."

"Yeah, I guess."

"That's quite sweet, actually," Shiv said, after a moment. "I *think*."

Turning to her, Nikos said, "So, when I saw all of you on the beach, I waited for a chance to speak to you, away from your mum and dad, and your brother. But"—he gave another shrug—"you were never on your own."

"How long were you watching us?"

"An hour. Hour and a half, maybe."

"Hm, Nikos, I think that probably counts as *stalking*."

"Oh sure, but I have to do my stalking on Kyritos, because on the mainland, I just have so many restraining orders." When they'd both finished laughing, Nikos said, "So, anyway, your brother went off by himself to the minimart and I decided to, you know, accidentally bump into him."

"That's so *sneaky*," Shiv said. "I'm impressed."

They were facing each other now, cross-legged. Nikos's fingers found Shiv's hand and he traced a spiral in the fine grains coating her palm. His knuckles were chapped from the seawater and there was a diagonal graze across his forearm. Shiv touched it gently with her other hand.

"Is that from one of the ninety-seven times you helped me back on the board?"

He watched her fingertips, following the line of the cut, then raised his gaze to hers. His eyes were too beautiful for a guy, so beautiful she hardly dared look at them.

"Is it okay if I kiss you?" he said.

She frowned, as though giving serious consideration. "Well, on balance," she said, "I think I'll be quite disappointed if you don't."

Shiv couldn't have said how long they kissed. First time she'd kissed a guy with proper stubble, who didn't treat her mouth like chewing gum, who *held* her rather than *pawed* at her. When they finally came up for air, they sat with their faces breathing distance apart, smiling, staring into each other's eyes as though searching for secret messages concealed in the patterns of their irises.

Had Declan seen them kissing? The thought jolted Shiv out of her trance.

She turned from Nikos and scanned the sailboards for her brother's orange-and-blue rig. It was nowhere in sight. She stood up. Nikos, too. No words had passed between them, but her anxiety had transmitted itself even so.

"I can't see him," she said.

Nikos was looking along the beach now, and Shiv's hopes leapt at the idea that Dec had come ashore and was walking toward them at this very moment.

But she couldn't spot him there, either. *"Nikos."*

"There." He was gazing out to sea again, pointing. "He's caught a riptide."

By the time Shiv located her brother, Nikos was already hauling the other sailboard into the shallows like it was the start of a race. Was it this that frightened her the most, or the sight of Declan so far out? He was almost clear of the headland that protected the cove from the rough waters of the shipping lanes.

She tried to call out after Nikos, but the words caught in her throat.

Shiv stood knee-deep in the sea, one hand clasped to her mouth, and watched, utterly helpless, as Nikos mounted his board and tacked into the breeze that would sail him right out to Declan. All around her, sunbathers, volleyball players, kids building sand castles, paddlers, swimmers, even the other windsurfers—carried on, oblivious to what was happening.

When Declan's rig collapsed, Nikos was still a hundred meters away.

He brought her brother in.

Declan had managed to scramble back on to his board and lie facedown on top of it, clinging like a limpet; somehow, Nikos hooked a line from his own sailboard to Declan's and towed it back into the calmer waters of the bay. Where her brother promptly stood up once more, raised his rig and sailed ashore looking so pleased with himself you'd have thought he was the one who had rescued Nikos.

"*That,*" Declan said, grinning all over his face, "was totally bloody *excellent.*"

SEVEN

"Why are you here, Siobhan?"

Shiv frowns. "You told us why we're all here. The other night, you said—"

Dr. Pollard interrupts. "No, why are *you* here? You, specifically?"

"That's obvious, isn't it?"

"Is it?"

"To stop doing the stuff I do. To stop being the way I am. And," Shiv adds, tapping her temple, "because the magistrates said I have to get this seen to."

The director shakes her head. "I didn't ask why you feel you *should* be here. I don't doubt that your mother and father, your social worker, the police, the juvenile court, your counselor, the people whose property you've vandalized, all want you to get well." The woman pauses, adjusts her glasses. "But do *you* want to?"

"Yes. Yeah, of course."

"Do you, Siobhan? Really, truly?"

Really, truly. The phrase sounds wrong, unprofessional, on the lips of someone running a psychiatric clinic. But Dr. Pollard has shown already that she doesn't mind doing things differently.

"*Yes,*" Shiv repeats, aware of sounding petulant. "Really, truly."

The woman looks a little disappointed, as though

she'd expected better of Shiv. But Dr. Pollard lets it drop. Switches to safer topics: does Shiv like her room, does she like the food, is she settling in okay?

They are sitting outside on a balcony at the front of the building, just beneath the domed clock tower, facing one another across a wrought-iron table laid out with tea and biscuits. The white table is too bright in the sunshine. It's the afternoon of Shiv's second full day at the Korsakoff Clinic, and the director is seeing each resident today for a one-to-one consultation.

The balcony is nothing like the one at the villa in Kyritos, but even so, as Shiv was led out here an image flashed through her mind of Declan in red swimming shorts, sunbathing on a wicker lounger.

"How were Walk and Make this morning?" Dr. Pollard asks.

"Okay, yeah." Shiv nods. Then, "Actually, a bit tougher than yesterday."

"Tougher how?"

Shiv explains that she was even more tired this morning, after being woken for a second consecutive night by a holiday photo of her brother on her bedroom wall. (Dec, playing beach tennis.) "Also," she says, "I couldn't get him in my head today. I was just walking and drawing, basically."

"It'll come," the director assures her. "This is only Day Two."

Day Two of sixty. Plenty of time for Shiv to attain what Dr. Pollard refers to as "immersion in her brother and in his death." At the moment, she's barely dipping her toes in the water. This is the Korsakoff method, it seems, or part of it, anyway: to *submerge* residents in the object of their loss, their grief, their guilt. But the director doesn't want to say too much about that just now.

"Lose yourself in the activities, Siobhan, and you'll find Declan soon enough."

"And the sleep deprivation?" Shiv asks.

"No one makes you look at those pictures. I believe that when the projections started last night, some of the others simply pulled the bedcovers over their heads and went back to sleep."

True. They were talking about it at breakfast. Shiv shakes her head. "If I know Dec's there, I can't *not* look at him."

The woman shrugs. *Then prepare to be tired,* the gesture says.

She is dressed for business again—black jacket and matching skirt, her white blouse fastened by a black bootlace tie held with a metal clasp in the design of a fox head. Whenever she takes a sip of tea or bites into a biscuit, she cocks her little finger.

"I heard about the incident at Write yesterday," Dr. Pollard says.

The water jug, she means. Shiv nods.

"You've had a few of those blank moments." A statement, not a question; it'll have been in Shiv's case notes, which she recalls the director saying that she'd read, before she trashed them. "And usually coinciding with one of your outbursts."

Outburst. It's a good word: it can feel like something's bursting out of her, or like she's bursting out of herself. If she's aware of it at all.

The sense of release never lasts very long, though.

"All those wine bottles I smashed in Tesco—I didn't even realize it was happening," Shiv says. "I *denied* it afterward. Couldn't figure out why this security guy was marching me off to the office." She almost laughs at the ridiculousness of the memory. "They had to show me the CCTV to make me believe I'd done it."

Dr. Pollard removes her glasses and sets them down on the table, their lenses casting two discs of rainbow-tinted light onto its white surface. "These lapses in awareness—in cognition—are not altogether uncommon in post-traumatic patients."

A pause in the conversation follows. Shiv wonders who's speaking in Talk. And how Mikey is getting on. His face looked worse, if anything, when he turned up for Walk this morning. He made it unscathed through Break and into Make, although still very much the loner in the group. A sullen, sulky presence.

At lunchtime, Mikey went off somewhere by himself.

"Now," the director says, "there's something I need to ask you."

Shiv expects it to be about what she wrote in Write. *I killed my brother.* From talking to those who had their one-to-ones this morning, she knows that Dr. Pollard has seen what they put in their notebooks at yesterday's session. But the woman asks, "Is it the lake?"

"What?"

"When you joined me just now, that chair was facing forward, looking out toward the lake." She pauses. "But you repositioned it so you'd have your back to the view. Was that a conscious decision. Hm?"

"So you throw my counselor's notes in a bin," Shiv says, half smiling, "but you're happy to borrow her theories."

"But it wasn't the counselor who repositioned your chair. And it wasn't me."

When Shiv doesn't reply, Dr. Pollard leans forward, as though the change of angle will offer her a better perspective. She looks much younger without her glasses. Friendlier, even though the conversation has taken a less friendly turn.

"Could you move your chair back the way it was, d'you think?"

"What is this, aversion therapy?"

The woman pulls a face, as though she just swallowed something bitter. Shiv can't tell if it's the sarcasm she finds distasteful, or the term *aversion therapy* itself, or the fact that a *resident* has used the jargon.

"It isn't that."

"What, then? You want me to look at the lake—I mean *really* look at the lake—until I can see that, hey, it's just a lake! Just a plain old English lake."

The director shakes her head. "I want you to see the lake for what it is."

"That's what I just—"

"What it is to *you*, Siobhan. Look at the lake and see whatever it is that you see there, in all its horror. Don't turn your back on it."

Shiv stays sitting right where she is, though, her back to the view.

Dr. Pollard puts her glasses on again. Leaning back in her seat, she looks at the place where her glasses lay a moment ago, as though perplexed by their disappearance. Shiv expects her to warn against "repression" or to ask Shiv once more to reposition her chair. She says, "You dream about your brother." Another fact from Shiv's file. But her tone is less confrontational. "You have flashbacks to what happened too."

Shiv nods. "They're sort of mixed up, though. A bit of nightmare, a bit of flashback—sometimes it's hard to tell which is which."

"Horrible, I imagine."

"Yeah, they are. Horrible."

Shiv had one last night, sometime after the picture show on her wall.

Declan, at the poolside, in a bloody, broken heap on a sun-lounger. Two dogs—feral-looking mongrels—sneak up on him, take hold of a limb each in their jaws, drag him off the lounger and across the flagstones, leaving a trail of smeared blood, before disappearing with her brother into a dense bank of rhododendron. Shiv woke at the moment when she heard the dogs feeding on him.

She describes the nightmare, or whatever it was, to Dr. Pollard.

"Is that a typical example?" As she speaks, a sudden breeze raises one corner of a paper napkin on the table, holds it there for a moment, then lets it back down.

Shiv lifts her gaze from the napkin to the director. "None of them are *typical*."

She tries to explain that no matter how surreal they might be—no matter how far removed from what actually happened to Dec—they are more real to her than some of her violent outbursts while she's wide-awake.

Shiv exhales, tips her head back. The sky is perfectly clear but for the vapor trail of an aircraft, like an unseen hand sketching a chalk line across a pale blue page.

For the next few minutes they talk more generally about Shiv's life since Kyritos, especially about the effect of Declan's death on Mum and Dad.

"They're going to miss you, these next two months," Dr. Pollard says.

"You'd think so, wouldn't you?" Shiv doesn't dilute the sarcasm. She thinks of Mum, so absorbed in grief she barely registers Shiv from one day to the next. As for Dad, he'll be "working late" again tonight, or planning his next trip to Greece in his quest for "justice." "Actually, they can hardly bear to look at me anymore."

The director studies her, her expression unreadable.

"So it's good if I'm out of the way for a bit. You know? They don't have to keep being reminded that if wasn't for me, their son would still be alive."

"You believe what you wrote in your book? That you killed your brother?"

"Yes. I do."

"It's interesting," Dr. Pollard says.

"What is?"

"Just how emphatic you are about that."

"It's why we're *all* here, isn't it?" Shiv says. "Lucy's baby niece dies because she doesn't check on her; Mikey's sister drowns because he can't save her; Caron kills her best friend by giving her Ecstasy." She stops, thinking about the other two. Helen's father died in a skiing accident after she fell and he swerved to avoid her; Docherty crashed a car—his girlfriend didn't survive.

Dr. Pollard spreads her arms. "Yes, you are all here for the same basic reason. Each one of you believes you killed someone you loved."

"Believes."

"Believes."

"And, what, you're going to make us believe we didn't?"

The director says, "Let me take you back to the question I asked earlier: Why are you here? What do you hope to get from us, from your time at the Korsakoff Clinic?" She wants an *honest* answer this time, her tone says.

"Do you want to 'get well'?" she prompts, when Shiv doesn't respond. "Do you want to 'move on'? Do you want to return to being the girl you were before, the kind of girl everyone else expects you to be? Is that it?"

"No," Shiv says after a bit. "That's not why I'm here."

The woman nods. "Of course not."

Shiv places her hands on her thighs to stop them trembling. Her gaze drifts to the biscuit crumbs scattered on Dr. Pollard's plate, to the napkin, flapping again in the strengthening breeze. She gives an involuntary shudder, cold all of a sudden.

"So why are you with us, Siobhan?" the director asks. Gently.

It takes Shiv an age to get the words out but, finally she says, "Because if I can't find a way to live—" She breathes.

"What?"

Shiv starts over. "I'm here because I don't know how to live with what I did to Declan."

After a picnic lunch on the beach they still had almost three hours before Shiv and Dec were due back at the villa. Nikos suggested they'd windsurfed enough for one day and how about a trip to "the most special place" on the island? Shiv, who'd windsurfed enough for one *lifetime,* was quick to agree and, for all his bravado after being rescued, her brother raised no objection.

"Thank you," Shiv whispered to Nikos as they loaded the rigs in the pickup.

"For what?"

"For giving him an easy out."

"I'm a guy too, remember," Nikos whispered. "We don't like to lose face."

He drove inland, following a zigzag route into the hills. Only a 4x4 vehicle and a driver with a steady nerve could handle those gradients, those hairpin bends on steep drops into the valley below.

"And this is safer than windsurfing?" Shiv said over the roar of the engine.

"It is so long as I keep my eyes on the road," Nikos said, turning to grin at her.

"Nikos!"

He looked forward again, laughing, swinging the pickup into another sharp curve. As he changed gear, Nikos let his fingers brush against the outside of her bare leg. Fleeting, but it sent a jolt through her. She shot a glance at Declan, beside her, but he was oblivious, hanging his head out of the open window like a dog, his hair whipped by the wind. Yodeling, for some reason.

At the head of the valley the road leveled off. They were following the line of a ridge that ran beneath the craggy cliff of the summit. It was quieter now the engine no longer strained against the incline.

Declan pulled his head back inside the cabin.

"Yodeling?" Shiv asked. "This is Greece, not Switzerland."

"I wasn't yodeling, I was shouting hello to the goats."

"The *ghost?*"

"*Goats,* deafo." He stuck an arm out the window as though signaling a turn. With his free hand, he punched some buttons on the radio. "Does this work?"

A man speaking in rapid Greek competed against a fuzz of static; it might've been a ranting politician, a sports commentator, or an ad for cereal. Nikos adjusted the dial to pick up a music station. And so, as they bumped along the mountain ridge, they listened to some kind of Greek techno-punk.

From where they left the pickup it was only a thirty-minute hike into the ravine, mostly downhill, but beneath the furnace blast of a midafternoon sun they were soon soaked in sweat. The idea of falling off a windsurfer into the clear, cool sea no longer seemed so unappealing.

Nikos led them along a dried-up streambed, flanked on either side by steep, rock-strewn banks. The ground was parched, fissured, and their feet were coated with dust. Shiv paused to swig from the bottle of water Nikos passed round, shuttering her eyes against the bleached glare of the hillside.

"It's like the moon up here," Declan said.

To Shiv the land was biblical, a desert wilderness where a bush might burst into flames at any moment.

"We're almost there," Nikos said.

"Where?"

He smiled at her. "The place where we're going."

As he took the bottle back and raised it to his mouth, the sun caught the hairs on his forearm, making them glisten. Shiv watched his Adam's apple bob as he swallowed the water. Watched his moist lips as he lowered the bottle and replaced the cap. She longed to kiss him again. More than she'd ever wanted anything.

But how could she, with her brother right there?

"Lizard!" Dec said, pointing.

The creature was as big as a squirrel, sandy-gray tinged with yellow, basking on a boulder. Studying them with its swivelly eyes. Raised on its forelegs, the lizard looked as though they'd interrupted it in the middle of a set of push-ups.

"Stellion," Nikos said. "It means 'star'—see the patterns down its back." Then, after a pause, "Very nice in a kebab."

"You *eat* lizard?" Shiv said.

"Mmm, much tastier than baby turtle."

At which point Nikos let slip a smile and Shiv whacked him on the shoulder for making fun of her. If Declan noticed the intimacy of the gesture he gave no sign, too preoccupied with the lizard. When the creature tilted its head to one side, Dec did the same; when it raised one foot, as though waving, her brother waved back.

"I think he likes me." But when Declan turned back the lizard had gone, not even the parting flick of a tail to suggest it had ever been there.

"Come on." Nikos gestured up ahead. "Let's get moving before we burn up."

Not that it was apparent how they might escape the sun; as far as she could see, the dry terrain shimmered with heat haze. They rounded an outcrop of rock a little farther along, where their route left the dried-up stream and forked sharply downhill.

Instantly, the three of them plunged into the coolest, sweetest shade. Not only that, the landscape was transformed into an oasis of green—a long stripe of lush grass and overgrown trees where a cleft split the hillside like a rip in the flesh of a ripe fig.

"Wow!" Shiv said.

Nikos turned to smile. "Beautiful, isn't it? I call this my Shangri-la."

They paused, standing on grass as vivid as an English lawn. "How come it's so *green*?" Shiv asked.

"There's water underground. In the rock."

"An aquifer," Declan said.

"*Yes*." Nikos looked impressed. "Just here, the aquifer is close to the surface."

Nikos's Shangri-la was no more than a hundred meters long and ten or so wide, following the course of a V-shaped channel overhung with the trailing branches of the willowlike trees that grew there. He led them farther along to a point where the water surfaced, briefly, forming a miniature waterfall over a waist-high shelf of rock.

"It's magical," Shiv said.

"Actually, it is. Even when there has been no rain on the island for months and everywhere is like dust, the water, the trees, the grass—they are still here."

They sat on the grass beside the small pool which fed the waterfall. Nikos removed his sandals and dangled his bare feet in the water, letting out an exaggerated sigh of bliss. Shiv and Dec dangled their feet too. The pool was only shin-deep but shockingly, deliciously cold. Shiv closed her eyes, let a smile spread across her lips.

"Now," Nikos said, "we lie back and watch the sky. The sky is the other reason I brought you to this place."

Nikos lay on his back, feet still in the pool. Shiv and Declan did the same. In a gap between the branches overhead, a swathe of cloudless sky hung blue and perfect. The three of them became still. All Shiv could hear was the miniature waterfall; all she could feel was the cool grass beneath her and the chill of her feet in the pool.

"Keep looking," Nikos told them. "She will come if we are patient."

"Who will?" Dec asked. But Nikos shushed him.

At last, a bird appeared, tracking left to right—not flying but gliding, a long, slow arc, its wings outstretched, head dipped. Dark grayish-brown with a lighter head, throat and belly. It was close enough to the ground for Shiv to make out black markings around the eyes and a rich cinnamon-red tinge on the breast. The largest bird she'd ever seen.

"What is it?" she whispered.

But Nikos shushed her, as though anxious that her words might scare the bird away. It *did* disappear momentarily, then wheeled back into view—higher than before, spiraling down from one thermal to the next. For several minutes, the creature circled above, diamond-shaped tail stark against the blue, putting on a majestic display as though just for the three of them. It let out a shrill, wavering cry that resounded off the hillsides.

Shiv watched, bewitched, almost forgetting to breathe.

Only once the huge bird had gone did she dare to speak again. "That was . . ."

"Too much for words," Nikos said.

"Yeah." Shiv smiled to herself.

After a moment's silence, Nikos asked, "You know this bird?"

"I do," Declan said. His voice came from a little way off, surprising her. She eased up onto her elbows to locate him—perched up a tree, in the crook of two branches. Shiv hadn't heard him move from the grass beside her, so engrossed was she by the circling bird. Dec was dropping twigs one after another into the pool and watching them drift over the waterfall. "Vulture," he said.

Shiv laughed. "Yeah, right. Like you know anyth—"

"Quite a rare vulture, actually," Nikos said. "A lammergeyer."

Shiv looked at him, incredulous. "But vultures are . . ."

"Are what?" Nikos had sat up and was smiling at her.

"I don't know. Horrible. Ugly."

"Why horrible?"

"Because they just *are*—because they eat dead things."

"And you don't?" His tone was gentle, teasing but not nasty.

"Okay, yeah, but—"

"And 'ugly'?" He gestured at the sky, as though the vulture was still there, performing its entrancing aerial display. "You thought she was *ugly*?"

Shiv fell quiet. Then, after a moment, "No. No, she was . . . beautiful."

A ballad played on the radio as they drove down from the mountain. The female singer's tone was sweetly melancholic, the voice of a broken heart.

"What's she saying?" Shiv asked.

Nikos raised the volume. "It's about a girl whose boy has gone forever." He listened some more. "She's saying, 'The hole alongside me in our bed is the . . . grave you dug to bury my heart . . . Tell me, please, do I fall'—no, 'climb'—'should I climb in the grave or live all my days with a hole in my breast where my heart was?' "

Her brother, beside her, failed to stifle a giggle.

"Shut *up*," Shiv said, jabbing him with her elbow.

Over the next lines of the song, Declan half sung, half said, "My breasts, my poor heartless breasts that once were twin moons orbiting the planet of your love."

"*Declan.*"

"And these eyes, without your face to gaze upon . . . I shall pluck them from their sockets and feed them to the dogs of grief who howl for your return."

Dec could barely sing for laughing. Nikos was laughing

too, running with her brother's riff. "My hair, shiny as silk with your fingers' touch will turn to . . . to . . ."

"Rope," Declan said.

"For me to hang myself—"

"From the gibbet of my despair."

"Piss *off*," Shiv said. "*Both* of you. This is a lovely song and you've totally ruined it." But she was laughing along with them. "Was that even true?" she asked Nikos. "Those lines you translated before Dec joined in?"

Nikos shrugged. "I've no idea. She's singing in Albanian."

EIGHT

"I sculpted your head in Make today," she tells Declan. "Started to, anyway. Some kind of modeling clay—dead easy to work with. They gave us these plastic scalpels, but you could do most of it with your fingers." She pulls a face. "Smelly, though—catch a whiff of that." She raises her hands to the picture on her bedroom wall. "And that's *after* I had a shower."

Dec just goes on standing there, his expression unchanged, offering an apple to the goat in the olive grove behind the villa.

"I haven't started on your face yet," she goes on. "Well, I *did*. Spent ages on your nose, then gave up and just squished it back in." She presses her thumb against his nose in the photo. "You have a very *difficult* nose, Declan Richard Faverdale."

Shiv has taken to doing this, lately—chatting to the nighttime projections of her brother. Telling him all about her day. Letting him know how she's getting on. With her voice kept low so as not to disturb Caron and Helen in the rooms on either side, Shiv's monologues remind her of the whispery conversations she and Declan had in the dark when they were still small enough to share a bedroom.

"Hey, it was *Day Ten* today," she says. "One-sixth of the way through. That's somewhere between ten and twenty percent, I reckon."

It was a standing joke between them that Shiv is rubbish at maths—always asking his help with homework, even though she was three school years above him. One time, when he was going through some geometry revision with her, Declan said,

"You know what *rhomboid* means, right?"

"Yeah, *durr*," Shiv replied, "it's a creature from the planet Rhomb."

Day Ten. Nine days of Walk, Make, Talk and Write, and one day off (most of which Shiv spent catching up on sleep or playing table tennis with Caron).

It's okay here. Kind of. She has taken Dr. Pollard's advice about losing herself in the activities. And, in a way, she has "found" Declan. Or he has found her. Through the walking meditation, the drawing and sculpting, the nighttime conversations, the speaking, the things she writes, Shiv is so immersed in her brother these days he is more of a presence in her life than an absence.

"I like spending time with him," she admits at her latest one-to-one.

"But?" Dr. Pollard asked.

"What d'you mean?"

"I felt a 'but' coming on. I could see it in your eyes."

Shiv went to deny it, then stopped herself. "I don't know, just . . . it isn't *right*."

"What isn't?"

"For one thing, it isn't real—me and Dec. And anyway, I don't deserve him."

"What *do* you deserve, Siobhan?"

"I don't deserve to forget he's dead. Even for a moment."

"I asked what you do deserve, not what you don't."

"I deserve not to be forgiven."

Whatever, the clinic must be doing something right because she hasn't smashed anything—or wanted to—in about a week.

She has never felt as close to her brother as she does right now.

"I spoke again at Talk today," she tells Dec. "I filled *four pages* at Write."

Shiv studies his outstretched arm, the apple resting on the flat of his palm.

Each night, without fail, her brother appears on the wall. A different one every time: Dec doing a handstand on the beach, Dec eating a slice of pizza, Dec poised at the end of a springboard, Dec bouncing a yellow tennis ball . . .

Caron talks to her pictures as well. In the dead of night, Shiv has heard her through the wall, murmuring to the girl—Melanie—whose life she took with the gift of one tiny pill.

"What d'you say to her?" Shiv asked one time.

"I tell her how sorry I am and how much I miss her. Or I just cry."

To begin with, the images upset Shiv, too. Now she looks forward to them. She likes this one. Dec looks natural, unposed; so intent on the goat he doesn't seem to realize he's being photographed.

When she's done taking him through her day, she fills him in on the others.

"Lucy binged again at dinner tonight," Shiv says. "Then someone heard her making herself sick in the toilet." She describes how Caron went to see if her buddy was okay and brought the girl out, pale and tearstained.

If Dec has an opinion about this, he keeps it to himself. Same when she tells him that Helen has started chanting under her breath during Walk.

He just goes on offering that apple to the goat.

Shiv tells him about Mikey making a formal request to be discharged.

"No sign of him at Buddy Time, of course," Shiv says. She has no idea where he goes between Write and dinner. He doesn't turn up in the rec room either, and her attempts to befriend him at mealtimes and Break are met with monosyllables, if he bothers to speak at all. "Caron reckons I should leave it," she says. "But I can't just give up on him, you know? There's a good kid buried inside him, somewhere."

She looks at Declan. "What d'you think?"

An enigmatic half smile. The apple fell to the ground when the goat went for it—her brother flinched at the last second for fear of getting bitten. She searches for signs of nervousness in the photo but he appears calm and unafraid.

"Remember the windsurfing? You acted like you weren't scared when Nikos had to rescue you, but I knew you were." Shiv wants to ask if he thought he was going to die at that moment. And the other time too, of course. But she can't bring herself to put it into words. "You were so *happy* that day, Dec. We both were."

She catches herself tracing a fingertip in her palm in slow circular caresses, just as Nikos did on the beach that day when her hand was grainy with sand. She stops.

Nikos. She doesn't let herself think about him anymore.

Shiv rubs her face, sits a little more upright to avoid dozing off. It wouldn't be the first time she's fallen asleep in front of Dec's picture and woken there hours later—cold, stiff-necked—as dawn seeps through the curtains.

"In the woods this morning . . . ," she begins, whispering, shutting out memories of Nikos and returning her attention to Declan. "Was that *you*?"

She glimpsed white in the woods at Walk. A shirt? A boyish figure? Closer than the other sightings (that first evening, by the rhododendrons, and a couple of times since), but it was gloomy under the canopy of leaves and it might have been nothing more than a flash of daylight between the trees.

"*Was* it you?"

Shiv rests her fingertips lightly against Declan's face and strokes his cheek—gently, as though afraid of smudging his features.

The projector shuts off just then and she is left sitting in the dark.

Her brother is everywhere.

Even in the dining room a few hours later, she's reminded of him at the breakfast buffet. In hotels, guesthouses and self-service restaurants, Dad and Dec would compete to bring the biggest haul of food to the table, then see who finished first. Dec usually won that one—even if it meant cramming an entire croissant in his mouth or almost choking on a sausage he tried to gulp down whole, in the style of a sword swallower. As for those egg-cup-sized glasses of fruit juice you get in B&B breakfast rooms, her brother's record was twenty-nine at one sitting.

"Gluttony is not a sin," he would say. "It is an art form."

Shiv takes her tray of food to the seating area—the tables are separated out for breakfast—and is about to join Caron and Lucy when she spots Mikey (by himself, predictably) in the far corner. She heads over there instead, mouthing a "sorry" to the two girls and earning a don't-know-why-you-bother look from Caron.

Mikey is sitting with his back to the room, shoulders hunched, fists clenched on the table as though gripping an invisible knife and fork.

"Mind if I join you?" Shiv says, sliding into the seat opposite. It's only now that she sees he's crying—soundlessly, great tears rivering down his face.

"*Mikey,* what's wrong?"

Shiv sets her tray down, unloads toast, grapefruit juice; reaches for his hand, then thinks better of it. She has seen him angry and agitated and impatient; she's seen him sullen and silent and withdrawn. But this is the first time she's seen him upset.

He raises his eyes to hers. He has no food in front of him, nothing. Just his bunched fists. His injuries from bashing his head against the tree are mostly healed—just a notch in one eyebrow and a reddish patch of skin on his forehead. From the expression on his face you'd think he has never seen Shiv before. Then, as though pulling her into focus, his gaze hardens and she braces herself for another rejection.

What he says, though, is "They won't let me leave."

His discharge request; he must've just heard the news. "I thought Dr. Pollard said she'd let your mum and step-dad decide?" Shiv says.

"They said no. They said I have to stick it out till I'm *better*."

Mikey wipes his face on his cuff. Turns toward the window. It's raining this morning, fat droplets of water patterning the glass. They'll be having Make inside the Portakabin. Would *her* parents let her leave, if she really wanted to? She has no idea. Mikey goes on staring out the window. Shiv eats her toast. Waits. Maybe he'll speak, maybe he won't.

Eventually, he says, "This place does my head in. Everyone's so *nice*." He faces her again, back in angry mode. "Everyone wants to be my *friend*."

"Do they?" Shiv can't help laughing. "I thought it was only me."

The next two days—Good Friday and Holy Saturday—Nikos couldn't see Shiv. Among Greeks, he explained, these were family days. He hoped she understood.

"You're not prepared to abandon your culture, your religious customs, your entire family," Shiv joked, "to spend time with an English girl you only just met?"

"I guess I'm just a total bastard."

"All guys *are*," Shiv sighed, affecting a world-weary air.

At which point they kissed again. Tricky, because Nikos was driving the pickup and the nearside wheels scuffed along the verge.

"Hey!" This was Declan, thumping on the roof.

Nikos had finally relented and let him ride in the back, with the windsurf rigs, for the last few kilometers of their descent from the mountain. It gave them some privacy, of course—a chance to talk, to hold hands, to swap mobile numbers, to *kiss,* without her brother knowing. She suffered a tug of guilt over Dec being kept out of their way like that, the unwanted kid brother. Not that *he* felt excluded—he sounded like he was having the best time ever back there.

When Nikos dropped them off in the lay-by at the end of the track leading to the villa, the reality of two whole days without him clenched a fist inside her chest.

"Sunday," he'd whispered as they said their goodbyes. *"Kalo Pascha."*

"Happy Easter," according to the phrase book.

Their plan was for Shiv to fix it so her family went to the Easter festivities in the largest of the villages on that stretch of coast. Hundreds of people would be there, and it ought to be easy for them to slip off by themselves for a while unnoticed.

If he thought it odd that a (supposedly) seventeen-year-old girl wasn't free to go where, and with whom, she pleased, he kept it to himself. Shiv had been sure to let him know just how strict Mum and Dad were—better for him to believe this than to suss the truth about her age. Or have him turn up at the door like a regular boyfriend.

"My parents are the same with my sister," he said.

All Shiv had to do now was persuade an atheist mother, agnostic father and spiritually comatose brother to watch the Greeks celebrate Jesus's resurrection.

For the next couple of days, the Faverdales slipped back into holiday routine: balcony, pool, terrace, beach, taverna. Shiv took care not to mention Nikos, except to answer—disinterestedly—any questions Mum or Dad asked about the windsurfing excursion. She didn't need to say all that much, as Dec said enough for both of them.

Her brother planned to take up windsurfing in time for the next Olympics.

"As well as emigrating to Greece to run boat cruises, or instead of?" Dad asked.

Dec answered sulkily, "As well as."

Then Mum chimed in, "Is windsurfing actually an Olympic sport?"

Shiv kept *her* excitement buried. The pleasure of their day out coursed through her like a slow-release drug, his kisses lingering on her lips as though they'd been brushed by butterfly wings. And while they couldn't meet again till Sunday, they could at least send texts—silly, funny messages, or sometimes just an X or a smiley—and twice, Shiv managed the briefest of whispered conversations.

Every minute of every hour, Nikos pulsed through her mind or ached inside her or prickled her skin or thudded her heart against her ribs.

She was *sick* with him. With longing. With missing.

Predictably, after forty-eight hours of doing very little, Dad proposed an outing for the next day. Just as predictably, Declan groaned. Shiv made a play of groaning too.

"Suggestions?" Dad said, ignoring their protests.

They were on the dining terrace, the evening air lemony with the scent of the candles Mum had lit to deter mosquitoes. From the olive grove beyond the garden, the cicadas laid down their nightly sound track.

"Oh, I don't mind," Mum said. "What haven't we done on our to-do list? In fact, where *is* our to-do list?"

"To do," Dec said, miming the writing of a note. "One, find the to-do list—"

"There's that fort we talked about going to." This was Dad. He liked forts, castles, that sort of thing. "Dec?"

"What?"

"Your thoughts."

"My thoughts on forts?"

Mum reappeared with the to-do list. "What about the turtle sanctuary?"

"Easter Sunday," Dad said. "It'll be shut." Then, turning to Shiv, "Any ideas?"

"There's a boy in my class who can light his own forts," Declan said.

Shiv laughed. Dad just gave him a look.

"Sorry," her brother said, "my mouth's still learning to type."

"Actually," Shiv said, "I saw something in the thingy." She pointed indoors. "You know, the information folder."

"What was that, then?" Dad headed inside to fetch the folder and Shiv called after him, "It's the red-egg game, or something like that."

"Red-*egg* game?" he called back, laughing.

"So." Declan clapped his hands. "Looks like we're off to the fort, yeah?"

When their father reappeared, flipping through the folder, Shiv said, "It's a bit like conkers, apparently, only with hard-boiled eggs."

"Red ones," Dec said.

"Yes. Red ones." Shiv mock-scowled at him. Then, addressing Dad again, "There's a picture somewhere—in the bit about festivals."

"Hey, you're right." He sounded suitably surprised. "'*Tsougrisma,* or the red-egg game. A traditional part of the Easter festivities here on Kyritos, it is played using eggs dyed red to symbolize the blood of Christ. . . . Participants play against each other in pairs, taking turns to knock the tip of their hard-boiled egg against their opponent's until one of the shells cracks. The victor goes through to the next round and so on until there is an overall winner. That person is destined to have a year of good luck.'"

"When is this?" Mum asked.

"Tomorrow, in . . . where is it . . . ah yes, Lackanack-athon." The village wasn't called that—it was the name Dec had invented after they visited the beach there, and whose real name was unpronounceable. "Anyone can watch or join in," Dad went on. "And"—reading aloud again—"'the Easter Sunday festivities also include lamb roasts, music, dancing, fireworks and devotional rites such as the burning of Judas.'"

"The burning of *Judas*?" her brother said, eyes lit up. "Oh, *please* tell me they sacrifice an actual villager."

Dad ignored this remark. "So, who votes for the fort . . . and who votes for red eggs in Lackanackathon?"

"*Whoa,*" her brother said. "Four-nil win for Shivolop-poulos!"

The beach was unrecognizable from their previous visit. Where there had been sun-loungers, there were rows of people sitting on benches in front of an open-air altar. Beyond the altar, a tall pole with a dangling Judas effigy had been planted in the sand.

With nerves knotting her stomach, Shiv located the stage at one end of the beach, behind which she would—somehow—sneak off for her rendezvous with Nikos.

In front of the stage, scores of picnic tables formed a U around a dance floor of wooden panels laid directly on the ground. To one side, eight, nine, *ten* carcasses roasted on spits above barbecue pits, tended by chefs in soot-stained white shirts. The air was dense with smoke and the aroma of cooked meat.

"Lamb of God and all that." This was Dad. "Apparently, the Greeks—"

"Factoid alert," her brother whispered.

"Shush," Mum said, "the service is starting."

They shuffled in among the tourists standing at the back of the congregation as a black-frocked priest began to speak. The service went on for what seemed like *hours*. Shiv spent most of it scanning the backs of heads for Nikos and wondering if she could text him without Mum and Dad noticing. She'd hoped to have spotted him by now, and the doubts crept up on her after another day, another night, apart.

Who knew what Nikos was thinking, caught up with his family all this time? Why hadn't he replied to the text she'd sent this morning?

At last, the priest brought the worship to a close. Raising both hands, he declared, *"Christos Anesti! Alithos Anesti!"*

"Christos Anesti!" the congregation responded. *"Alithos Anesti!"*

Declan tugged out the phrase book and thumbed it open.

But before he could make up some daft translation, the priest extended his arms and—in fractured English—said, "Christ is risen! Truly He is risen!"

"Spot on," Dec said, snapping the book shut. "This guy knows his stuff."

She'd never felt like this about anyone. Less than a week ago she didn't even know Nikos existed, and now it was as though he was the only thing that did. The pain of wanting to see him and the dread that he wouldn't come combined to torture her.

They were sitting at one of the tables, cardboard plates loaded with roast lamb, salad and bread. Shiv's was untouched, with Declan already casting covetous glances. Around them, the din of chat and laughter.

Under the table she checked her phone. No messages.

"I wouldn't mind wandering up to the church in a bit," Dad said, pointing at an ancient-looking white building perched on a hill overlooking the village.

Mum was the only one to show any enthusiasm. Dec was too busy eating.

The red eggs were ceremonially produced after lunch and distributed among the revelers. Most people took one, Greeks and foreigners alike—Dad and Declan included. What followed was too confusing for Shiv to make sense of, but at some point, her brother and father returned, defeated, and eventually a winner was declared, the master of ceremonies holding his arm aloft as if he were a champion boxer.

Shiv had paid little attention to the tournament, too distracted by the musicians setting up their equipment on the stage.

"You okay?" Mum had said while it was just the two of them.

"What? Oh, yeah. Fine."

Mum rummaged in her bag. "Here." She smiled sympathetically, placing two painkillers in front of Shiv. Her coded way of saying *Time of the month?*

"Thanks," Shiv managed to say, going along with the misunderstanding. Then, blinking away the tears, flapping a hand in front of her face, "Eugh, smoke."

"Do you have any—"

"Yeah, yeah." Shiv indicated her bag, down by the side of her seat. Then, with Mum studying her, she popped the pills in her mouth and swallowed them.

"Headache?" This was Dad, suddenly reappearing at the table, Declan in tow.

Before Shiv could reply, there was an announcement over a loudspeaker and, onstage, the musicians started to play.

"Can I help burn Judas?" Declan pointed toward the pole, where twenty or so children were being organized to fetch wood from a nearby stack to make a bonfire.

"You don't want to see the church, then?" Dad said, pretending to be serious.

Dec pulled a face.

"Okay, then. Shiv?"

She looked at her father. "What?"

"Mum and I are heading up to look at the church," he said. "You coming?"

"I might just watch the dancing," she said. "I don't feel too good, actually."

She saw her mother mouth *PMS* at Dad.

"Oh. Oh, right."

Mum told Shiv to sit where she could see the stage and keep an eye on Dec at the bonfire building. "See you back here," she said. "We won't be gone too long."

And so Declan and their parents headed off in different directions. Shiv ought to have been delighted at the

123

stroke of luck in losing all her family at once, but by now she'd convinced herself that Nikos wouldn't be waiting for her.

All the same, she slipped out from the table and picked a route through the crowds toward the rear of the stage.

NINE

It's a stiff pull to the high ground beyond the copse at the rear of Eden Hall. Worth it, though, for the view across the valley. Forested hills lie in all directions, so you can almost imagine yourself back in a landscape from the time before humans.

Shiv sits down. Her breathing steadies. Green is meant to be good for you, she recalls, gazing out over the countryside—soothing for the spirit. Lying back on the grass, she shuts her eyes, sleepy and a little weepy after Write, setting down page after page about Declan. The whole reason for coming up here was to leave him behind for a bit. She visualizes a locker, her thoughts of her brother as so many school books scattered on the floor. Pictures herself picking them up one by one, stowing them away in the locker, closing the door and snapping the lock shut.

It's an *old-style* counseling technique, not Korsakoff method.

With each passing day, Shiv finds herself more confused by the contradictions between the two therapies, old and new. The previous counselor encouraged Shiv to separate herself from Declan, but it didn't help at all; if anything, it made her worse. This place, which *is* helping, wants her to fill every minute of every day with him. Which is all very well, but when she eventually checks out of the clinic and returns to her *real* life, Dec won't be there. He won't be anywhere.

Shiv drops off. Not that she's aware of doing so, only of waking up afterward. Gummy-mouthed, panicky. It's okay. Checking her watch, she sees there's still time to hike back down and freshen up before dinner.

She stands up. Yawns. Stretches. Glances up to see a figure at the end of the ridge. The Declan-like boy. He is descending the slope at the back of the escarpment, oblivious to her.

Too late, she calls out, "Hey! Hey, wait!"

But he is lost from view over the brow. Without a thought, she follows him.

Over the ridge the ground drops to an area of woodland. The boy has already entered—she can make out his white shirt between the trees. Again, she calls, but the breeze whips the words from her mouth so that she can barely hear them herself.

In the woods the ground is choked with ferns and brambles. She pauses to call again, seeking another glimpse of him. Nothing. Just trees and more trees. Venturing deeper, forcing her way through the undergrowth, she heads first this way, then that. But he has vanished. Even so, Shiv presses on into the heart of the woods.

Catches herself yelling, "Declan! Dec, where are you?"

Close to tears, breathless, Shiv finally gives up. She looks around to get her bearings and figure out a route back to the ridge—but this part of the woods looks much the same as any other. She is lost.

Idiot. Stupid, stupid idiot.

On all sides, the towering trees stand in silence, like troops waiting for Shiv to issue orders. She picks a direction at random.

The woods must connect with the ones she knows from Walk because Shiv eventually finds herself on the bark-chip trail that leads to the Make area.

Good. She isn't lost anymore.

She hears a grunt, a little way off. Fox? Badger? There it is, along with scuffles of movement, of *exertion,* that mark the sounds as human. Curious, Shiv follows the trail toward the Break clearing. Entering the glade, creamy in the early evening light, she doesn't see anyone.

Then—Mikey.

He's wearing his yellow jumpsuit, standing hands on hips at the base of the steep mud bank that runs along one edge of the clearing. He has his back to her and is breathing heavily. He bends down to grapple with something at his feet—a sawn-off chunk of tree trunk, big as a car tire, which he raises with a grunt. The log clutched tightly into his midriff, he sets off up the slope, legs bent, straining with each clumsy step. She's sure he'll drop the log or stumble to his knees, but he makes it all the way to the top of the bank and lets the log thud to the earth.

After a moment to recover, he stoops to pick up the log and sets off back down the slope.

"Mikey." She's waited till he's at the bottom.

He spots her across the clearing and glares. "What're *you* doing here?"

"I was about to ask you the exact same thing."

He's drenched in sweat, hands torn and blistered, twitching. He must've been up and down that hill quite a few times.

"Sisyphus," Shiv says.

"What?"

"The guy who had to keep rolling a rock up a hill. In Greek mythology, yeah?"

Mikey clearly has no idea what she's talking about.

They're sitting on a felled tree at the edge of the clearing. She starts to explain how she came to be here—the hike, then getting lost in the woods, but not about the boy—but Mikey doesn't seem interested. Was it him she saw up on the ridge? No. He's been here for a while, as far as she can tell; besides, he's wearing a blue T-shirt and yellow jumpsuit, not white.

Her eyes are drawn to his hands again. She points. "They must hurt."

"A bit," he says, looking at his hands as though they don't belong to him.

"A bit of a bit, or a lot of a bit? Or a lot of a lot?"

He plays along. "A bit of a lot."

"That wasn't one of the options."

Mikey gives her a look.

"For a second there, I thought you were going to crack a smile," Shiv says.

"You thought wrong, then."

After a pause, she taps her watch. "Technically, it's still Buddy Time. You're meant to be nice to your buddy."

"You ain't my—"

"Yeah, yeah, you already said. I *could* be, though—if you'd let me. Cos, I dunno, it must be bloody lonely being you, Mikey."

He goes to speak, then falls quiet. His grubby blond hair is tousled, his face paler than ever in the gathering dusk; his eyes give no clue to his feelings. She knows that Mikey wouldn't hesitate to get up and leave or tell her to sod off. That he does neither, she takes as a good sign.

She wants to fill the silence but can't think what to say for the best. Talking to Declan could be like verbal chess; with Mikey it's more like a game of tetherball.

She gestures at the surrounding woods. "Dec loved to climb trees."

"Your brother?"

"He was like a monkey."

Mikey just nods, studying his tremulous hands.

"Without the tail, though, obviously," she adds, giving him a sidelong look. "And not so hairy. And he *hated* bananas."

A definite smile this time; he turns away to hide it. She lets another hush settle, not wanting to push. Mikey folds his arms, shoves a hand in each armpit and clamps them to his sides; leans forward, then back again, sets up a rocking motion.

She wants to tell him to stop, but she says nothing.

Eventually, he becomes still. "You know the rope pyramid—in playgrounds, yeah?" he says. "Feebs could climb right to the top of it when she was six."

He turns to look directly at her, as though daring her to disbelieve him. Shiv nods, tries to appear suitably impressed. She *is* impressed—when *she* was six years old, she cried if Mum pushed her too high on the swings.

"What color hair did Phoebe have?"

He goes on staring. Suspicious. "Brown, like Mum's. Sort of wavy."

"Was she pretty?"

"Pretty? She was my *sister*."

Shiv changes tack. "What did she like to do? What was she into?"

Mikey thinks about that. "Sylvanian Families," he says. "She used to play with them in her room for hours." He starts to explain but Shiv interrupts to say that she collected the little animal dolls too. "The squirrels were her favorites," he says.

"I made houses for mine out of old shoe boxes," Shiv says.

Feebs didn't do that. "She got too grown-up for them in the end," he says. *In the end.* When she was nine, he means. By the time she died. "So she *said*," he adds. "She kept them hidden in the bottom of the wardrobe in case her friends came round after school." He smiles. "But I knew she still played with them sometimes."

Feebs was the fastest girl in Year 5; a better runner than most of the boys, too. The best in her class at maths. She got a merit in her Grade 1 piano.

Shiv listens. Nods, smiles.

Mikey hasn't spoken about his sister at Talk; has broken the silence just once, to rant at Assistant Sumner about what a waste of time Talk is. Some of the others resent him for it: *We speak, why should he be any different?* Shiv wishes she could've recorded what he just said and play it back to everyone. *See, he is the same as us.*

Shiv could easily set herself in opposition to the whole regime here, as he has done. Detach herself. Give in, smash things, lash out. But she doesn't want to be that person anymore. She doesn't want Mikey to be either.

"I almost got her." He mimes grabbing something, his messed-up hands raised like a pair of monstrous paws. Then, shaking his head, as though a wasp is bothering him, "I *should've*. I should've held on to her."

With a bit of prompting, he tells Shiv about the river. How it was Dazza's idea to wade out to the island but that didn't count for shit cos Mikey was meant to be watching out for Feebs and he ought to have said no to Daz. Or just told Feebs to stay put. Not to follow them. Cos him and Daz, the water only came up to here—he does a karate-chop motion at his belly—but with Feebs it was right up to her armpits.

"And the current . . ."

Mikey can't finish. He doesn't need to.

Shiv can picture it as clearly, as horribly, as if she was there on the riverbank, watching a nine-year-old girl with wavy brown hair losing her footing, being swept away, shrieking, her brother diving after her, grabbing hold of her arm with both hands . . . but not strong enough. Nowhere near strong enough. Pictures him clutching at nothing as the fast-flowing water carries Feebs off, then under. Did he swim after her? Did he almost drown trying to find her, pull her to the surface, save her?

She imagines he did.

Maybe that's what the log was all about—hauling it up and down the hill to prove his strength; the strength that wasn't enough when he really needed it. Or he was *punishing* himself for failing to save her.

She thinks of how Declan died. Her part in it. Her failure.

"*You're* not s'posed to cry over Feebs," Mikey says, looking oddly at her.

Shiv wipes her face. "No, I know. Sorry."

He goes on studying her before shifting his gaze again. Toward the base of the hill, the log on its side where he left it. For a moment, she thinks he's about to go over there and carry it up the slope once more.

"It's all over in a few seconds, isn't it?" Shiv says quickly. "They're there, and then they're not—and you can't ever have those seconds back. That moment when you could've made things turn out differently."

Mikey won't meet her gaze; she can tell she has his attention, though. She starts to explain what happened the night Declan died but he cuts in.

"I know. It was on the news."

Shiv shakes her head. "What they said on TV and in the papers—" She breaks off. Tells him the true version—the one where she's to blame.

They are silent afterward. She checks her watch; late for dinner, but so what? She could go on sitting with him like this for ages—until it's cold and dark and they'd merge into the gloom of the woods as surely as if they were draped beneath a cloak of invisibility.

"We should go back," she says reluctantly. "Before they send a search party."

Mikey frowns, as though only vaguely aware that someone is speaking to him.

"They didn't find her for two days," he says. "Some bloke fishing spotted her—nowhere near where she went in." He sniffs, swallows. "First off he thought it was a dead dog. 'Swhat he said. A dead dog floating in the water."

That night in her sleep she is in the woods near Aunt Rosh's place, with Dec. They've run on ahead of the adults, scouting for trees to climb.

It starts off as an actual memory from two summers ago: Declan picking out a large sycamore and making it almost to the top before panic sets in. Shiv has already scrambled back to the ground and is gazing uselessly up into the canopy. He doesn't call for help—just clings to a high branch that bows with his weight, like he's in a trance.

When the others catch up, Shiv expects Dad to kick straight into action, or Aunt Rosh, the athlete, but before either of them grasps the situation, Mum has shrugged off her rucksack and is hauling herself up the tree.

"I'm coming, Dec. You just hold on tight as you can and I'll be right there."

Positioning herself below Declan, Mum reassures him, coaxes, reaches up to guide first one foot, then the other to a lower branch—again and again, all the way down to the ground. Where Dec stands stock-still, face bleached with shock, while their mother tidies his clothes and hair, like getting mussed up is the worst of it.

In her dream, though, things happen differently.

Shiv is the one on the high branch, not Declan. The tree sways in the wind and an icy, numbing rain lashes down and—bizarrely, impossibly—there are no lower branches by which she might climb back down. Or by which anyone might clamber up to rescue her.

Worse, two large dogs prowl around the base of the tree, lean as timber wolves—baying dementedly, waiting for her to fall.

"I could've *died*," Declan said that evening, back at Aunt Rosh's.

Dad shook his head. "Not today, Dec. It wasn't your turn."

Nikos wasn't there.

It was private, at least—nobody to witness her humiliation. A cool space, shaded by the trees that fringed this end of the beach, and screened off from the Easter festivities by a huge billboard at the rear of the temporary stage. The ground was strewn with cans, food wrappers, cigarette butts and stinking debris (bits of plastic and rope, driftwood, seaweed) dumped by the tide. A rusted oil can. A used condom. With no one to mock her, their meeting place had taken on the task. Along with the jaunty music and the sounds of dancing and singing.

He stepped out from among the trees.

If he hadn't smirked, she might not have hit him so hard in the shoulder. If he hadn't tried to grab her hand, she might not have wrenched herself free and stormed off.

How *dare* Nikos just turn up like that—late, looking so pleased with himself?

How *dare* he not notice she was upset, or understand why?

Shiv half walked, half jogged out of there. At the edges of her vision, blurred by tears, she saw people dancing, sitting at picnic tables, standing around chatting and laughing and having a good time—but they could all go to hell.

Nikos was coming after her, calling her name.

She kept going, jostling her way through the revelers outside the tavernas that fronted onto the beach. Blind to their glances, deaf to their comments. She broke free of the crowds at last, hurrying along one of the narrow passages that led back to the village square. After the gloom of the passageway, the plaza was drenched in sunlight.

Nikos finally caught up with her by what must once have been an ornamental fountain but which now stood dry, its stonework blotched and flaky.

"Shiv, please. Stop."

She wheeled round, shaking her wrist free from his grip. "Don't *touch* me."

"I don't get why you're angry with me." He sounded more out of breath than she did. He was wearing one of his basketball jerseys—the blue-and-white one—sweat pooling in the dent at the base of his throat, his chest heaving. "Was I so very late?"

"I thought you weren't *coming*," Shiv said. "And then you just stroll out of the trees with that stupid grin on your face, like everything's all right now you're here."

"I was grinning because I was pleased to see you."

Shiv refused to be mollified. "And why did we have to meet *there*?"

"Because nobody would see us," he said, shrugging. "Your parents."

"It stank. It was disgusting."

"Shiv—"

"I didn't see you *anywhere*." She gestured toward the beach. "You didn't even text or anything."

Nikos let out his breath, looking exasperated but trying not to show it. "You were with your family—I didn't think you'd be okay to check for messages."

She stood there, glaring at him, only just beginning to calm down. Why did he have to be so bloody reasonable? Tentatively, he stroked her bare arm.

"Shiv, please don't be like this."

Her immaturity struck her then. Her wrongness. How childish she must have seemed to him—crying, storming off, acting stroppy. And for what? He hadn't stood her up, or even been all that late, really. She'd simply got herself so convinced he wouldn't show that, when he *did* turn up, the relief overwhelmed her. Just then, the age gap between them seemed greater than ever.

"God," she groaned, "you must think I'm such an idiot."

He smiled. He hadn't shaved and his teeth looked so white against the dark stubble. "What I think," he said, flexing his shoulder, "is you punch *really* hard."

He took her to a café down a shady side street. A sanctuary from the blistering sun. They sat at one of the tables lining the pavement, sipping black coffee from tiny cups.

"You like it?" Nikos asked as Shiv set hers back in its saucer.

"Mm," she said, trying not to grimace. She'd never tasted anything so bitter.

"English people don't usually like our coffee."

"Yeah, well, it's not a skinny latte."

Shiv took another sip, hoping it might taste better than the first. It didn't. She glanced at the bottle of chilled water Nikos had ordered for them to share.

He unscrewed the cap and filled their glasses. "Go on, I won't be offended."

"Have I failed some kind of test?" she asked, smiling.

"Yes, absolutely."

She laughed; they both did. It was okay, being here with him like this. It was good. The scene behind the stage, Shiv running off, the quarrel in the square—all of it had begun to recede like an outgoing tide. The street was deserted; she and Nikos might've been sharing a table in a ghost town, the sole survivors of an apocalypse.

"Won't your folks wonder where you are?"

She told him where they'd gone but didn't mention that she was supposedly keeping an eye on Dec while he helped to build the bonfire. They fell quiet, settling into each other's company—learning how to *be* together.

"D'you miss home when you're away at uni?" she asked.

"Yes and no." He ran his finger up the condensation on the side of his water glass. "I like being here, but also I like going away again."

They talked about his life on the mainland—his studies, his friends, his part-time job in a bar, the things he missed about Kyritos. It wasn't a conversation Shiv could have with a boy at school. And though Nikos was talking about the difficulties of adjusting from island life to city life, the insecurity of living away from home for the first time, he seemed at ease with himself. It was a different confidence from the kind she was used to in guys her own age. Less showy, less needy of her approval.

"Will you move back after your degree?" Shiv asked.

"To Kyritos?" He thought for a moment. "I doubt it. Maybe I'll leave Greece altogether. No money, no jobs."

"But what about your family? Don't you—"

"They are my family, sure, but they aren't my life."

"I thought you were very close to them?"

"I am. But . . ." He left the thought incomplete.

"But what?"

"In such a close family—especially a big one—you are tied up in lots of little knots. Like a prison, but where everyone loves you and you have to love everyone back. And sometimes you just want to . . . *untie* yourself." He gave a shrug. "That's one reason I was happy to go to Thessaloniki."

"So where would you go next, if you could live anywhere in the world?"

"America." Plucking at his jersey. "All I need is to be twenty centimeters taller and I can play for the New York Knicks."

She laughed. Took a swig of water.

Leaning back in his seat, Nikos gave her a long, appraising look, a hint of a smile on his lips. She tried not to stare at him or let him see how sexy she thought he was. "What about you?"

"What about me?"

"Will you live in another country? *Would* you? The conditional tense," he said. "I think the English invented it to make foreigners seem stupid."

She smiled. "I don't think so. Live abroad, I mean."

"Why not?"

"I haven't really thought that far ahead." It was out before she realized.

Nikos rescued her. "Yeah, you have college first. Do you start in the autumn?"

Did she? If she was seventeen . . . "Yes. Yeah, in September."

"Oxford?" he asked, deadpan. "Or Cambridge? It must be so hard to choose."

Shiv stuck out her tongue. (Jesus, she *stuck out her tongue?*) "Depends on my grades—but no, neither of those." She was trying to recall a conversation she'd had with Laura's older sister. "I've applied to Leeds and Nottingham." Which led to a brief but hazardous discussion about why Leeds was her first choice, and what subject she'd study, and will (would) she have to get a part-time job as well, seeing as how expensive it was to go to university in England?

Shiv winged it. She hated deceiving him. But if you lie about your age, you have to lie about a load of other stuff as well.

"So, just a few months," Nikos said, "and you'll be leaving home."

"Yep." She tried to look excited and apprehensive all at once.

"Would you miss your family?"

"*Will* you."

Nikos frowned. "Will I miss your family?"

"No, it should be—" Then she saw he was making fun of her. She laughed. "Don't take this the wrong way, Nikos, but you really remind me of Dec sometimes. Same sense of humor."

He nodded. "I can see that."

"That's why he likes you."

"Maybe it's why *you* do too."

Shiv snorted. "I *like* you because you remind me of my *brother?*"

"I don't mean in that way. I mean . . ." Nikos frowned. "You and Dec seem like good friends. Like you'd hang out with him even if he wasn't part of your family."

"Yeah. Yeah, I would." She laughed, self-consciously. "Is that *weird?*"

"No, it's nice. It says you're an okay kind of person." Nikos tapped his chest. "In *here,* you know?"

"In my *lungs?*"

They laughed. Shiv wondered how his cheesy compliment managed to make her so warm inside.

"I bet he was *really* glad about visiting the church," Nikos said.

"Oh, no, it's just Mum and Dad—Dec stayed behind to help build the bonfire for the Judas thing. He'll have made about ten new friends by now."

After a pause, Nikos said, "You're going to miss him, I reckon."

"What?"

"When you go to college."

She lowered her gaze, drank more water. She would miss *Nikos.* It suddenly hit her—this was a holiday romance, doomed to end when she set foot on the plane in *five days.* He would return to uni after his brother's wedding and she'd go back to the UK; maybe there'd be texts and emails—Skype, even—but sooner or later it would fizzle out. Wasn't that how these things went? Anyway, she'd go back to being a *schoolgirl.* So even if they were still in touch by September, Shiv would have to explain why she wasn't starting university. Or go on lying to him, make up a fantasy life for herself in Leeds, Nottingham, wherever.

No. Today, these next few days, were all she could hope for with Nikos.

She shivered, as though a breeze had whisked along the street. "Do you have a girlfriend in Thessaloniki?"

She hadn't planned on asking the question—had known that she *shouldn't*—but blurted it out.

He took a moment, his eyes not leaving hers. "No," he said at last. "I did have, but not anymore." He continued to hold her gaze. "How about you?"

Shiv shook her head. "Same."

Just then, her bag buzzed, startling her. She pulled out her phone. "It's from Mum. They're leaving the church and heading back to the beach."

He checked his watch. "They'll be lighting the fire soon. There are fireworks later, once the sun goes down."

"I don't know if we'll be staying that long."

"I was hoping we could dance." Nikos finished his coffee.

"Tonight?"

"Just now, when we met. I was going to drag you out onto the dance floor—I won't care who saw us. *Wouldn't* care."

"You should've said something before I ran off."

She thought he was about to say she shouldn't have run off in the first place. But, indicating the deserted street, he said, "We could dance now. Right here."

Shiv laughed. "There's no music."

142

"Listen." In the quiet, the sounds of the band playing on the beach whispered a melody that floated through the village. "There," he said. "Music." He was out of his chair and drawing Shiv to her feet.

In a moment, they would head back toward the beach. They'd say their goodbyes—kiss for as long as they dared—before going their separate ways. Shiv would slip back into the Easter crowds and reach her seat at the picnic table, just in time to be there to greet her parents, hot and sticky from their long walk. When they asked where Dec was, she'd point to where her brother and some Greek kids (she imagined) played beach volleyball. They would ask if she was feeling better and she'd say yes, thanks.

All of that was to come, though. For now, there was just Nikos and an empty street and the ghosts of distant music.

TEN

Dinner has already begun. The supervisor takes one look at Mikey's injuries and orders him to see the nurse.

"Only if she comes with me," Mikey says, with a jerk of the head toward Shiv.

In the sick bay, he won't let Nurse Zena touch him, so Shiv gets the job of bathing his hands, using liquid soap and the softest of sponges.

"Go easy," Zena says as Shiv lowers the first hand into the warm water.

Mikey hisses, stiffening like he's been electrocuted, and fires off a volley of swear words. "Sorry, Mikey," Shiv says.

He stands rigidly, jaw clenched, trying so hard not to cry it's pitiful. The washing reveals the extent of the damage to his hands—swollen, scored with cuts and grazes, popped and unpopped blisters, flaps of shredded skin; like something from the gift shop in a horror museum.

"Sweet God," Zena says under her breath, "what've you done to yourself?"

The nurse sits him down with a soft towel on his lap and Shiv dries each hand as gently as if they were newborn babies. Strangely, given how much it's hurting him, Shiv finds it soothing. Pleasant. When she's finished, Mikey finally agrees to let Zena take over.

"You're not going to like the next bit," she tells him.

Shiv grips his shoulder but by the time the nurse is through with dabbing antiseptic on the wounds, Mikey has given up on holding back the tears.

The following morning, the familiar Wake-Up buzz on the intercom signals the end of another night's Shut Down. Shiv is dressed when Caron appears at her door, hair still damp from the shower, for their routine of heading down to breakfast together.

Caron gives the subtlest of nods along the corridor. *Meltdown,* she mouths.

Leaning out, Shiv sees a pile of stuff outside a door at the end. Desk, wooden chair, armchair, bedside table, lamp, sheet, duvet, pillows, curtains. Another item lands on the heap—a red vase, tossed out of an open doorway to spatter the wall with water and bits of flower. A moment later, a lightshade spirals through the air.

Mikey is struggling to shove the wardrobe across the room when Shiv and Caron appear in the doorway. The bandages on his hands are working loose, stained with blood.

"Hey, Mikey," Shiv says.

He gives her a nod. Gets back to work, even though the piece of furniture is too heavy for him. Apart from the bed and its stripped mattress, his room is bare.

"Need a hand with that, mate?"

Docherty. The commotion has drawn Lucy and Helen, too. Mikey says he can manage but Docherty eases past Shiv and Caron and takes hold of the other end of the wardrobe. The boys maneuver it through the doorway to join the rest of the stuff. Assistant Webb arrives just then, too late; all he can do is stand and look.

Caron surveys the room. "Nice one," she says. "Like a bloody prison cell."

Shiv nods. *"Exactly."*

At Walk, Shiv doesn't *try* to think about her brother. She has found that the surest way to let him enter her head is not to force things but to clear her mind, to think of nothing at all. To create a space for Dec to fill. Or not.

Crossing the rough pasture behind the main house, the single file of walkers still finding their rhythm, Shiv shutters her eyelids, leaving enough of a crack to see Caron's green boots directly in front. She shuts out everything else, synchronizing her footsteps with those of her friend. One by one, she lets the distractions surface: Mikey, stripping his room; his bandaged hands; the spider's-web tattoo on Docherty's elbow; the chafing of the jumpsuit against her skin; the smell of stale sweat from the Salinger T-shirt; an aftertaste of breakfast— each thought neatly parceled and set aside.

Her mind gradually empties of everything but the placing of one foot, then the next, on the ground, in time with the drawing of her breath.

Minute after minute after minute.

After a while, Dec is there. She's aware of his breathing, the scuffing of his (she pictures them) red Converses in the thick, dewy grass, feels his right hand in her left.

They *never* held hands that she can recall. Even as small children walking to primary school, Shiv would hold one of Mummy's hands, Dec the other.

Shiv wraps up this thought as well; removes it.

His grip is casual. Ironic. He is making a game out of holding her hand. *This is fun and we are unembarrassed.* Playing along, Shiv squeezes his fingers. *Don't worry, Dec, I've got you.* How she longs to give a sideways glance. She daren't, though—afraid that the touch of his skin, the swish of his feet, the whisper of his breaths, will disperse on the morning air like so many specks of pollen. Besides, she can't be certain which Declan it is:

The one in her memory.

The one in the images projected onto her wall each night.

The one she sometimes glimpses in the grounds of Eden Hall.

Worst of all would be to turn her head and see none of these three but the dead brother from her most terrible nightmares.

At some point near the end of Walk, he is gone. Shiv panics, has the urge to call his name—wonders if she actually *has.* But none of the others seems aware of her; they plod on, lost in their own worlds.

She tries (by *not* trying) to lure him back. No use. She wants him too much.

At Break on Day Thirteen, Shiv flops down on the ground beside Caron and watches Hensher make his circuit of the clearing, doling out water and granola bars.

When he reaches them, Caron, as usual, tries to wind him up.

"Assistant Hensher, can I ask you something about these snack bars?"

"Go on, then." He sounds resigned to his role as the butt of her daily joke.

"Are they made with hamster *food*—or the *scrapings* from their cages?"

"Scrapings," he says, deadpan.

"*Told* you." Caron nudges Shiv, as though they've had a bet.

"And it's rats," Hensher adds, "not hamsters." With that, he moves away.

Shiv looks at what she thinks of as Mikey's Hill. Not that he comes here anymore—when Dr. Pollard heard about the state of his hands from the log-hauling, she ordered him to be supervised during "free" time.

That suits him just fine. He wears the yellow jumpsuit all day—not just for Walk and Make. His prisoner's uniform, he calls it. The staff keep putting his room back the way it was but, each morning, he strips it bare.

"Are you trying to make them discharge you?" Shiv asked him one time.

He shook his head. "If they won't fix me, I'll fix myself."

As usual at Break, Mikey remains standing—turned away from them all on the far side of the clearing, hands behind his back, head bowed.

"What is it with him?" Caron asks, impatient.

"He thinks he should be punished, not treated. Says it's what we deserve."

"We?"

"Helen, Docherty, Lucy—you and me—we've all got off way too lightly for what we did."

"Our messed-up lives—you call that getting off *lightly*?"

"They *died* because of us. Melanie, Declan, Phoebe—"

"Zuss, girl, you think Mikey's *right*?" She fakes a swoon. "I need to sit down."

"You are sitting down."

"Then I need to stand up so I can sit down." Theatrically, she does.

"Caron, I'm trying to have a serious conversation here."

"So, what—you going to turn *your* room into a cell too? Dress like a convict? Shave your head? That would look quite cool, actually."

There's no reasoning with Caron when she's like this. She steers them on to safer topics, tries to lighten up; all the while, though, Shiv is aware of Mikey at the edge of the clearing. It's so black-and-white for him. So uncompromising. Caron might be more laid-back, but Shiv knows that this is an act. For all that Mikey is four years younger than Caron and about a hundred times more uptight, there's an honesty to him that cuts right to the heart of things.

This is what I did. This is who I am. Don't tell me any different.

It's the voice Shiv has been hearing in her own head and the voice she came here to silence. How else is she meant to live with herself?

In her first two weeks at the clinic, that voice *has*

begun to quiet. Or be drowned out by the "noise" of her treatment. The hum of *DeclanDeclanDeclan* that envelops her and which seems designed to erase her brother's death, replace it with the illusion that he's alive, and with her, walking beside her every step along the path to recovery.

"Are you going to eat that?" Caron indicates Shiv's granola bar.

Shiv manages a smile.

"What?" Caron asks.

"Dec was always doing that—troughing up anything I didn't eat."

"I do *not* 'trough,' thank you very much."

"Anyway, it's hamster scrapings, isn't it?"

"Rat. That's an entirely different snack-based concept."

Shiv hands her the bar.

"You sure?" her friend says.

"Go on. I'm not hungry."

Actually, the idea of food sickens her all of a sudden. Along with the thought that, in a moment, she'll have to head to Make, then lunch, then Talk, then Write, then dinner, then another night with Declan on her bedroom wall.

The day after she danced in the street with Nikos, Shiv was eating with her family on the patio. The sun hung over the bay like a great golden balloon. Its slow descent would mark another day apart from Nikos, another day of failure to meet in secret.

Dont worry ill think of something, his last text had said.

Tuesday evening. They were going home on Friday morning.

Shiv had little to say at dinner; her pasta lay mostly untouched. Mum and Dad were reminiscing about a previous holiday when a knock at the door interrupted them.

"It'll be the concierge," Dad said, going off to investigate. "Concierge" was what other, less expensive holiday agencies called a "rep."

"Can I fill in the evaluation form?" Declan asked.

"No," Mum said. "Not after last year."

"Hell-*o*." Dad: too loud, too friendly. "*Kalimera, kalimera.*" Then two sets of footsteps approached on the path that ran down the side of the villa. Dad was the first to appear. "We have a visitor."

And there was Nikos.

For a nanosecond, Shiv must've done the cartoon-shock thing: dropped jaw, raised eyebrows, eyes on stalks. Then she got a grip, composed herself, acted like Nikos's arrival was the *least* surprising event in her entire life.

She speared a pasta shell and popped it in her mouth. It tasted of rubber.

"Oh, sorry." Nikos gestured at the table. "I'm interrupting your meal."

"Not at *all*, Nikos," Mum said with her warmest smile. She tapped the dish. "There's plenty left, if you'd care to join us."

"Can we spare it?" Dad said, laughing. "Dec hasn't had his third helping yet."

"*Dad*." Her brother looked cross.

Nikos smiled politely. "It's okay, thanks. I ate already."

He was standing awkwardly, clutching a brown paper parcel in both hands like someone had just given it to him and he wasn't sure what to do with it.

"So, young man," Dad said, "to what do we owe the unexpected pleasure?"

Shiv tried to catch Nikos's eye, to flash him a warning. If that parcel was for her, if he'd turned up to make some kind of declaration (*I realize you may not approve, but your daughter and I . . .*), she would just crawl under the table and *die*. But he wasn't looking at her, hadn't looked at her the whole time.

"I just came by to give this to Declan," he said.

It was her brother's turn to look panicked. Confused.

Nikos handed him the parcel. "You said how much you liked mine, so I figured you'll like one of your own."

Shiv recalled Dec complimenting Nikos's shirt the other day, in the pickup, then blushing fiercely. He was blushing now as he pulled out a green-and-gold jersey. For once, he was at a loss for words. Shiv couldn't tell if he was pleased or mortified.

"Actually, it's an old one I grew out of," Nikos said, when Mum protested that he really *shouldn't* have. "Clean, of course."

"Nikos, it's very kind of you," Dad said. "*Isn't it,* Declan?"

Her brother looked up, startled. "Oh, yeah. Yeah. Thanks."

"I hope it fits," Nikos said.

"It looks *perfect,*" Mum said, when Dec clearly had nothing else to say. "They both had such a great time windsurfing with you," she went on. Shiv smiled inside at the kissed daughter and nearly drowned son that their mother had no idea about. "This one," Mum said, nodding at Declan, "hasn't stopped talking about you."

Dec shot Mum a furious glance.

"I had the best time too," Nikos said.

"Your English is *very* good, Nikos."

"Mum," Shiv cut in, "d'you think you could be just a *little* more patronizing?"

"I'm only saying—"

"If we can't give you something to eat," Dad said, "how about a beer?"

Nikos hesitated, flicked a look at Shiv. *Please say no.* It wasn't that she didn't want to see him, but the thought of him (them) enduring an evening with Mum and Dad . . . What had Nikos been *thinking,* turning up here like this? If he stayed, Mum or Dad were bound to say something that gave away Shiv's age.

"That's nice of you, sir, but I'm meeting with some friends. Beach football. Just a kickabout." Then, a little sheepishly, "Actually, we could use a couple of extra players . . . if anyone's interested."

"You *hate* football," Declan hissed at her as they followed Nikos along the narrow track through the sand dunes.

"*Someone* has to chaperone you."

It was true, kind of. Choosing their words carefully to avoid offending Nikos, Mum and Dad had made it clear that they didn't mind Declan playing—seeing as he was so keen—but, well, he *was* only twelve and, much as she didn't want to, would Shiv mind going along as well? And they both had to be back at the villa before dark.

Her brother was wearing the green-and-gold basketball jersey. It was too big but, even so, she had to admit he looked pretty cool. "I should warn you, Nikos," Dec called out, "that Shiv's even worse at football than she is at windsurfing."

"Hey," Nikos said, "who needed rescuing?"

"For your information, I didn't *need* rescuing, you *chose* to rescue me."

Nikos laughed. "Is that right?"

"Yes, it is. It was a massive overreaction on your part."

The game was already under way, the lines of the pitch scored in the flat sand vacated by the tide. Four motorcycle helmets marked out the goals. Three guys and a girl on one team, three guys on the other—all about Nikos's age, as far as Shiv could tell. The game paused so Nikos could introduce everyone. Declan joined the team with the girl; Nikos and Shiv made up the other five. Shiv was aware of one or two curious looks being directed at Nikos for bringing them along.

Just then, she wished she hadn't agreed to come.

But once the game resumed everyone forgot about her and Declan and just got on with hoofing the ball about. Shiv wasn't even the worst player—that honor went to a guy on her team, Nikos's cousin, Joss. He was shaven-headed, belly flopping out from under his T-shirt, and he cavorted about the pitch like a lunatic.

"Team joker," Nikos remarked, when Joss broke up an opposition attack by picking up the ball, shoving it under his shirt and running to the other end of the pitch.

For much of the game, Shiv could barely kick the ball for laughing.

The other team won 15–9 (or 14–10, no one was sure) and Declan scored four goals, celebrating them with acrobatic high fives with his teammates.

"You're *crazy*," Shiv whispered to Nikos during a time-out. "Turning up like that."

He grinned. "Yeah, crazy to see *you*."

"Oh, please. Who writes your scripts?" Inside, though, she was delighted.

"You handled it well. Little Miss Cool."

Shiv pushed her hair back from her sweaty face. "So where's *my* present? Dec gets a basketball shirt, what do I get?"

"You get to see me."

"I get to play *football* with you. You and eight other people."

"Let's sneak off to the dunes, then—nobody will notice."

Of course he was teasing. In any case, the ball was back and play was ready to continue. For the rest of the match Shiv ached with the thought of them slipping off—and of what they might get up to, hidden away in the sand dunes.

By the end of the game it was dusk and hard to see the ball. Trainers and sandals were retrieved; water bottles shared out. Eventually, only Shiv, Dec, Nikos and his cousin Joss remained, the golden sand turned to oatmeal gray in the failing light.

Joss and Nikos had reclaimed two of the helmet "goal-posts."

"You have a motorbike?" Dec asked Nikos.

"Moped, yeah." He pointed out two bikes on the road fronting the beach. "Fifty cc. It sounds like a really cross mosquito."

Beside him, Joss stood with his crash helmet under his arm. His bald head was waxy with perspiration and his thick, dark eyebrows looked like they'd been stuck on.

"Decalan, maybe one day you plays to Manchester Unite. Yes?" Dec grinned self-consciously. Turning to her, Joss said, "Sheev, sorry, but I think you not ever plays to Manchester Unite." He patted her shoulder.

Shiv couldn't help laughing. "Thank you, Joss. I appreciate your honesty."

The four of them headed toward the mopeds; in Shiv and Declan's case, to the track that branched off just before. At a beachside taverna, fish were being grilled. The drifting smoke conjured up an image of the bonfire at Lackanackathon on Easter Sunday, the flames consuming the effigy of Judas so completely Shiv could believe she'd imagined him. Just charred scraps fluttering above the crowd, like black moths.

"I'll walk up with you," Nikos said.

Handing his helmet to Joss, he spoke to him in Greek, and then the three of them were weaving a route through the dunes.

Shiv scrolled through different, impossible, ways to edit Declan out of the scene so that she and Nikos might be alone. Might lie in the sand together.

All too quickly the evening was coming to an end.

They reached the road to the villa. It was almost dark and the outside light glinted off the rental car. They stood around, unsure what to say or do.

Please, Dec, just go indoors.

Nikos said goodnight, pulling Declan into a manly hug—Dec, stiff as a shop-window mannequin. Then, with mock formality, Nikos took Shiv's hand between his.

"See you around," he said. Just like that, he was gone, fading into the gloom.

Shiv waited till they were inside, till Dec had gone out to the terrace to find Mum and Dad, before slipping away to the bathroom. With the door bolted, she opened her hand to see what Nikos had pressed into her palm as they'd said goodbye.

Carefully picking apart the pink tissue-paper wrapping, she eased the gift open.

It was the preserved remains of the baby turtle which Nikos had passed round on the boat trip and which Shiv had told him was the most beautiful thing she'd seen.

ELEVEN

At breakfast on their second Sunday at the Korsakoff Clinic—officially a rest day—Assistant Sumner informs them that a group picnic has been arranged.

"Miss," Caron says, hand raised, "can I have *jam* in my sandwiches, please?"

Sumner, smile fixed, ignores the question. They are to meet on the front steps at noon, where she and Dr. Pollard will escort them to the meadow next to the lake.

The lake. Shiv isn't going anywhere near the lake. But when she stays in her room past noon, Sumner comes to fetch her.

"You've listened to me in Talk," Shiv says. "You've read what I've written in Write. You *know* why I don't want to go down there."

"And *you* know why Dr. Pollard wants you to."

They spread out on tartan rugs around a wicker hamper and a cooler, Sumner and her boss handing out food and drink, plates and plastic beakers.

Shiv glances at the chain-link fence with its sign—DANGER: DEEP WATER.

She shares a rug with Caron and Lucy. Sits with her back to the lake.

But it's right there, on the other side of that fence.

She can hear it lapping. Can smell its odor of damp earth and vegetation. Can picture its bluey-pewter surface stippled with sunlight and a scattering of coots and mallards. Her mind conjures another version too: rocks and crashing waves, the stink of salt and seaweed, the terrifying darkness of night. Her own screams.

"Ew, *tuna*." Caron peels back the top of her sandwich.

Mikey is the only absentee. "Unwell" is the official explanation; but he seemed okay at breakfast. And he was fit enough to strip his room bare again. Shiv wonders if he hates water as much as she does and has snuck away somewhere—or simply did a better job than Shiv did of saying no. But she recalls that time she saw him down here from the window, gripping the fence, staring at the lake. Shiv figures he wanted the sight of the water to remind him of his failure to keep Phoebe safe. Confronting the lake was another self-inflicted punishment. Or maybe he wished the fence wasn't there so that he could throw himself in. Did he hate himself that much?

There was a time when Shiv's counselor worried that *she* might be suicidal. The woman was cautious in raising the subject—presumably for fear of planting the idea in Shiv's head. Her line was to find out if Shiv had ever thought ending her life would free her from having to cope with the enormity of what had happened. Suicide as a *release*.

Suicide as a means of *self-punishment* didn't seem to occur to the counselor.

"It's a flooded gravel pit, actually, not a natural lake," she overhears Dr. Pollard telling Helen, the words drawing Shiv from her thoughts. "Very cold and *very* deep."

"No good for skinny-dipping, then?" Caron calls over.

The director laughs. "I wouldn't recommend it."

Somehow, this spins off a discussion about the Loch Ness monster.

Shiv focuses on eating, not looking at the lake or thinking about it. Or about Mikey and suicide. She listens to a monologue from Lucy about how homesick she is, and how she's going cold turkey from two weeks without texting, Facebook or phone calls. Shiv doesn't miss any of it. She thought she would, but she doesn't. If they relaxed the rules and let the residents phone their parents, Shiv isn't at all sure she'd make the call—or what she'd say to Mum or Dad if she did. It'd be Dad she phoned; no point talking to her mother these days. *How's it going?* Dad would ask. Meaning, *Are you getting better?* What would she tell him? *Yeah, I talk to Declan all the time. Hey, and guess what? He held my hand at Walk!*

When everyone has finished eating, Assistant Sumner produces a Frisbee and organizes people into a circle on the grass. Shiv goes to join Dr. Pollard on her rug.

"Frisbee not your thing?" the director asks.

"No. I mean, yeah, but . . . not just now."

She used to love throwing a Frisbee with Declan— they'd stand farther and farther apart, competing to make the most acrobatic catch. Her brother split his lip one time on a beach in Sardinia, trying to catch the disc in his mouth like a dog. Shiv is about to share this memory with Dr. Pollard but decides not to.

"Am I making progress?" she asks.

"Progress?"

"Am I getting better?"

The woman looks at her appraisingly, like she's searching for clues. For once, Dr. Pollard is not in a business suit but a pink polo shirt and white chinos. No glasses. Her bare arms are stick-thin and freckly.

"Do *you* think you're getting better?" she asks.

"I'm asking *you*. You're the expert here."

Dr. Pollard gives a slight nod. "Your response to the program is pretty much on track."

"What, you think I'm *improving*?"

"Ah, now, 'progress' and 'improvement' aren't necessarily the same thing."

"What does that mean?"

"Take your friend." Dr. Pollard points to Caron, bending to retrieve the Frisbee she's just dropped. "At Make, her collection of artwork is progressing, but there's no obvious improvement in her artistic ability."

"I don't understand. Are you saying I'm—"

"But in your case, Siobhan," the woman continues, "yes, I do believe you are progressing *and* improving. In your treatment, I mean." Then, smiling, "And in Make, as well, as it happens. You have quite a talent for art."

Shiv ignores the compliment.

She plucks at the rug beneath her, works a fingertip into a small tear in the material. "Sometimes," she says, after a deep breath, "I think he's here."

"Your brother?"

"It's like I have him back again. All to myself."

"And you like that?"

Shiv nods. "My other therapy, it was all about learning to let him go."

The woman studies Shiv, her expression unreadable. Shiv is cross-legged; Dr. Pollard, her legs stretched out, is massaging her knees. "Poor circulation," she explains, catching Shiv watching. Then, "So, tell me about it."

About having Declan back, she must mean. So Shiv does.

"How is that 'getting better'?" Shiv says when she's through. "It's not exactly normal, is it? Seeing someone who isn't there. Holding his hand, talking to him."

"Hmm, normal." The director gestures toward the rest. "I'm sure you know you're by no means alone in experiencing these . . . let's call them encounters."

"Oh, so I'm as normal as every other patient in a psychiatric clinic. Great."

Dr. Pollard laughs.

It's true, what she said. Caron speaks every night to the friend she lost; Lucy says that when she's sculpting her niece's face in Make, the modeling clay feels like flesh—that the baby girl *smiles* at her; Helen has confessed to being "visited" by her dead father. If the therapy is meant to reunite the living with their dead, it's working.

Except for Mikey, if he can be believed.

Shiv shakes her head, serious again, still picking away at the rug, widening the rip. "I'm not *entitled,* though. Why should I get to have Declan back?"

As she says it, she realizes she has pretty much repeated something Docherty said at Talk the other day. He'd been telling the group about Natalie, his girlfriend he killed in a car crash: how the re-creation of her likeness at Make is messing with his head; how he has tried to quit thinking about her at Walk or writing about her at Write; how he can't bear to look at the pictures of her on his wall anymore.

I don't deserve to have Nat back.

Shiv glances over at the game, locates Docherty just outside it—half turned away, head down, hands in pockets.

"Shall we go for a stroll?" Dr. Pollard says, reclaiming Shiv's attention.

"A stroll? Where?"

"Just round the lake." She pats her stomach. "Work off some of that lunch."

Shiv fixes her a look. "You can't make me go round the lake."

"No, I can't *make* you." She pauses. "But I'd like you to come. Please."

W

Dr. Pollard uses a key to let them through a gate in the fence and onto a dirt path that follows the shoreline. Beside them is a wooden post hung with an orange-and-white life belt, one of several around the perimeter of the lake. Shiv fixes her gaze on the ground. With Dr. Pollard keeping to the inside of the path, closest to the water, Shiv could almost make believe the lake isn't there at all.

She is shaking.

From nervousness? Anxiety? Fear? What she feels is cold—as though she's *in* the water. Her hands are numb, her fingers icy-stiff.

It brings to mind her "tree" nightmare, sitting on a high branch, wet and frozen, no way to climb down or for anyone to reach her; those vicious dogs circling, waiting for her to lose her grip.

Shiv relates the dream to Dr. Pollard, aware that she's talking to distract herself.

"Ah, dream interpretation." Does she notice Shiv shaking, the voice tremor?

"It felt more like a memory than a dream." She tells the director about Mum rescuing Dec from the sycamore and how that morphed into her nightmare.

"Was your brother there, in the dream version?"

Shiv is about to say no, because she's fairly certain he wasn't—not at the end, anyway—but, picturing it now, she sees him at the base of the tree, waving to her. Signaling, though she can't tell what. The two dogs weave back and forth, ignoring him, raising their heads to howl.

"I'm not sure if he was there or not."

They're halfway round the lake and she realizes she has lifted her eyes to look ahead, along the path. Still not letting her gaze stray to the water but conscious of it at the periphery of her vision. She isn't as cold now, and the shaking has almost stopped.

"Your friendship with Mikey," the director says, out of nowhere.

"What about it?"

"What draws you to him, do you think?"

"I don't know," she says. "I just like him. When he hurts himself it reminds me of me, when I smash stuff."

"You want to help him. Protect him from himself."

"*You* made us buddies." Then, with a shrug, "He just needs a friend."

"A friend? Or a surrogate sister?"

"Feebs was way younger than me," Shiv says. "That's not how he sees me."

"What about Declan—was he way younger than Mikey?"

Shiv flicks the woman a look. "I'm not looking for another brother."

They fall quiet, continuing round to the side of the lake where an old wooden jetty—rickety, missing a few planks—extends ten meters or so out over the water. Although the setting could hardly be more different, it reminds Shiv of standing on the jetty at Kyritos, waiting to board *Poseidon IV*.

"You okay?" Dr. Pollard asks.

"Yeah . . . yeah, I'm fine."

The director gives Shiv a moment. Then, "I'm thinking of un-Buddying you."

"Me and Mikey? Why?"

"His attitude toward what we're trying to do here—it's not helpful. Not for him. Or for you. I might have to keep Mikey apart from all of the other patients."

"So you lied when you said he was 'unwell' today."

She turns to face Shiv. "Siobhan, it's vital that you *want* to be helped."

"I wouldn't be here if—"

"Because, you see, Mikey *doesn't*. Not yet. Possibly, he never will." Dr. Pollard goes to put a hand on Shiv's shoulder, then seems to think better of it and lets her arm drop to her side. "If he derails his own treatment, that's one thing. But I won't allow him to jeopardize yours."

"I do have a mind of my own, you know." Even as she says this, Shiv knows the seeds of some of her doubts about the clinic have been planted by Mikey.

Dr. Pollard smiles. "Mikey is a force of nature," she says.

Having paused by the jetty, they continue on the final short stretch along the path toward the gate where they started. As their *stroll* comes to an end, the director asks Shiv how she has found being so close to the water. The question catches her by surprise. Shiv has been so preoccupied with her friendship with Mikey that she forgot all about the lake and Dr. Pollard's purpose in inviting her to walk round it.

Her eyes are drawn to the surface of the water. Smooth and calm. Even so, she begins to tremble and has to look away.

"Two steps forward, one step back, eh?" Dr. Pollard says kindly.

"My counselor used to come out with crap like that too."

The director seems taken aback. "*Is* it crap? Sometimes, you have to—"

"My *treatment*," Shiv says, cutting in. "How is that taking me forward?"

"This is only Day Fourteen, Siobhan. Be patient with us. Please."

"Can you fix it for me to take Declan with me when my sixty days are up?" Shiv goes on, her fists clenching and unclenching. "Cos that's really going to make me well again, I reckon—going home, going back to school, and right through the rest of my life, tricking my head into believing my brother's still around." She glares. "Do you give us a lifetime's supply of paint and modeling clay to take with us? A pile of those exercise books? Am I meant to go down the park every morning for a couple of hours' walking meditation? Do I get to keep the projector so I can have a slide show of Dec on my bedroom wall every night for the next sixty years?"

"Have you finished?" Dr. Pollard asks, once Shiv's breathing has steadied.

Shiv just wheels away and makes for the gate.

The message said, *can i see you this pm 7+?*

Shiv replied to say she'd sort something out and text him back.

"Laura or Katy?" Mum said, indicating the phone.

"What? Oh . . . Laura." Shiv pressed "send." "Boy-friend trouble."

"Which one's Laura?" Dad asked.

"The one you always call Lorna," Mum said.

"I thought Katy was the one I call Lorna."

"Oh, wow," Declan said, swirling honey into his third bowl of yogurt, "did I just teleport to an old people's home?"

They were on the balcony, finishing breakfast. Shiv watched a red-and-white ferry cross the bay, trailing a long arc of surf like a rip in a turquoise dress.

See me where? And how?

"Are you going to finish that?" Declan said. Her toast, he meant. He was wearing the green-and-gold basket-ball jersey Nikos had given him. Dec hadn't taken it off; he'd even slept in it.

Shiv smiled inside at her own gift—the baby turtle—carefully rewrapped and concealed in her socks-and-knickers drawer.

"Shiv?" Declan pointed. "Your toast."

"Help yourself."

She met Nikos outside the minimart where he'd "bumped into" Dec that time.

He was sitting on his moped, sipping beer from a bottle and chatting to a couple of guys—one, Vassos, she recognized from the football. Nikos instantly switched his attention to her and gave the broadest of grins. They looked at Shiv, too. Vassos smiled and said hi, and the other spoke a few words of Greek to Nikos which made Vassos laugh. Nikos said something sharp to them.

"I was at school with them," Nikos said as the two guys drifted away.

He produced another Mythos from a bag looped over the handlebars and popped the cap with the bottle-opener tool on a Swiss Army Knife.

"What did that one say to you?" Shiv asked.

"Andreas?" He handed her the beer. "He said you're very pretty."

"No he didn't." She could tell from the way Vassos had laughed that the remark was something crudely sexual. "You don't have to protect me," she said, taking a slug of beer. It was startlingly cold and fizzy. "I know what boys are like."

Boys. Why did she say *boys*?

"Andreas is okay, really. Don't think badly of him."

Unsure how to respond, she drank more beer. This might be their last chance to be together; the tension was making Shiv edgy.

"Officially, I'm on an emergency mission to buy milk," she said. She'd *caused* the emergency by tipping a carton down the sink while no one was watching.

Nikos frowned. "That doesn't give us much time."

"Ah, but now I'm going to text them to say the shop has sold out of milk and I'm off to the big supermarket along the main road." She grinned. "That's got to be twenty minutes there and twenty back? Longer if I stop to admire the view."

Nikos laughed, chinked his bottle against hers and leaned in for a kiss.

"Mm," Shiv said, "I'd forgotten how nice you taste."

They went down to the rocks she and her brother had explored. Scrambling over them with Declan had been like a scene from a Famous Five novel; now, Shiv tried not to wonder how many other girls Nikos had brought to this spot. He was there with *her* now. That was the thing.

"When my grandmother was younger and my grandfather was still alive, they used to take us here for picnics." Nikos sat down. "Me, my brothers and sister."

Shiv sat beside him. "Is she very old now, your grandmother?"

"When I visit, she thinks I'm my father. Or shouts that I've come to rob her." He set the carrier bag of beer down carefully. "My grandfather used to catch fish and fry them in a big pan just over there."

"Sounds good." She could picture Nikos as a young boy.

"The fish were disgusting, really. But if I come here I can smell them, and the pipe my grandfather used to smoke. You know?"

Shiv nodded. "If I smell peaches I think of my gran, from her hand cream."

They fell quiet. Then they kissed for a while.

When they broke for air, Nikos repositioned Shiv between his legs, her back against his chest. He had one hand pressed against her belly, the other held his beer. Shiv was pacing herself; she'd started off too fast, out of nerves, and didn't want to get drunk. His hand felt warm against her stomach. She liked it there, liked when he kissed her cheek, her ear, her neck. She also knew where it would lead, if she let it continue. Preoccupied with *how* and *where* they were going to meet, she hadn't considered what she and Nikos were meeting *for*—what he might expect of her.

He's nineteen. He thinks I'm seventeen.

Shiv felt seventeen just then. Twenty, twenty-five; older and wiser than she'd ever felt. Was it because of Nikos, or did it come from inside her? Whatever, she knew no boy her own age would've sat like that for long without groping her.

"How'd you hurt yourself?" Nikos asked, stroking the bump on her forehead.

"Volleyball. On the beach today—me and Declan against Mum and Dad."

They raised their beer bottles simultaneously, sipped, lowered them again. "Synchronized drinking," Shiv said. She was gently raking the fingernails of her free hand though the hairs on Nikos's forearm.

"You like being with your family?"

"When we're like that I do. Even Dad, wanting to win so bad."

"Your brother likes to win too. Last night—at the football."

"I guess. Not like Dad, though. Declan wants to do

well to prove to himself that he can. Like with the wind-surfing, yeah?"

"He must not be beaten," Nikos suggested.

"Exactly."

"And you?"

She shook her head. "Not really."

They fell quiet, sipping their beers. Across the water, a house on the opposite shore appeared to move; no, it was the lights of a fishing boat heading out to sea.

Nikos held her tighter. His cheek pressed against hers, so that when at last he spoke, the words vibrated on her skin. "I think your brother has a crush on me."

Shiv twisted to look at him. *"Declan?"*

She laughed. But as soon as he'd said it, she knew he was right. Of *course*, Dec had a crush on him. A harmless crush. "He likes you, that's for sure," she said. "A lot. You're the big brother he never had."

Nikos produced two more bottles. "The big, cool, handsome brother."

"Arrogance alert!" Shiv said, poking him in the ribs.

He sighed melodramatically. "I can't help it if I'm a Greek god."

"Yeah—half man, half bullshit."

They kissed. When they stopped, Shiv groaned. *"God,* I can't believe I'm going home on Friday."

"I know."

"When d'you go back to the mainland?"

"Sunday," Nikos said. "The day after the wedding."

"Oh, you will be *so* hungover."

"I hope so."

Shiv smiled. Then, serious again, "It's weird to think

we're so close like this and in a few days we'll be on opposite sides of Europe."

Nikos held her tight.

"Sorry," Shiv said. "I promised myself I wouldn't get all heavy tonight."

"What will you do tomorrow?"

"We're going to some fort, I think. On the other side of the island."

"What about the day after, in the evening?"

"It's Mum and Dad's wedding anniversary. They're going out for a meal."

"Just the two of them?"

"Yup. Last night of the holiday, I babysit my kid brother."

"That's tough."

"Too right." Then, "How about you?"

"We're having a beach party for my brother. Just down the coast."

As they talked, she was conscious of time ebbing away. Soon, she would have to head back to the villa before her parents wondered where she'd got to. The dread of parting, of never seeing him again, was an actual pain in her throat.

"Nikos—"

"Shh." He touched a fingertip to her lips.

They kissed again; a long kiss that crackled with danger. Shiv didn't want to stop but also didn't want to go further; not then, not there on the rocks. Not yet. But there could be no "not yet" for them. Just now, or never. They went about as far as it was possible to go without removing clothes and Shiv knew they were close to the point where he wouldn't stop and she wouldn't want him to.

"You okay with this?" he whispered.

She just breathed against his ear, his cheeks, his lips.

Then, as Nikos began easing her shorts down, a scene popped into her head: that guy outside the minimart saying something to him in Greek about her. The other friend's laughter.

"Sorry," she blurted, grabbing at his wrists. Making him stop. "Nikos, I'm sorry. I'm so *sorry*, but I can't do this."

They called in at the shop for milk, and mints to mask her beery breath. He gave her a ride home on his moped, lending her the only helmet. He didn't speed, or try to scare or impress her; she held on to his waist, and he steered one-handed on the straight so he could rest his free hand on her thigh.

Nikos hadn't taken it too well. But better than Shiv expected.

A little pushing, a little coaxing and wheedling . . . but he stopped. And, for all his obvious frustration, he hadn't said anything to make her feel it was her fault.

Still, she blamed herself.

With the scent of flowers and the dusk gathering around them like a soft cape, Shiv clung to him on that moped. If she shut out what had just happened, she could easily convince herself it was the perfect end to a perfect evening.

He braked to a halt in the lay-by where the track from

the villa joined the road. She thought he would simply let her get off, then drive away without saying goodbye.

But he killed the engine, dismounted with her and eased the moped onto its stand. Unhooking the bag containing the milk from the handlebar, he handed it to her in exchange for the crash helmet, which he set down on the saddle.

"You okay?" he said.

"Yeah, fine." She made herself look at him. "You?"

Nikos nodded. Then, gesturing at the dilapidated bus stop and the big stinky, wheelie bin, "A nice romantic spot to say goodnight."

"You know how to show a girl a good time, don't you?"

They were trying to put things back the way they were. The unnaturalness was worse than anything. She started to apologize again.

"It was just—" *Too much, too soon,* she wanted to say.

He shushed her. "You don't have to explain."

Shiv blinked away the tears. Almost whispering, she managed to say, "It would've been my first time."

His face, in shadow, was unreadable. "You're cold," he said, tracing his fingertips over the goose bumps on her arm. She shivered, as though the word "cold" had made it so.

"Hold me," Shiv said. "Please."

They were still hugging—kissing, softly, tentatively—when they heard the creak of the wheelie-bin lid and a plastic sack being swung inside.

Shiv and Nikos broke apart and she turned to see Dec staring at them. In the fading light, the gold stripes of his basketball jersey looked luminous.

"Declan, hey . . ."

But her sentence trailed off. He wasn't gazing at her, but at Nikos. In his eyes was the truth of what Nikos had said down at the rocks—a different, more potent truth than the one she'd allowed. This was no mere crush.

He looked like someone catching a lover cheating on him.

"I, um, bumped into Nikos at the shop," she said. "He gave me a lift home."

Dec glanced at her, then at Nikos. His expression had shifted from bewildered hurt to spite. He stood rigid, arms straight down at his sides and fists clenched.

"I should go," Nikos said, giving Shiv's arm one last rub.

As Nikos remounted the moped, Declan said: "You do know she's *fifteen*?"

Over the next two weeks, Shiv sticks with the program, immerses herself deeper still. Or tries to. Each day is tougher than the last.

The routine has grown tiresome, Shiv's energy and commitment starting to dissipate. Instead of throwing herself into it, she does what is required but no longer with confidence that the treatment will work. Even the time spent with "Declan" is losing its appeal.

Be patient, Dr. Pollard urged, down at the lake. It has been a recurrent theme of their one-to-ones since then. The routine will change soon, the director promises— the daily activities, the *therapeutic focus,* will be radically different. This is just Phase One.

"What's Phase Two, then?"

"Phase Two is what comes next."

"Is that meant to be funny?"

"It means Phase One is laying the foundations for what we do in Phase Two." As for exactly what *happens* in Phase Two, "All I ask, Siobhan, is that you stay strong and, when the time comes, be open to the possibility that it will help you."

Trouble is, once Doubt whispers in your ear it's hard to shut the words out.

Other therapies haven't worked, why should this one?

They want you to feel good about yourself—but you don't deserve to.

You killed Declan. You should suffer for it. You should never stop suffering.

Reducing Mikey's influence hasn't prevented Shiv's decline, although they haven't isolated the boy altogether, or forbidden Shiv to speak to him. But he no longer joins them for Walk, Make, Talk and Write; at Buddy Time and evening rec, he is confined to his room. The only time Shiv or the others get to see him is at meals. Mostly, he eats by himself, but sometimes Shiv joins him, careful not to crowd him or to abandon Caron too often.

If it's nice enough to take lunch outside, they'll share a bench in a sunny spot. Sometimes they talk; sometimes they just sit and eat. An orderly is never too far away from Mikey—but even so, Shiv is glad of their snatches of time together. Apart from anything else, she doesn't like being told who she should or shouldn't be mates with.

"What do you *do* all day?" she asked not long into this new routine.

"I have to run in the woods with Assistant Webb," he told her. "Or they get me to help out the gardener. Push a wheelbarrow, pull up weeds and that. And I have one-to-ones with Pollard." Then, shrugging, "Mostly, they just leave me in my cell."

It *is* a cell now; at least, the staff agree to let him keep his room stripped right down, so long as the bed is made up properly, not just a bare mattress.

"They're letting me play at being a convict."

The tactics seem to be working. While Shiv grows disaffected, he is more cooperative, more at ease with himself.

179

Shiv gets the impression it's a front, though—he's simply biding his time.

Until when? To do what?

Breakfast, Day Thirty-One. Shiv and Mikey, at a table in the corner of the dining room.

Last night marked the halfway point of the program, and when Shiv woke this morning she hoped for an announcement over the intercom. *Good morning, everyone. We are pleased to inform you that, from today, you will enter Phase Two of your treatment* . . . Or something like that. The intercom remained stubbornly silent.

Mikey is trying to cheer her up with a series of terrible impressions: Hensher, Sumner, Dr. Pollard. If he didn't name them, Shiv would have no clue. They're so bad they're funny. Despite herself, she starts to smile. He's on to TV characters now.

"Who's this?" he says, pulling a face and making an odd slurring sound.

"Someone having a stroke?"

"*Homer Simpson.*" Mikey is indignant. "You know, when he drools down his chin. Look." He repeats the mime. "Beeerrr. Aarrgghh. Dooonuuuutsss."

Shiv lets out a snort of laughter. "How did we get to the stage where *you* have to lift *me* out of a grump?"

Mikey looks pleased with himself.

As they finish their cereal, her mood is already dipping. In a moment, Mikey will go, and Shiv will head off to the assembly corridor for yet another Walk.

"If you're thinking of digging an escape tunnel, let me know," she says.

He gives her an odd look. "Seriously?"

She keeps forgetting that Mikey doesn't do irony.

While they're at the counter, tipping food scraps into the bin and stacking plates, Assistant Webb enters the breakfast room. With a single loud clap, he says,

"You are all to report to the Blue Room. Right away, please."

The buzz of speculation is still crackling when Dr. Pollard enters the Blue Room, flanked by Webb, Hensher and Sumner, as she was way back on Day One.

"Good morning, everyone."

"Good morning, Dr. Pollard," they chorus.

"I'm gonna divide you into two teams," Caron chips in, putting on a gruff, blokey voice. "And in the losing team—one of you will be fired."

Her wisecrack sends a wave of laughter along the residents. The director and her staff remain straight-faced; even Assistant Sumner's perma-smile is switched off.

"You have reached the midway point of your time with us," Dr. Pollard says, once the amusement has subsided. "This marks the conclusion of Phase One of your treatment." She eyes each face in turn. "Today you start Phase Two."

Lucy raises a hand.

"No questions," the woman says.

No questions, no more interruptions. She hasn't even started to explain what Phase Two consists of, but already, her tone—her whole manner—prickles Shiv's skin with apprehension. They're into the serious stuff;

like the first month has been some kind of psychiatric kindergarten.

"Thank you," Dr. Pollard says as Lucy lowers her hand.

"So, Phase Two." The director clasps her hands, fingers interlocked in the way that a small child might pray. "Thirty days ago, when I stood here to welcome you to the clinic, you'll recall me saying that each of you had suffered a significant traumatic bereavement?"

Some nod; there's hear-a-pin-drop silence along the row.

"In Phase One, as you know, we have focused on the *object* of that bereavement: the person you lost. We have encouraged you to re-create a very strong sense of him or her. Your niece, Milly"—she gestures at Lucy, then at Caron and Docherty in turn—"your best friend, Melanie; your girlfriend, Natalie."

Each name resonates. Docherty actually flinches when his turn comes. Like she's slapped him.

"Your brother, Declan," Dr. Pollard says, indicating Shiv, then Helen and Mikey, "Your father, Peter; your sister, Phoebe."

Mikey's face is stony-blank. If he seemed surprised when Webb said the summons to the Blue Room included him, he has pulled the shutters back down now.

"When a loved one dies," the director goes on, "it is not unreasonable for us to wish they were still with us—even to imagine that they *are*." Dr. Pollard's gaze alights briefly on each resident. "We see them, talk to them. Our heads fill up with thoughts of them so that they seem to be more present than absent." She pauses, fingers still interlocked, her knuckles white. "Some bereaved people find this a comfort, some a torment. For some, it is both."

Shiv catches herself nodding. Dr. Pollard holds her gaze so that what follows appears to be addressed solely to Shiv.

"Comfort or torment, either way it is delusional. If it takes root, it can go from being a perfectly normal *stage* in the grieving process to something that stalls, or even *replaces,* that process." She unlocks her gaze from Shiv's—releasing her, it feels like—and turns to the group. "Each of you, to some extent, came to us in this condition."

"So why—" Caron begins. Dr. Pollard cuts across her.

"As you'll know by now, Phase One of your treatment has been designed, as far as possible, to indulge you—to encourage you, to *immerse* you—in the delusion that the person you lost is not lost at all. That you can still maintain some semblance of a genuine relationship with them." Another pause. "Why do we do this?" She looks at Caron. "Is that what you were going to ask?"

Caron nods.

"Perhaps you can answer that for me. All of you." Finally unclasping her fingers and lowering her hands to her sides, Dr. Pollard asks, "After thirty days of this—hour after hour, day after day, night after night—how many of you still hold to the delusion? How many of you believe your loved one is present, is with you?"

No hands go up.

"And how many of you wish to continue indulging yourself in the delusion of a relationship?"

Again, no hands are raised. Not a single one.

"You have your answer."

It's like the *ta-daaa* moment at the end of a conjuring trick and Shiv almost lets out a gasp of startled, appreciative laughter. From the murmuring along the line, the others are similarly impressed. Can it really be so simple, though? So clever? So *easy?* She isn't sure what to think, but what she does know is that it's been at least a week since she regarded "Declan" (in any of his various forms) as remotely *real,* rather than someone she created for herself.

Dr. Pollard resumes. "Phase One, the *object* of your bereavement. In Phase Two, we shift the focus to the *nature of your trauma.* That is, from the person who died to the circumstances of their death. Trauma Centered Therapy, or TCT."

She lets that sink in.

"I won't say too much more at this stage because it's best that you enter TCT without knowing exactly what to expect. Some therapies train you to rationalize your trauma, to detach yourself from it—as though it happened to someone else or to an earlier, obsolete 'you.' In TCT, you are plunged right into the trauma." She makes a fist, a plunging motion. "Face to face with what happened, with where it happened. With *how* it happened."

For the first time, she smiles her gap-toothed smile.

"It's the difference between lighting a prayer candle for someone possessed by a demon—and conducting a full-blown exorcism."

No one says a word as Webb and Hensher escort them along the corridor. Too shocked, is all Shiv can think. Too scared. No Walk; no Make, either. From now on, they've been told, each of them will spend their mornings in a specially designed Personalized Therapy Unit, or PTU. Four hours, every day. Alone. Locked in.

Shiv's palms are clammy, her breath hot in her throat.

They're taken upstairs to a first-floor corridor Shiv hasn't seen before. It must be directly below the patients' bedrooms and, with its green decor and sequence of doors along the right-hand wall, looks the same.

At each door, Assistant Webb stops to swipe it open with a key card and usher the resident inside. Helen, Caron, Docherty—one by one, they disappear.

It's Shiv's turn.

Webb lets her in and closes the door without a word. She hears the electronic click of the lock. As though the shutting of the door triggered it, the darkened room blooms into light.

Whitewashed walls, tiled floor, plain blue curtains, a set of asymmetrical shelves lined with books, a blue-and-white checkered rug, a cream leather sofa and chairs, a low coffee table—the room, her *Personalized Therapy Unit,* is more or less an exact replica of the lounge in the villa at Kyritos.

The morning after the roadside encounter, Declan didn't surface until the rest of them had eaten breakfast and were preparing to go out.

Dad was in the lounge, a map spread out on the coffee table, plotting their route to a fort on the other side of the island. Shiv was in the kitchen area, helping Mum to make up a picnic, the floor tiles deliciously cold beneath her bare feet. Every now and then she glanced at the stairs, where Dec might appear at any moment.

Actually, he could sulk in bed the whole day for all Shiv cared, but mixed in with the anger was dread. Of what he might say to their parents.

"Fifty minutes, I reckon," Dad called out, tapping the map. "An hour, max."

"Good-oh," Mum said, buttering bread.

She had picked up on the atmosphere, even if their father hadn't. "What was all that about last night?" she'd asked earlier, while Dad was in the shower.

"All what?"

"Dec stomping off to bed early, you moping around like a ten-year-old."

"I wasn't *moping*," Shiv had said.

She opened three cabinets before she found the sandwich bags. Greek music played on a radio outside, where the maintenance guy was servicing the pool. For no other reason than he was old and Greek, he put Shiv in mind of Nikos's granddad and the tale Nikos told of fried fish and boyhood picnics down at the rocks.

Nikos. The look he had given her last night as he climbed onto his moped.

So what if you're only fifteen? That was what she sought in his expression in the wake of Declan's revelation. *It's okay, Shiv, we're still good.* In the countless replays of that scene in her mind over the past twelve hours, she almost convinced herself she'd seen exactly that look in his eyes in the moment before he rode off.

But she no longer trusted herself to distinguish between what she's seen and what she'd hoped to see.

In another version, she saw him dismiss her as a kid, a stupid, lying, jailbait bitch. Saw his relief that he'd learnt the truth before things had gone any further. Saw that he couldn't mount his bike and get away fast enough.

If only Nikos had *said* something. If only he hadn't just flicked her a look—the briefest unreadable glance—before veering off with a spurt of grit and dust that left Shiv alone with her brother in the twilight. Then alone altogether as Dec, without a word, returned to the villa. Shiv had stared for ages at the point where the gloom swallowed the moped's taillight before she turned to follow her brother.

Shiv had texted Nikos that evening. Three, four times. She'd left a whispered message on his voice mail. She'd texted again, twice, in the morning.

Nothing.

If his look as he'd left was open to interpretation, his silence was clear enough. Nikos was gone and Shiv would never see or hear from him again.

Afterward, she'd found Dec at the pool, cross-legged at the end of the diving board and gazing blankly at the water. He'd removed the basketball jersey Nikos had given him and was shivering in the night air.

"Why did you tell him?" Shiv said, furious, but keeping her voice low in case Mum and Dad overheard through the open patio doors. From inside came the sounds of food being served, a wine bottle being opened.

"*Why,* Declan?"

Her brother just sat there, the board bowing beneath his weight. The pool lights on the rippling water illuminated him from below like the reflection of so many silver coins. He ignored her so totally you'd think he hadn't even registered her at the side of the pool. Her arms hung straight down at her sides, as Dec's had done earlier, in the lay-by; her hands, as his had been, were bunched into fists.

He was crying, but Shiv said it anyway: "I'll never forgive you for this."

"Does his lordship intend to grace us with his presence today?" Dad said. He had folded away the map and come to stand on the other side of the kitchen counter, picking an olive out of the tub of salad and popping it into his mouth.

"Who knows?" Mum said, shooting a sidelong glance at Shiv.

Dad looked at his watch. "Only, we could do with—"

The slap of bare feet on the stairs and there was Declan, with slept-in hair, crumpled boxers and a very creased and grubby Salinger T-shirt. So, he was wearing that again. *"What?"* he said crossly as three pairs of eyes tracked his arrival.

"We're meant to be going to the fort," Dad said.

"And your point is?"

"We've wasted half the morning already."

Declan crossed the room, barging past Shiv, and raided the fridge for orange juice. He drank straight from the carton. "This fort is, like, a thousand years old," he said, wiping his mouth. "I don't reckon it'll fall down before we get there, do you?"

Before the bickering escalated, Mum intervened. "Eat something," she said, handing Declan a bowl, "then get showered and changed, please."

Dad muttered something and left them to it. Shiv watched her brother tip cereal and milk into the bowl and eat standing up at the counter. She thought he might continue to blank her, as he'd done last night, but he looked directly at her, his expression indecipherable.

Mum busied herself loading the cooler. "Do something with that, can you, Shiv?" she said, nodding at the chopping board, strewn with salad trimmings.

Shiv went to scrape it into the bin, but her brother was in the way.

"'Scuse me," she said.

"I'm *eating,*" he said, mouth full of half-chewed cornflakes.

"Go eat someplace else, then."

"For crying out loud!" That was Mum, banging the cooler lid down so hard the bottle of washing-up liquid toppled into the sink. "I don't know what's going on between you two, but we only have two days left of this holiday and you're not going to ruin them." She glared at them in turn. "Understood?"

Neither of them responded.

"I mean it," Mum said. "The pair of you, just grow up."

"Oh, *Shiv's* all grown-up. Aren't you?"

"Shut up, Declan."

"What's the problem?" Dad said, reappearing in the lounge.

"Nothing," Shiv said, widening her eyes at Declan, daring him to contradict her. He set the bowl down on the counter, slopping milk, and headed out of the kitchen.

"And don't take all day in the shower," Dad called after him.

"*No,* I *won't.*"

"And what's with the T-shirt—I thought the basketball top was glued on?"

Declan paused, hung his head a moment—as Nikos had done last night—then carried on out of the room without a word.

In the car, she expected Dec to slide back into a silent sulk. But he was something like his usual self, making up silly "facts" about the fort as he pretended to read aloud from the guidebook or singing along (intentionally badly) to the CD. *Too* normal. Like this was a reality TV show and he was playing an exaggerated version of himself for the cameras.

Shiv wasn't sure if she preferred this Declan to the one who had frozen her out or the one who'd sniped at breakfast. She wasn't sure what to expect.

She sat, half turned away from him, staring out the window as they snaked through the interior of the island. The sunlit hillsides, littered with huge boulders and twisted old olive trees, were almost stunning enough to lift Shiv out of her black cloud. Almost, but not quite.

They couldn't have been too far from the place where Nikos had taken them to see the vulture.

She checked her phone for messages. No signal.

Whether it was this that caught Declan's eye, or whether he'd planned to say something all along, she had no way of knowing. Maybe he'd just noticed where they were and remembered the vulture trip too. Whatever, he quietened again. She slipped the phone back in her bag.

Five minutes, ten—the silence in the rear seat was so profound Shiv couldn't believe their parents were chatting away about the passing scenery. Then, as they rounded a bend and the island's eastern coastline swung spectacularly into view far below, her brother said, "Don't worry, Shivoloppoulos," plenty loud enough for Mum and Dad to hear. "I won't tell them."

"Tell us what?" Dad frowned into the rearview mirror.

Mum sat dead still, eyes fixed on the road as though

she was the driver rather than the passenger. Like she dreaded where this was leading as much as Shiv did.

Shiv turned to her brother. "Dec, please—"

Dad repeated his question. "Won't tell us *what*?"

"I won't *tell* you," Declan said, "that your lovely daughter is shagging Nikos."

THIRTEEN

Shiv realizes immediately that the re-creation of the villa's interior is virtual rather than actual. That what she is seeing isn't a room furnished and decorated to resemble the lounge in Kyritos but photos of the original, enlarged to life-size and projected onto the floor and walls of an otherwise bare room. The clinic must have downloaded the images from the holiday company's website.

What doesn't happen so fast, or for several minutes, is the steadying of her breathing, or the return to a regular beat of her *thump-thump-thump*ing heart.

Or the lessening of the urge to hammer on the door and scream to be let out.

They won't let her out, though. For four hours, Shiv is stuck here with . . . whatever this is. A psychological experiment. Her very own Room 101, like in Orwell's *1984*. Trapped inside—*enveloped* by, taken back to—the place where her brother lived his last days.

Well, they can lock her in, but they can't make her look.

With nowhere to sit but the floor, she settles down in a corner, cross-legged, tips her head back against the wall and closes her eyes. She'll keep them closed the whole four hours, if necessary.

But her eyes have been shut for just seconds when an unbearably loud buzz breaks the silence, insistent, drilling into her ears—right into her brain, or that's how it feels. The moment she opens her eyes again the noise stops. She closes her eyes once more. The noise kicks back in. Opens them. The noise stops.

So, they *can* make her look. And if they know when she opens and closes her eyes, they must be observing her.

There are a several bug-eye lenses set into the ceiling—projecting the images that fill the room. Any one of them could house a camera to spy on her—not just to ensure she keeps her eyes open but to monitor her behavior, her reactions. She feels like a laboratory rat.

When she has calmed a little (and unable to avoid looking at it), Shiv studies the photomontage more closely, picking out details she missed at the first, shocking sight. The flat-screen TV in one corner, the books—some Greek, some English—lining the shelves, the framed print of an old woman in traditional costume hanging on the wall. She can almost picture her father at the wood-and-glass coffee table, a map spread clumsily across it as he plotted their route to the fort. Can almost see Mum's postcards propped on the mantelpiece. Dad's Stieg Larsson novel wedged down the side of a cushion. Dec's stinky flip-flops and sodden swimming shorts strewn about the place and the regular trails of biscuit crumbs he left across the floor.

Can almost feel the ceiling fan losing its battle against the heat of a new day.

Can almost smell the suntan lotion she's massaging into her skin.

Can almost hear the *thud-thud* of the tennis ball against the wall outside.

How long it is before the pictures change, she isn't sure. But, after she's been adjusting to them, making them less upsetting, the room plunges into darkness, and an instant later, the walls and floor light up again. She's outside, on the patio, gazing through the dangling vines at the pool, shimmering beneath a perfect Mediterranean sky. And at the olive grove and the bay and the pinkish hills, blurred by heat-haze.

The pool nearly does for her, with its springboard and the unbidden image that fills her head: Declan, in his red swim shorts, performing a clownish, acrobatic leap, soaking the patio's pink-and-white flagstones with a great plume of water. Another one: Dec, sitting cross-legged at the end of the board, shirtless, head bowed, mottled in the pool lights, the night he caught her with Nikos.

Instinctively, she shuts her eyes. The appalling buzzer snaps them back open.

For the rest of the morning—apart from a five-minute "comfort break," which Assistant Hensher escorts her to and from—Shiv is confined to her Personalized Therapy Unit. Throughout this time, the projections cut back and forth between the inside and outside of the villa. Boredom should have set in. The images should have lost their power to upset her. This *does* happen, somewhere around the middle of the session. But the picture show regains its intensity—its hold over her—as the sheer monotony of sitting for so long, staring at the same scenes, acts like a kind of water torture.

Or it may be that however hard she tries to resist it, Shiv's imagination takes over—filling in the gaps, scripting the story that the pictures leave untold. Resuming the countdown of the days, hours, minutes to Declan's death.

For the next few days, the projections remain the same.

Shiv starts to believe she can handle it. The mornings become an exercise in forcing her mind to look away, even if her eyes can't.

Then a whole new set of images appear.

At first, Shiv can't understand how the clinic obtained them. She has never seen them before, or even knew they existed. But it dawns on her that, of course, the photos must've come from the files of the police investigation. From Dad's lawyer out in Kyritos. Which means that Dad arranged for them to be copied to Dr. Pollard.

That he has agreed to let the clinic use them.

The first is a shot of the place where Declan died. Several shots. A sequence of digitally sharp photographs from every angle, super-enlarged—a relentless slide show that lasts the full four hours.

The next day, a different slide show: the place where Dec's body was found. She knows it's the place because his body is right there in the pictures, covered in a blue tarpaulin sheet. The sequence of images stops at the one where a Greek police officer is about to pull the sheet away.

She finds Caron next door, in her bedroom. It's lunch-time, but neither one can face eating. Shiv came up here to be by herself for a bit before Talk but heard sobbing as she passed Caron's door and couldn't just walk on by. She knocked, and after a moment, the older girl let her in.

They're sitting at opposite ends of the bed, struggling for words. Caron looks as though she might start crying again.

"It was Mel," she manages to say. "Just after she collapsed."

Thinking she was goofing around, a guy at the party had carried on filming Melanie on his phone, Caron explains. The clinic must have got hold of the footage and produced stills from it. In the first few days of PTU, the images of Mel at the party *before* she took the pill—laughing, dancing, singing along to a song—have hit Caron hard enough. Today, she's pale and shaky, eyes underscored by dark shadows, hair hanging limp and greasy. "How about yours?"

Shiv tells her about the latest pictures and Caron puts a hand to her mouth as though she's about to vomit.

"How can you bear to—" But she can't finish the sentence.

"I guess it was always going to come to this," Shiv says.

"Come to *what*?"

"Just—death."

Melanie and Declan, dying. For thirty days they were brought back to life; now they're being brought back to death. But she can't find a way to say this that won't sound brutal. She studies Caron. Where's the sassy girl in the scarlet dress? The girl who stashed cigarettes in her knickers?

"I don't know if I can face Talk and Write this afternoon," Shiv says.

"No," Caron says after a moment. "Me neither."

The afternoon sessions have continued as before, with the difference that each resident is required to speak—no exceptions—and to read out what they have written. They must speak and write about the death, nothing else. As Assistant Sumner puts it, they have to "sift the psychological rubble" created by the morning picture shows. Talk and Write strayed into this terrain, in Phase One, but never with such intensity.

Sumner probes, digs. Insists on details, however gory. *Where did they die, exactly? What happened, exactly? Tell me how, exactly, it was your fault?*

"Will you write me a note to say I'm sick?" Shiv asks, hoping to tease a smile from her friend. To conjure up a flash of the old Caron.

Caron lets the remark go. Talks about something else but stops at the sound of feet scuffing along the corridor. The footsteps pass Caron's door and halt outside Shiv's. Silence. As though the person is listening, trying to figure out if Shiv is in her room. Then the familiar *rat-a-tat-tat* of knuckles on wood.

"Mikey," Caron says, her voice flat.

"He'll be wondering why I'm not at lunch." Shiv wants to find out how he is after this morning's PTU, but not if it means making Caron feel abandoned.

"That's nice of him." Toneless again.

Shiv can all too easily imagine the shots of the river where Mikey's sister drowned, the muddy bank where her body was dragged ashore. He has taken surprisingly well to Phase Two, the tougher line. Like finally, the clinic gets the *point*. Call it treatment, but to Mikey, the pictures are a form of punishment. She wonders if today's images will be enough, or how much farther he needs to go before he finds the right kind of tree, the right way to bash his head against it.

She turns to Caron. "Don't be like that."

"I'm not being like anything."

Rat-a-tat-tat next door. "Shiv?" Mikey calls.

Her eyes flick toward the sound, then back to Caron. "I should—"

"Yeah," her friend says, "you don't want your little brother to worry."

Shiv glares at her. "He's *not* my brother."

"Whatever you say, Shiv."

The images undergo another change. Still the slide show of death, but gradually some living versions of Declan appear in the mix. More holiday photos, overlaying the ones of him beneath that tarpaulin, so that she can see the living brother through the outline of the dead one or the dead brother through the living.

It doesn't stop at photographs.

On Day Forty or Forty-One (she's losing track), the moving images start to appear. She'd forgotten about the clips Mum filmed with her phone in Kyritos.

Declan, performing handstands on the beach.

Declan, doing a backward flip off the springboard.

The clinic has chosen ones that show her brother at his most energetic, most vital. *Look how alive he is! How happy!* She didn't mind the nighttime picture shows in her bedroom, but these moving images of the life she snuffed out are unbearable, especially right after the days of death shots.

With them comes sound. Dec talking, shouting. Laughing.

Hearing his voice shocks Shiv into the realization that she will never hear him speak again. Never hear his silly jokes, his clever riffs, his witty sarcasm, his funny accents, his stupid yodel-singing. Never hear his voice break from boy's to man's. Never hear him at the end of a phone, pretending to be the answering machine. Never hear him shout at her to hurry up in the bathroom. Never hear him say her name.

Of course, she hasn't heard his voice in all the months since the night he died, except in her dreams and her imagination. But it has taken till now—taken *this,* Declan yelling "Watch and weep, Shivoloppoulos!" as he backward somersaults into the pool—to lay it bare for her.

She has condemned her brother to eternal silence.

FOURTEEN

Dec looks well. Tanned and smiley, spinning a volleyball on the tip of his middle finger. For a second, it looks as though he's mastered it; then the ball reels off and thumps onto the sand.

"You were such a pain that day," Shiv says. "D'you remember?"

Over and again, he tries to perfect the trick, Mum recording every attempt. You can hear her in the background, alternating between words of encouragement and bursts of laughter. They're meant to be starting a game, two-a-side, but her brother insists on keeping them waiting while he shows off his ball-spinning skill.

"It made you so cross that you couldn't do it."

There he is, being cross. "I could *do* it before," he says, on the footage.

Like it's their fault—Shiv's for watching, Mum's for filming, even though he nagged her to. The clip ends with a freeze-frame: Dec's face half obscured by the volleyball, the ball and his hand blurred, the forearm encrusted with sand, as though afflicted by some strange skin condition.

"Then Dad took the ball off you and did a perfect spin. D'you remember?" She laughs; on the wall, he does too. "That *really* pissed you off."

Shiv gets up, crosses the room.

Touches the image. Tries to brush the sand off his arm. As she does so, the picture dissolves beneath her fingertips, mutating into a photo of her brother's lumpy, tarpaulin-covered corpse.

Like the wall's electrified, Shiv jerks her hand away. Almost immediately, the freeze-frame of Dec with the volleyball reappears.

"Dr. Pollard reckons I have a demon inside me," she says after a moment, trying to steady her breathing. "Reckons I have to be exorcised." Declan passes no comment. Shiv smiles to herself. Then, serious again, "They never *blamed* me."

Who? he doesn't ask.

"Mum and Dad. The police. Anyone, really." She realizes she is about to touch the wall again and stops herself before the image changes. *"It's your fault. If it wasn't for you, he'd still be alive*—they all think it, but no one has ever said it to my face."

Dec is quiet still.

"Do *you* think it? Do you blame me?"

Silence.

"You do. Why wouldn't you?"

A partially obscured smile. A ball. A blurry hand. A sand-encrusted arm. A flare of irritation ignites inside her; she snuffs it out. He's only twelve years old, after all. Dec should be angry with her, not the other way round.

"When I came here, I told Dr. Pollard I had to find some way to live with what I did to you." Her voice is breaking up. "But how can I? How *can* I live with it?"

Declan has nothing to say to her.

The next day, in PTU, there are no images at all. Just a sound track.

Barking dogs. For ten minutes at a time, every half an hour for four hours.

Not just any barking, but a ferocious din so loud, so *savage,* the beasts might burst into the room at any moment and tear her to pieces. Shiv can't see them, but she's sure they're the ones from the tree dream, waiting for her to fall from her branch.

Shiv talks about the dogs in Talk, writes about them in Write. Explains to the group about her nightmare and how the dogs fit into the events of Dec's last night. His very last moments. It doesn't help; if anything, she's more traumatized by them than when she was in that room. From what the others say and read out, the morning sessions are pushing all the residents into what Dr. Pollard calls the "endgame"—forcing them to relive the last hours and minutes of their lost ones' lives. In Kyritos, the dogs were an odd but irrelevant detail; nothing to do with Dec's death, really. Or so it felt at the time. Now it's like they go to the very core of what happened. Like the dogs are outraged by Shiv, driven demented by witnessing what she did to her brother. Like they're *judging* her.

Of course, she knows the sound track isn't the actual dogs from that night. But it might as well be.

Looking around the circle of haunted faces in S-10 as Sumner calls Write to a close, Shiv sees she's not alone in being taken to the darkest, deepest reaches of herself. If

203

this stage is meant to drive out her demons, to exorcise her guilt, it's having the opposite effect. At no time since Declan died has Shiv hated herself as much as she does right now.

Back in her bedroom, she aims to take a long shower with the water full-blast, in the hope it will wash away the dogs' stink and drown out their relentless barking. She twists the dial to let the water run hot while she strips off. But the glimpse of the Salinger T-shirt as she unzips her top stalls her in the middle of the bathroom.

Don't ever tell anybody anything. If you do, you start missing everybody.

"Why did you even wear this shirt, Dec?" she says. "You were always talking to people, making friends. Telling them stuff."

A memory comes back to her. She's about three years old, maybe three and a half, and she's in the back lounge with its scratchy red carpet, dressing her dolls for a tea party. Declan toddles over with his shape-sorter, wanting her to play. She's playing with her dolls, she tells him. He starts to cry. And that's it—the dolls are set aside and Shiv sits on the floor with her brother, taking turns to slot colored wooden blocks into the round, the square, the triangular, the diamond-shaped holes, then tipping them all out and starting over again.

Shiv continues standing there for a moment. Then she finishes undressing and steps into the shower cubicle and stands under the water for the longest time.

And then this: Declan on board *Poseidon IV*.

Even though he's sitting on one of the benches, he

sways exaggeratedly with the motion of the boat, as though it was being tossed about in a typhoon. He's in his red swim shorts, his skin the color of honey. Mum, filming, tells him to "stop jigging about," her voice fractured by buffeting wind and the *swish-swoosh* of the sea. Just then, one of the other passengers—the old English lady—passes Dec something and an uncertain smile flickers across his lips.

"Hold it out," Shiv can hear her mother say.

Her brother extends his hand toward the camera, palm up. The picture jerks a bit, fuzzing in and out of focus as Mum zooms in for a close-up.

The dried-out corpse of a baby turtle.

Shiv puts a hand to her mouth. How have they managed to mend it, to make it whole again after she—but, of course, that happened later. When they were back home, just the three of them, and she finally got round to unpacking her suitcase. She'd forgotten the creature was there, buried among her clothes, in its pink tissue-paper wrapping. The moment she came across it, Shiv carried it out to the bathroom, snapped the turtle into little pieces and flushed them down the toilet. Three flushes it took, to get rid of them all.

Even as she tells herself the footage on the boat was shot *before* she did that—and that it's perfectly rational for the turtle to be intact in this film—a part of Shiv's brain can't make any sense of these images at all.

On the wall, Mum zooms in closer still.

So close, so super-enlarged, Shiv can make out individual scales of blackened, desiccated skin and partially formed shell, the tiny pits where its eyes would've been. And the backdrop (filling most of the space between floor and ceiling): Declan's hand, the creases in his palm and the joints of his fingers encrusted with grains of sand, or maybe salt, that wink like diamonds in the sun's sharp glare . . . the whorls and swirls of his fingerprints . . . and where the base of his thumb meets his wrist, a bluish-white artery pulses beneath the skin with the *beat-beat-beat* of his blood.

All morning, the film is replayed. Over and over. Its images, she knows, will worm their way into her dreams tonight (if she sleeps).

For the rest of the day, Shiv can't erase them from her mind—like when you look directly at the sun, then look away, and spots of light and color swim in your vision for a few seconds afterward. Except these images stay with her for hours on end, as though the dazzling Greek sunshine in that footage has burned the pictures onto her retina.

"How was your session?" Shiv asks.

Mikey shrugs. "Same."

Sometimes he tells her about the pictures and footage he sees during PTU, but mostly, he doesn't. He shoves his fingers roughly through his hair. They're in his room (no longer a "cell" but a bedroom again), sitting at opposite ends of the bed, Mikey in his yellow jumpsuit—the one throwback to his convict period.

"How about yours?" he says.

Shiv describes the film of Declan on *Poseidon IV*. Mikey knows all about the boat trip from the stuff she's said in Talk and read out in Write.

"I should've guessed they'd show that sooner or later," she says.

Declan's death began there, on that beautiful, perfect day. Everything that followed over the days and weeks and months to come started with her snorkel kit snagging in her hair; with Nikos fixing it; with where that led. Where Shiv led it. If they hadn't gone on that boat trip, Declan would still be alive and Shiv wouldn't be sitting here in the Korsakoff Clinic, talking to Mikey.

But they did.

"D'you ever think of the thousands of ways it might've happened differently?" Shiv asks. "With Phoebe, I mean."

Mikey looks at her. "All the time."

"My old counselor used to go on about that. Like Dec dying was just a fluke—as random as being struck by lightning. Like I wasn't *responsible*, I was just *unlucky*. I swear, she actually expected me to believe that."

"It's why they show us all this stuff in PTU," Mikey says. "From back before it happened, you know?"

"What, to torture us with all the moments when we could've stopped it?" Shiv shakes her head. "I don't need their help to do that."

He taps his skull. "She likes to mess with our heads."

She. Dr. Pollard. When it's just the two of them, he often lets slip his true feelings about this place. Publicly, though, Mikey is a *good boy* since the switch to Phase Two. No resistance, no kicking off, no trying to hurt himself. The clinic is giving this new Mikey the benefit of the doubt—putting him back on the same daily routine as everyone else, lifting the restrictions he'd been under, scaling down the supervision.

Shiv suspects that he hopes to lull the staff into lowering their guard. Part of his master plan, whatever that might be. If she asks what he's up to, he acts like he has no idea what she's on about.

"I still talk to Declan," she says. *Despite Phase One,* she doesn't need to add.

Mikey just waits for her to say something else. He has always denied talking to his sister, or "seeing" her, but Shiv isn't sure she believes him.

"That's messing with our heads, isn't it?" she goes on. "They spend the whole of Phase One making us see how delusional we are, then they lock us in a room for four hours a day with wall-to-wall movies of the people we're supposed to let go of."

"What would you do different?" Mikey asks.

"What?"

"On that boat. If you could go back in time, like."

"Oh." The sudden switch back to their earlier topic throws her for a moment. The question *itself* throws her. "I, um, I guess . . ." She's about to say she wouldn't go on the boat in the first place, or that she'd make sure not to come on to Nikos, but she knows neither answer would be true. The thought of erasing the time she spent with Nikos—the turtle trip, the windsurfing, heading up the mountain to see the vulture, playing football on the beach, dancing in the street, drinking beer and kissing on the rocks . . . They were the best, the happiest, days of her life.

"The last evening," she says, trying to keep her voice steady. "That's what I'd do differently. I'd stay in, playing cards." She nods, wipes her face, takes a deep breath. "That's what I'd do. I'd play cards with my brother."

Most people look away when you cry in front of them; Mikey goes on gazing at her face. No telling from his expression whether he's sympathetic or what he's thinking. Shiv likes his matter-of-factness. If she has to cry, he lets her get on with it.

"How about you?" she says at last. "What would you do differently?"

"I'd keep hold of Feebs' hand."

"Even if it meant you got swept away too? Even if you *both* drowned?"

He nods. "Even if."

That silences them for a while. Mikey sits at his end of the bed, gnawing a thumbnail. Avoiding eye contact, self-conscious all of a sudden. Hunched up like a skinny Buddha or some homeless kid begging in a shop doorway. The big brother with no little sister to be big brother to.

She told him, right after it happened, what Caron had called him that time. "Your little brother." And what Dr. Pollard suggested down at the lake, about Shiv and Mikey being drawn to one another as surrogate brother and sister.

"Is that how you see us?" Shiv asked him.

"No," he replied, once she'd explained what "surrogate" meant.

"Good. Me neither."

Even so, they were awkward with one another for a couple of days after that. Looking at him now, Shiv finds herself mentally ticking off all the ways in which Mikey is nothing like her brother, or any kind of brother to her. But if Declan were here, in this place with her (how could *that* ever happen?), she knows they would be sitting at opposite ends of his bed, or hers, talking like this.

"I wanted to be sent to prison." She gestures at Mikey's jumpsuit. "Wanted to make a confession so they'd have to charge me with something. The Greek police." Mikey is studying her intently. "But the lawyer Dad hired—he wouldn't let me."

"It's not up to him," he says. "Not up to any of them."

Any of them. Lawyers, police, social workers, magistrates. Psychotherapists. Counselors. Parents. This clinic. Who were *they* to absolve, to forgive, to *choose* for her—to choose treatment over punishment?

It was too hot to spend another moment on the lounger. Shiv sat up, sweat trickling down her back. She squinted at the pool's dazzling surface; the thought of plunging into the water sent a cold thrill through her veins.

Mum called over to her from the shade of the pergola, where she and Dad were playing quoits. "Sure you won't join us?"

Shiv shook her head.

Dad, collecting the hoops for his turn, didn't look up. He'd hardly spoken to Shiv since the furious quarrel that followed his return from confronting Nikos.

Jesus, the thought of him at the jetty, waiting for the boat to come in.

A couple of hours later, he'd come back. Through her open bedroom window she'd heard her parents talking down below, on the patio.

"You didn't *hit* him, did you?" Mum had said.

"No, of course not. But I thought his father was going to."

There was a pause. Then Mum again, "So, what did Nikos say?"

"He says it didn't go any further than kissing."

When Mum asked if he believed him, Dad said he did—*the lad* had looked genuinely shocked and remorseful.

Shiv went downstairs then—*ran* down, banging the patio doors open and yelling, tripping over her words. "You didn't believe *me*, did you?"

"Siobhan—"

"You believed Declan and now you believe Nikos, but when I—"

"He said you lied about your age." She had never seen Dad so angry. "Said he wouldn't have come anywhere near you if he'd known you were a child."

"A *child*? He never said that!"

"Those were his exact words. And, like it or not, that's what you are—a child, a fifteen-year-old girl. And fifteen-year-olds on holiday with their family do not sneak off at night with nineteen-year-old men. Christ, Shiv, anything could've happened."

"You know what, I really wish it had."

Dad thumped one of the dining chairs. "He could have *raped* you!"

Declan was standing there. Shiv hadn't even heard him come outside. "Happy now?" she said, rounding on him.

Her brother shrugged. "I wasn't the one who went off with Nikos."

"Why should it bother you so much what I get up to with him anyway?"

"It *doesn't*." But she saw his fear over where she was going with this.

She went there even so. "Unless you're *jealous*, of course."

"Shut up."

"Yeah? Is that it? Do you wish—"

"Siobhan," Mum said, "that's *enough*."

Declan had tears in his eyes. "Just . . . shut *up*!"

Shiv stood up, her skin unpeeling from the plastic surface of the lounger, and stepped gingerly across the hot
flagstones to the poolside. She dived right in.

The shock of the cold was exhilarating, just the best
feeling.

She could gladly have stayed there. Down in the
depths, among the bubbles and eddies, with the thrum-
ming in her ears, and the shafts of sunlight glimmering
on the pale blue sides of the pool. She surfaced with a
gasp.

"Don't burn up there, will you?" This was Mum, stepping out from under the pergola to call up to Declan,
one hand raised to shield her eyes. "Dec, love?"

No answer. He was there, on the balcony—Shiv
could see his feet resting on the wooden rail. Declan had
skipped breakfast altogether this morning and finally
appeared on the balcony after the rest of them had retreated to the poolside for what Mum called "a lazy last
day" of the holiday. After yesterday's truncated trip to
the fort, and what followed, none of them was in the
mood for going anywhere or doing anything as a family.

"Leave him be," Dad said. With Dec it was "leave him
be" but whenever Shiv acted like that it was "let her sulk."

She disliked hating her brother. Or hating herself
for hating him, which was much the same thing. They'd
had their bust-ups before but nothing on this scale, or so
malicious. Yes, she had felt pure malice toward him. For

ruining everything with Nikos. For saying what he'd said in the car on the way to the fort. She had wanted to say something to get back at him. To *hurt* him.

Well, she'd done that sure enough.

Shiv continued to stare up at her brother's feet, the white soles stark against the tanned insteps. The rest of him was obscured by the towels draped over the rail to dry—or that he'd put there to hide himself away from them all. From *her*.

One more afternoon, one more evening, one more night. This time tomorrow, they'd be on the flight home. The thought sank a dead weight of sadness into her.

It was all she could do to stop herself climbing out of the pool and jogging out to the road to flag down a car to take her to the harbor where Nikos and his father ran their boat trips. Instead, Shiv pushed off and swam— length after length after length.

Declan didn't join them for lunch. He didn't eat the plate of food Mum took up to him.

"Can't you go up there and try to make peace with him?" Mum said.

"*Me?* He's the one who said I'd been *shagging* Nikos."

"Shiv."

"His word, not mine."

They were sitting in the shade of the tree at the far end of the pool—Shiv, texting Laura and Katy about meeting up when she got back; Mum, playing patience, the cards warped with heat and moisture. Dad was inside the villa, having a nap.

"Who are you texting?" Mum asked.

"Not Nikos, if that's what you're thinking."

Her mother turned a card over. The jack of hearts. She looked at it as though she'd never come across that card before. "You know, Shiv, saying that to Dec . . ."

She let the sentence trail off.

"He *lied* about me," Shiv said, aware how sullen she sounded. She didn't want to think about the look in her brother's eyes after what she said to him.

"Look, you have strong feelings for Nikos," Mum said. "I can see that."

"Can we not talk ab—"

"But Declan is your *brother*, Siobhan." She paused to let that register. "He will be your brother for the rest of your lives—long after me and your father are gone. And long after you've forgotten Nikos."

Shiv stared out over the olive grove. The solitary goat was there as usual, lying in the shade beneath one of the trees. Across the bay, the windsurfers were out, their sails like scraps of bunting torn loose by the breeze.

She recalled Declan's face when Nikos rescued him from the riptide. She had never seen him so happy—so besotted, now she thought about it.

She'd been too wrapped up in Nikos to notice that Dec was as well.

He will be your brother for the rest of your lives.

"I'm going for a dip," she said, the lounger creaking beneath her as she got up.

Mum started to speak, but Shiv wasn't listening. She was in the water before her mother finished the sentence and before her own tears had properly begun.

She swam till her breath was ragged and her whole body tingled.

Flipping onto her back, exhausted, Shiv spread her limbs and floated like a starfish. Her brother's feet were still there. Gazing up at the balcony, drifting, she had the illusion that she was the one remaining still while the building spiraled into the sky like a gigantic villa-shaped helium balloon, carrying Declan away.

Shiv was sitting on the edge of the pool, legs dangling in the water, the heat of the afternoon sun on her shoulders, when she spotted the tennis ball among the shrubbery. That first day of the holiday, when Dec had surprised her with a wet splat in the head, seemed an age ago. They'd got each other a couple of times since then.

Shiv glanced up at the balcony. Those feet, that screen of towels.

Retrieving the ball, she leaned over the side of the pool to give it a good long dunk, smiling to herself at the idea of the sodden ball making Declan jump half out of his skin. If he was asleep, better still.

Underhand or overhand? Underhand, she decided.

Shiv positioned herself beneath the balcony, the tennis ball streaming water onto the flagstones, took aim, and sent it high into the air. Too hard. She'd thrown the ball so far it cleared the balcony altogether and hit the front edge of the pantiled roof . . . then rebounded and dropped onto her target. The yelped expletive told her all she needed to know.

She did the clenched fist thing, the *yesyesyes!* thing.

On the balcony, nothing. Silence.

Everything returned to the way it was before she threw the ball, except that the feet had disappeared from the rail. Dec could still have been hiding up there, or maybe he'd slunk off indoors. The thrill, the sense of fun, ebbed away. It'd seemed like a good idea at the time. Now, she couldn't have said for sure why she'd thrown that ball or what she hoped might come of it.

Did she really believe things would just click back into place between them?

Shiv looked over toward Mum at the far end of the pool, still playing patience. She'd paused mid-deal to watch the goings on. "Talk to him," she mouthed. But Shiv wouldn't go up there. She had made her gesture of conciliation and, stupid as it was, she'd been ignored—left standing there like an idiot.

Turning from the balcony, she headed along the side of the pool toward the patio doors. Go in, out of the sun. Make a start on packing her case.

"Did he give you that?"

Shiv started, almost dropping the baby turtle. She hadn't heard her mother's footsteps on the stairs or had any idea she was standing in the doorway. "Yeah," Shiv said. She was sitting on the bed, a half-packed suitcase yawning open beside her.

Mum came over. "Can I see?"

Shiv handed the turtle's tiny corpse to her. Mum asked if it was the one from the boat trip and Shiv said she supposed it must be.

"Poor little chap," Mum said, returning it.

Shiv wrapped it up again, stowing it between layers of clothes in her case—for protection, but also to hide it from Dad. And from Declan, for that matter.

"That was a *lovely* day on the boat, wasn't it?" Mum said.

Shiv nodded. "Uh-huh."

She'd half turned away but Mum noticed her crying even so. "Oh, sweetheart," she said, pulling Shiv into a hug—Mum standing, Shiv sitting on the bed, face pressed against her mother's stomach. Her shoulders, her whole body, shuddered with sobs. "Let it out," Mum said, stroking her hair. "Let it all out."

"I *love* him, Mum."

"I know, I know."

"I do. I really *do*."

They were going out for dinner, Mum and Dad. Mum had tried to talk him out of it—in *the circumstances,* she'd said, perhaps it might be best if they stayed home? Dad wasn't having any of it.

"I'm not letting her spoil our anniversary."

Shiv had eavesdropped on the argument. It had been obvious her father would win. Now, there they were, ready to go out: Dad, in the doorway, keeping an eye out for the taxi; Mum, putting the finishing touches to her makeup—talking to Shiv but aiming the words at her own reflection in the mirror by the foot of the stairs.

We'll be back about eleven-ish. . . . I've got my mobile with me. . . . There's pasta in the cupboard and cheese in the fridge that needs using up. That sort of thing.

Shiv was sitting on the sofa, surfing Greek TV channels with the sound muted. Dec was upstairs somewhere.

"Taxi's here," Dad said.

"You sure you two are going to be all right?"

"*Mum.*"

"Right, right—we're going."

Once they were gone, Shiv mooched about for a bit before deciding to give it another go with Declan. But when she went to the landing and called his name, asking if he wanted her to knock him up something to eat, she got no answer.

"Dec?"

Silence.

"I . . . I'm *sorry*, Dec." She paused, listening hard. "For what I said, yeah? I shouldn't . . . have said that stuff. And," she puffed out her cheeks, "I'm *really* sorry."

Still no response.

"Dec, *please*. Please don't be like this."

In the end she gave up and returned downstairs to the kitchen. While the pasta was cooking, she checked her phone again. Nikos wasn't talking to her either.

As last evenings of holidays went, they didn't come much more crap than this.

She ate on the terrace, citronella candles scenting the air. She tried not to think of Nikos, just along the coast, at the beach party that was a forerunner to his brother's wedding. There was a second bowl of pasta keeping warm inside but she didn't suppose Declan would show his face. She didn't want *hers*, particularly. In the guttering light from the candles, the penne looked like severed fingers. She speared one tube after another, robotically placing them in her mouth and chewing, swallowing,

219

sipping from the glass of white wine she'd snaffled from the nearly full bottle in the fridge.

Dad might notice some was missing, but so what? She could hardly be in his bad books any more than she was already.

Not that she got to finish her drink.

Because, at that moment, a yellow tennis ball landed on the glass from above, glancing off the rim, knocking the glass over so that it shattered against the dish and spewed wine and broken shards all over the food, the table—all over her lap, too.

"Oh, *yyyeessss*," came a voice from the balcony.

FIFTEEN

"Go on, Shiv! Do it!"

How does she hear him when he is so far below her, way down at the base of the tree, his tiny figure waving up at her, beckoning? But, somehow, Declan's voice reaches her, perched on her impossibly high branch.

"Go on!"

Jump, he means, because there are no lower branches by which to climb down. All she has to do is lean forward, let gravity do the rest. If he got down okay, then so can she. She imagines herself floating like a leaf, spiraling gently to the ground where her brother is waiting, arms outstretched, to catch her.

"Shiv! Do it!"

She does. She shifts her weight, loosens her hold on the branch. Drops.

The fall lasts forever and yet it is over in seconds and, although she knows she is plummeting at great speed—can see the ground accelerating toward her—Shiv has no sensation of movement. So the impact, when it comes, surprises her. Literally takes her breath away.

Water.

What she thought was solid ground is water and she is plunging into its depths.

Then, bursting to the surface once more. Swimming for the shore. Calling out to Declan to help her.

"I'm here, Shiv. I've got you."

She turns toward the voice. "Dec?"

"This way." Hands reach into the water, pull her out, drag her onto the muddy bank at the base of the tree—a face looming into her field of vision as she blinks the water from her eyes. A boy's face. Not Declan.

"Mikey?"

He smiles. "You're safe now."

"Where's my brother?"

"There."

Shiv turns to glimpse a figure floating on the surface—limbs disjointed, neck at a strange angle, clothes soaked in blood—and she sees that the water is glass. A great sheet of glass, shattered to a thousand pieces.

To reach him she must—

Frantically, she starts to repair the damage; picking up one glass fragment, one shard after another and trying to fit them back together like pieces in a jigsaw puzzle. It's no use. Her hands are bleeding and the bits of broken glass refuse to attach, to re-form into their once-smooth, flawless surface.

Shiv looks up at Mikey, standing over her, watching.

"Help me!" she cries. "Mikey, please, you have to show me what to do."

Most of her nightmares are like this now. A terrifying mix of old dreams and new, garbled flashbacks to her brother's death and the surreal images of her unconscious, with Declan and Mikey so interchangeable she can't always tell them apart.

In some of the nightmares, the dogs are there: chained up, barking, snarling, trying to get at Shiv or at whichever boy's body she's stooped over this time.

The visions come while she's awake, too. More and more, they come. They're worse at night, though. So bad, so *real,* she's petrified of letting herself fall asleep.

Dr. Pollard has spoken of residents reaching a "tipping point" in this stage of the program. A point where, instead of staring down into the blackest abyss, their faces begin to tilt—slowly, hesitantly—toward a bright blue sky.

The mind can only take so much darkness before it demands light.

So she would have them believe.

If this is a tipping point for Shiv, it's not the kind the director imagines. No gradual rising up toward the heavens but more like a sudden plunge over the edge, into the depths of hell.

She knows the darkness for what it is, now. Knows herself for what she is.

He can't move, she puts in her notebook in Write.

He can't run.

He can't swim.

He can't throw balls, can't climb trees, can't dive off a springboard.

He can't see.

He can't hear, smell, taste, touch.

He can't think, can't speak.

He can't laugh or cry.

He can't drink. Can't eat.

He can't feel anything ever again. Love, hate. Pain, comfort. Joy, sadness. Hope, despair. Nothing.

He can't breathe.

He can't grow up, grow old.

He is nothing. He is nowhere. For all eternity.

I. DID. THIS. TO. HIM.

The passing of time has become difficult to track—she counts the days in "sleeps," like she did when she was a small child.

Three sleeps since she woke from another nightmare to find her bed soaked in urine. Two sleeps since they showed her the film of Nikos, hands under Dec's armpits, lifting her brother back onto the boat. One sleep since Shiv retrieved her old Walk jumpsuit from the utility room and started wearing it instead of her regular gear.

Dr. Pollard will want to discuss all of this at their next one-to-one.

She is concerned about Shiv. "You seem to be straying off course," she said, the last time they spoke. Four sleeps ago? Three?

"Whose course?" Shiv asked. "Yours or mine?"

Shiv stops eating.

Once she's thought of it, the decision seems so obvious she wonders why it has taken her till now. So, from here on, she will eat nothing, drink only water.

Day after day, this is what she does.

There's something *purifying* about going without food. With each hour that passes, she grows more acutely conscious of the toxins leaching out of her body. Out of her mind, too—the poisoned thoughts slowly draining away. Right after Declan's death—in the days on end when Shiv forgot to eat, or skipped meals, or left food unfinished—she was starving herself out of neglect or inertia, because eating (along with everything else) seemed so pointless. This time is different. Now she's doing it deliberately: cleansing herself, emptying herself, focusing herself.

Punishing herself.

It's tough, at first. Really tough.

But by the third day she is learning to ride out the hunger, and how drinking lots of water can fool her stomach into feeling full. She knows to clasp a pillow to her belly to ease the cramps that sometimes double her over, and when she stands up or moves about, she takes care to hold on to something until the dizziness passes.

She has to be clever, of course. Devious. No clinic lets a patient starve.

At mealtimes, she helps herself to the smallest portions, then sneaks some of her food onto Mikey's plate, or Caron's, while the dining-room supervisor isn't looking. She leaves as much as she can get away with or hides bits in her pockets to dispose of later. When it's okay to eat lunch outdoors, she'll take a sandwich into the garden, away from prying eyes, and feed it to the birds that gather near her bench. The little food that does pass her lips she makes sure to puke back up as soon as she can.

At the daily activities, she wears extra layers of clothing to hide her weight loss; rubs her cheeks to make them less pale, less gaunt-looking. In front of staff, she forces herself to act like nothing's wrong, to move and speak and behave normally.

Mikey understands. But Caron tries to talk her out of it, threatens to tell. So Shiv has to conceal her fasting from Caron, too; difficult but not impossible.

Shiv ought to be wiped out. But she has never felt so alert or so energized. At PTU, the photos and film footage are sharper than ever; in Talk and Write, she gets straight to the heart of things—she speaks, writes, listens *brilliantly*.

"The monks fasted," she tells Mikey. "The ones who lived here back when this place was a monastery. It brought them closer to God."

"Is that what you want?" he asks.

"No, I'm just saying."

"I don't believe in all that." Does he mean fasting, or God? "One of my aunts, right, she comes up to me after the funeral and takes hold of my face in both hands and says, 'Phoebe is playing with the angels now.'" Mikey sniffs, swallows. "Is that what you think—that your brother's in heaven, waiting for you?"

Shiv shakes her head. Pulls the pillow into her belly. They've been in her room most of the afternoon—another Sunday with no sessions, nothing to do. They haven't spoken all that much. Sometimes it's enough for them just to sit in silence.

"Day Fifty tomorrow," Mikey says.

"Really?"

It doesn't seem possible that they'll be leaving the Korsakoff Clinic in just eleven days. Can she get away with starving herself for that long?

Her head aches. Her *eyes* ache.

She closes them. Leans back, hoping the wall's cold surface will ease the knot of pain that's been nagging away inside her skull all day. Bad idea. The thump of her headache grows worse; turns, in her mind, to the *thud-*

thud of a tennis ball—so that she can almost believe if she went next door right now she'd find her brother playing bounce-and-catch in Caron's room.

Four sleeps since she stopped eating.

Today, things are not so clear anymore, not so sharp. The corridors and rooms of Eden Hall are too gloomy, the daylight from the windows too harsh; a doorway, a banister, a chair, a face, float randomly into view, then out again—blurred, as though by tears—and she can't judge their distances. She stumbles on the stairs. Cracks her shin on the low table in Talk. Drops the plastic cup of water when she sets it down. Can't make out the words she writes in Write.

Is this where she blacks out?

She can't be sure. She thinks she might've left S-10 *after* Write—yes, she did, she was walking along the corridor (or was that during the mid-session break?)—anyway, she was walking, or possibly still sitting down, *somewhere*, when her head went swimmy and her ears filled with the sound of crashing waves.

Shiv doesn't recall actually fainting, or falling, or her face hitting the ground, or any of that—just the second or so beforehand, and the absolute certainty that it was about to happen. Then nothing.

SIXTEEN

A smiling face appears in front of her—chalky skin, too-pale blue eyes, flyaway fair hair; the face of a fairy. Of an angel. It takes her a moment to recognize it as Zena's.

"Where is he?" Shiv asks, panicky, trying to sit up.

The nurse's smile crinkles into a frown. "Who?"

Shiv can't recall. She's in a bed, in a light white room, and the bed is so soft, so comfortable. "He climbed too high," she says.

"Here, you're all unwrapped." Zena tidies the covers, straightens the pillows behind Shiv, helping her to sit up a little. "Drink this."

Blue beaker, green straw. *Blue and green should never be seen.* Where does Shiv know that from? Mum, she supposes. Or is it red and green? Shiv fumbles with her lips for the tip of the straw and for some reason is reminded of a giraffe's rubbery mouth as it plucks at a leaf on a high branch.

"Go easy," Zena says. "Just small sips."

Fruit juice. It's so unbelievably *delicious.* Shiv has already swallowed several mouthfuls before she remembers she's only meant to drink water.

"I shouldn't be dr—"

"You're in the sick bay," the nurse says. "*My* rules, not yours."

The sick bay. She looks around. Yes, she knows this room—she's been here with Mikey. Mikey—*that's* who she was asking about just now. "He got stuck in the tree," she says, urgently, batting away the straw as Zena offers her the beaker again. "I went up after him and . . . I must've fallen."

"You fainted."

"No, I was—"

"You passed out as you were leaving Write." The nurse touches her own chin. "Got yourself a bit of a bump—a carpet burn."

Shiv mirrors the gesture, wincing at the sticky, tender skin. Lowering her hand, she realizes—although it must've been there all along—that an intravenous drip is attached to her arm. The IV stand beside her bed holds a plastic pack of clear fluid.

Zena follows Shiv's gaze. "We had to get some nutrients into you."

"Did Caron tell you?"

"You did a very good job of hiding it from us. I'm impressed."

It's clear from her tone that the nurse isn't at all impressed; that she thinks Shiv has been stupid but, also, that the staff have been stupid not to realize sooner.

Shiv examines the tube taped to the back of her hand, where it enters the vein.

"If you pull it out," Zena says, as though reading her thoughts, "I'll just sedate you and put it back in again. *Keep* you sedated, if I have to."

The hours in the sick bay drag and drift. Nothing to do but doze, or stare at the ceiling, or lie there watching the fluid bag slowly drain into her body.

Are they trying to bore her into submission?

In an often-repeated family tale, Mum tells of the time when everything went quiet in the delivery room while she was in labor with Declan. A temporary lull in the contractions, that was all. But as it dragged on, her mother, woozy with pain-relief drugs, looked at Dad and the midwife and asked, "What are we all waiting for?"

"For *you*," the midwife said, laughing.

Dec took twenty-seven hours to be born. He lived twelve years, six months, seven days.

How Mum was, that's how Shiv feels: in suspended animation, with everyone (including Shiv herself) waiting for her. To *do* something. To see what she does next.

Right now, she has no idea what that might be.

Toward evening, judging by the failing light at the window, Zena announces that she has a visitor. Not Mikey—they've told Shiv she can't see him—but even so she half hopes he'll step into the room.

"Hey," Caron says, smiling, but looking uncertain.

"Oh, hey." Shiv sits up; manages to smile back.

"Now, I'm a bit out of practice with you," the older girl says. "*So,* is that your good-to-see-you-please-come-in smile, or your piss-off-and-leave-me-alone smile?"

"Both."

"Zuss, girl, you were nowhere *near* this complex when I first met you."

Actually, Shiv *is* glad to see her. The hours by herself with no one to talk to have worn her down. Her eyes well up.

"Hey, hey." Caron crosses the room, takes up the hand that isn't snagged with an IV tube and massages it between both of hers.

After a moment, she pulls up a chair and sits beside the bed. They don't have much to say at first; at least, they have *lots* to say but leave most of it unsaid. They just sit there like two women working on a patchwork quilt, sharing odd scraps of conversation between bouts of silence. At one point, Caron says, "I was going to wear my red dress, for old time's sake."

In fact, she's in a navy sweatshirt and her faded, ripped-at-the-knee jeans. She points at Shiv's pajamas. "You not wearing your—"

"Underneath," Shiv says, tugging the pajama top. "Fifty days out of fifty."

Even on laundry days, Shiv has got them to tumble-dry the Salinger T-shirt so she could put it back on as soon as possible.

"Was your brother wearing it when he died?" Caron asks.

An image comes to her: yellow T-shirt. "No," she says. "He wanted to wear it on the flight home, so Mum put it in the wash."

It was still pegged on the line at the villa the morning after; Shiv took it down, stashed it in her case—to stop Mum from seeing it more than with the intention of keeping it for herself. That came later, back at home.

"I used to imagine it smelled of him," Shiv says. "But it didn't. It smelled of Greek soap powder." She stifles a yawn.

"Bored of me *already?*" Caron asks. "Or just tired?"

"Bored, definitely."

They smile. It feels good to share a smile with her. Caron looks better, the shadows under her eyes nowhere near as bad as they were. PTU seems, finally, to have begun working for her.

"Actually," Shiv says, "you've lasted longer than my other visitor."

"Who was that?"

"Dr. Pollard. I totally blanked her and after about five minutes she gave up."

Shiv frowns. Was that today, or another day altogether? No, it must've been here, because Nurse Zena was changing her IV bag at the time. But then, *Declan* was standing across the room earlier, when she surfaced from a doze—doing his wave, like there was a window between them and he was wiping a hole in the condensation.

She can't tell things apart anymore: five minutes ago and five hours ago; being awake and being asleep; what's in the room and what's in her head.

For all she knows, she could be imagining *Caron*.

"So, *have* they?" The girl's voice tugs at her attention. Shiv gets the impression she's repeating a question Shiv must not have heard.

"Have they what?"

"Said when they'll let you out of here." The sick bay, she means.

"Not today, they want to fatten me up some more— also, they think I might've knocked myself out when I fainted," Shiv says. "Dunno, maybe tomorrow."

"Then what?"

Shiv shakes her head.

"Only, we're so close to the finish line," Caron says, leaning forward.

"Finish line. You think there's a finish line?"

"There can be, Shiv. If you—"

"Did Pollard put you up to this?" Shiv asks, suddenly cross. "Eh? *Let's send Caron in, see if she can talk some sense into her.* Is that why you're here?"

"No, I *asked* to come." She's annoyed. "If you want the truth, you're 'at such a crucial point in your recovery' I had a job getting Dr. Pollard to let me near you."

"Recovery. That's a laugh."

"'Swhat she said."

Shiv fixes her a look. "So why *did* you want to be anywhere near me?"

"Bizarrely enough, because I *like* you. And I'm worried about you."

"Yeah, well, don't be. I feel good. I feel strong."

"Sure." Caron gestures at her. "I can see that."

Shiv taps her head. "Up here, I'm talking about."

"Right. Cos of course what Declan would've wanted—"

"Don't tell me what my br—"

"—is for his sister to starve herself to death for him."

"Oh, like you never tried to kill yourself over Melanie?"

"That was before."

"Before? Before what?"

"Before I came here."

Shiv shakes her head. "All therapy comes down to the same thing in the end."

"What?"

"You have to learn to think like your therapist. Same in school—'right' is what the teacher says is right, 'wrong' is what the teacher says is wrong."

"No. It's true, what I just said. It's what I believe."

"Really? Or is it just what you need to believe to get yourself through this?"

Caron leaves. No big scene or stropping out of the room—she even finds another smile for Shiv and gives her hand one last squeeze. Then she lets herself out of the sick bay and Shiv is alone once more.

Shiv calls after her, shouts out that she's sorry. Too late.

Her gaze settles on the hand Caron just touched—it was the one with the tube. Shiv looks at the tube, where it goes into the vein. Then she yanks it right out in one quick rip, releasing an arc of startlingly bright red blood across the sheet and, with another swipe of her arm, sends the IV stand crashing to the floor.

It's another couple of days before Shiv's considered well enough—reliable enough—to be discharged from the sick bay.

She's barely in her room ten minutes when Hensher appears at the door.

"Dr. Pollard wants to see you."

Shiv follows him. When she realizes where Hensher is taking her, she begins shaking. Stops in her tracks, starts to turn back. Not until he assures her that the room won't be "active" does she finally agree to step inside.

"You know why this place is called the Korsakoff Clinic, I take it?" Straight in. She hasn't even said *hello* or *how are you?* or anything like that.

Shiv nods. "I read the stuff you sent my dad. Googled it and that."

"So, you'll know Dr. Sergei Korsakoff was a *neuro-*psychiatrist. Psychiatry examines *what* we think and *why* we think it," Dr. Pollard says, "while neuropsychiatry looks at *how* we think. In particular, the effects of neuro-logical damage or disorder."

They're sitting on the floor in Shiv's Personalized Therapy Unit—facing each other across the room, backs against the walls, voices echoing. The projectors are switched off, the walls, floor and ceiling a uniform off-white. Stripped of its picture show, the PTU looks smaller, ordinary. Nothing to fear.

Why has she been brought here, of all places?

The director is talking about Korsakoff's Syndrome.

"Also known as amnesic-confabulatory syndrome. Amnesic, as in memory loss; confabulation, as in false memories or perceptions. In basic terms, sufferers of this disorder not only have gaps and lapses in memory or per-ception, they *create* memories of things which didn't hap-pen in the past and perceptions of things which aren't happening now."

"*Seeing things?*" Shiv asks.

"Hallucination can be a symptom, yes."

Shiv thinks of all those sightings of "Declan" in the grounds. The holding of hands during Walk. The other day in the sick bay.

Dr. Pollard sits up a little straighter, like a propped-up Barbie. Smart, suit-wearing, psychiatrist Barbie. "In some of the incidents after Kyritos—whether or not you realized it, it's probable you were experiencing amnesic-confabulation."

The vandalism, she means. The violence.

Shiv is about to deny it but, no, of course, there was that time she smashed up the bottles of booze in the supermarket and, afterward, had no recollection of doing so. There've been other episodes, now she thinks about it. Blank moments when she has zoned out of conversations or blacked out altogether.

"It's involuntary," Dr. Pollard adds. "A misfiring in the brain that causes you to confuse imagined perceptions with actual ones, whether it's a remembered event or something happening—or seeming to happen—right now, in front of you."

"Why are you telling me all this?" Shiv asks.

"I'm right, aren't I?" the woman says. "You *have* experienced confabulation."

Shiv nods, conscious of being observed. Dr. Pollard's face is creamy, yellowed by the spotlights. It could be made of wax. Shiv is tired. She planned on being asleep in her bed right now, but she knows she has to focus on what the woman is telling her—to try to make sense of it. "Korsakoff says this falsification can also apply to what people *believe to be true*. About themselves, or others. In how they interpret things."

"Like what?"

"Okay, so, even when they remember a true event, they create a false narrative from it. A boy tries to save his sister from drowning, but to his mind, he failed not because the sheer force of the water made it impossible but because he didn't have the courage to take the ultimate risk. To *die* in his attempt to save her, if needs be."

"Mikey."

"To anyone else," Dr. Pollard adds, "the boy did everything he could. But to his way of thinking, he didn't do enough."

"I don't blame myself for not saving Declan," Shiv says. "I blame myself for—"

"False narratives, Siobhan." She holds Shiv's gaze. "They come in different forms—the belief that your loved one is still alive, that you might have prevented their death, that you *caused* their death, that *your* life has no point without them—but essentially, they are all rooted in amnesic-confabulation. They are all fictitious."

"What if you *did* cause their death? Fact, not fiction."

"An illusion is a belief derived from human wishes. D'you know who said that?" Then, "Sigmund Freud."

"What—you're saying I *wanted* to kill Declan?"

"No, of course not. But you want it to be true that you killed him."

Shiv bangs the back of her head hard against the wall. "Because it *is* true."

"Is it? You *literally* kil—"

"What happened happened because of me."

"And if that means 'I killed him' you must be made to pay for his death. Yes?"

Shiv doesn't answer. Just sits there, staring at the floor between her splayed feet, the boards patterned with tiny woodworm holes like a crazy dot-to-dot picture waiting to be filled in. Her head smarts from where she banged it.

"Not everyone who's bereaved suffers illusions," Shiv says sullenly.

"That's true. But, at this clinic, we specialize in treating people who do."

"So why me? Why do I . . . confabulate?"

"There are two main causes," Dr. Pollard says, adjusting her glasses. "One is organic: a thiamine deficiency. Then there's your sort, caused by trauma. It could be physical, such as damage to the brain's prefrontal cortex, or due to a sudden, extreme shock. An Acute Stress Reaction."

"Post-traumatic stress disorder," Shiv says. "That's what my counsel—"

"PTSD's not quite the same. In PTSD people tend to have repressed memories or intense flashbacks of the traumatic episode. Or both. I know this applies to you, but what you *also* display is the amnesic-confabulation we've been talking about."

"Seeing things that aren't real."

"Yes. And believing things which aren't true."

Dr. Pollard explains that, in Acute Stress Reaction, the patient can't make sense of what has happened or what's going on around them. "So they rewrite the story in their unconscious," she says. "And what you end up with is *two* realities—the real reality and the false reality—merged into one."

Like this room, Shiv thinks. This is real reality: blank walls, no audio, an empty, neutral space; the false reality is the one she experiences in her PTU sessions—that this room is a portal to the time she killed her brother. Perhaps that's why the director chose it today—to demonstrate its harmlessness.

Who knows? Shiv isn't sure she knows anything anymore.

A thought strikes her. "How do the film shows and photos help me to sort out the real from the false?" She gestures at the walls. "Surely they'd just make it worse."

"They do. That's the point."

"*What?*"

"In the First World War, a lot of soldiers suffered terrible facial injuries," Dr. Pollard says. "The medics in the battlefields patched them up as best they could, then sent them home for proper reconstructive work—the pioneering experiments in what we now know as plastic surgery. But before—"

"What has this got to do with—"

"*Before* the surgeons could operate to repair and rebuild, they had to break apart the patch-up and return the face to its original, damaged state, let the wounds heal again and start from scratch. If they didn't, the reconstructive surgery would be a botch job, causing even worse disfigurement—not to mention the risk of infection."

The director pauses, studying Shiv's reaction.

"So, the PTU sessions—" Shiv begins.

"Are the psychiatric equivalent of reconstructive surgery, yes. D'you recall, at the start of Phase Two, I described it as Trauma Centered Therapy?"

Shiv nods.

"Well, this stage of your treatment is designed to

break apart all the therapy you've had before, to strip away the scar tissue of your grief, cut through the layers of confabulation—take you right back to your original traumatized state."

"And then what?"

"Let you see the truth of it."

After Declan had helped clear up the mess and Shiv had changed out of her wine-soaked shorts, they sat on the low wall to watch the sun setting over the bay.

A chance to talk. To make up.

They were both still too raw, though, to set the ill-feeling aside completely. It would take more than a tennis ball. But after the last couple of days, the simple act of sitting side by side—gazing at the shifting colors of the sky, the warm breeze bathing their faces—was a kind of healing. Or the start of one.

"What happens if Mum and Dad see there's a glass missing?" Dec asked.

"We deny all knowledge. Anyway, it's not my problem," Shiv added, teasing. "I wasn't the one who broke it."

"No," Dec said. "And I wasn't the one drinking wine."

Another silence gathered round them. "It *was* a good shot, though," Shiv said at last, smiling.

"I thought so."

They were still sitting there when the drone of a pair of mopeds disturbed the evening hush, turning off the main road and coming along the track.

Shiv glanced at Dec. "It won't be him," she said, her mouth dry.

Shiv met Nikos coming the other way along the path down the side of the villa. All the strength had drained from her legs. But she would not allow herself to be weak.

"Hey, there you are," he said, his face unnaturally white in the glare of the security lamp. He was smiling, but tentatively. It was the first time she'd seen him so unsure of himself. "I thought nobody was home."

She tried to keep her voice steady. "What are you doing here, Nikos?"

"I, uh"—he spread his hands—"I remembered what you said about your parents going out tonight. For their anniversary."

"That doesn't answer my question."

They were a couple of meters apart, hemmed in by shrubbery on one side and the whitewashed wall of the villa on the other. Nikos hung his head, as though accepting that he deserved to be spoken to like that. "I had to see you," he said quietly.

Had to. "Suppose my mum and dad had been here?"

He gestured back toward the rental car. "I thought they *were*, at first."

"Dad would've *killed* you." The idea of her father killing anyone was ludicrous. Nikos just nodded, though. "Who's with you?" Shiv said, refusing to soften her tone.

"My cousin. Joss. We're on our way to my brother's party."

"Uh-huh." They continued to stand there, facing one another. He looked at a loss to know what to say or do next. "Well, have a nice time," Shiv said, turning to go.

"*Shiv,* I wanted to say sorry."

She turned back. "For what?"

"For everything. I . . . I'm sorry the way things worked out."

"You told Dad you didn't know I was a *child*. Was I a *child* to you, Nikos?"

"No. You weren't."

"So why did you say that?"

You lied about your age, he could've said. *You deceived me. You could've got me arrested, thrown in jail, branded a sex offender.* Nikos might've said any of these things, she realized. But he didn't.

"I told your father what he wanted to hear."

Shiv frowned. "What does that mean?"

Nikos rubbed his face, the stubble rasping against the palm of his hand. "It means you don't stop liking someone just because they're younger than you thought."

It had been so black-and-white before he turned up, but now he was confusing her. "I texted you," she said. "I left messages on your voice mail."

"I know. I'm sorry. That was the deal with your dad."

Shiv laughed despite herself. "So, you thought it'd be safer to *visit* me?"

Nikos took a moment to answer. Finally, he said, "You go back to England tomorrow. I came because I can't bear not to see you again. *Couldn't*. Couldn't bear."

With that, the last of her resolve fell away. Almost. She took a step toward him and, as he opened his arms to hold her, she thumped him hard in the shoulder.

"What was *that* for?" Nikos said, steadying himself against the wall.

"I don't know. I just . . . bloody felt like it, all right?"

Whether they would have hugged then, she never found out. Because at that moment, Joss appeared at the end of the path. "So," he said, grinning over Nikos's shoulder, his bald head as shiny in the security light as the silver crash helmet tucked under one arm. "Do they coming for the party?"

Declan wanted nothing to do with it—with them, the party, anything. If Shiv wanted to go, it was up to her.

"I'm not leaving you here by yourself."

"I'm nearly thirteen," her brother said. "Not seven."

"Dec, I'm not going if you're not. End of."

"Fine. We don't go, then."

And so on. In truth, it was a crazy idea—at best, they had two hours before Mum and Dad got back. But the alternative was to say goodbye to Nikos right there and then. Watch him leave her life. Then spend the rest of the evening—the last night of the holiday—at the villa with Declan. Playing cards. Or quoits. Or watching Greek TV or CNN. Finishing her packing. Killing time till their parents came home in their taxi, squiffy with wine.

Whatever, Declan refused to go. And Shiv refused to go without him.

She left Dec sitting on the wall while she went back out to the front of the villa to break the news to Nikos and his cousin.

"Sheev, you waits," Joss said, tapping the side of his nose. "I go speak him."

A couple of minutes later, he returned, beaming. Giving the thumbs-up. Then Declan appeared, a pace or two behind, wearing the silver crash helmet.

"Mum and Dad don't get to know about this," Shiv said, above the music. "Not *ever*."

"Not ever," her brother repeated. "There must be a simpler way of saying that. Like, I dunno, 'never.' You'd think someone would've invented that word by now."

She pointed at the can of Coke in his hand. "Has Joss put anything in that?"

"No," Dec said. "Anyway, *you* can talk."

He was right. If Shiv drank much more wine, her parents wouldn't need Dec's help to figure out where they'd been. She set the plastic glass down, twisting the base into the sand to keep it from tipping.

"I'm going to dance a bit more," she said.

"Shiv, you don't have to keep coming over to check I'm okay."

"I know." She held his gaze. "I'm just . . . I know. Sorry."

They stayed longer than they'd intended, but that was okay—Shiv got a text from Mum saying the prebooked taxi had failed to show and they wouldn't get back to the villa till eleven-thirty at the earliest.

No worries, Shiv texted back.

All ok with u?

Gin rummy. I'm winning!

Shiv shut the phone off, only the tiniest bit guilty at the deceit. She made a mental note to settle on the final score at cards with Dec so he didn't contradict her.

Pitching up at the party hadn't been as awkward as she'd feared—a brief flurry of attention when the four of them arrived, that was all. The about-to-be-married brother set the tone by greeting her in an *if it's cool with Nikos, it's cool with me* way. Shiv and Nikos danced barefoot in the sand. Even Declan (who never, not ever, danced) joined in toward the end, after a third raid on the barbecue. Joss, too, pogo-dancing like a flabby Tigger, spraying froth from the neck of a bottle of Mythos. His shirt was saturated with sweat or beer, or both.

"What's with your cousin's name?" she asked Nikos, mouth against his ear to make herself heard. "'Joss' doesn't sound very Greek."

"Short for Giorgios." Her hair snagged on his stubble as he spoke. His breath was bittersweet with beer. "His surname's Giorgios as well," Nikos said, laughing.

"Really? That's hilarious."

"No, *that's* Hilarios, in the green shirt, standing over there by the barbie."

Shiv looked where he was pointing before realizing he was making fun of her.

"Not the bad shoulder!" Nikos cried, moving swiftly out of range.

They left the beach, Joss and Declan leading the way, Shiv and Nikos following, hand in hand. Nikos and Joss would rejoin the party once they'd taken Shiv and Dec back.

"Can I ask you something?" Shiv kept her voice down so the two in front wouldn't overhear.

"Depends what it is." It was Nikos's teasing tone, but she detected a heaviness underneath. The end of the evening, the holiday, hung over them both.

"You brought me here to dump me, didn't you?" she said.

He walked quietly beside her, barefoot, his sandals and motorcycle helmet dangling by their straps from the fingers of his free hand. "Shiv, for us to finish the way it was—just *pfft* . . . I didn't want that."

"But you do want it to finish." She made it a statement, not a question.

He exhaled. "You live in England, I live in Greece. You have, what? Three more years in school. Then university. You know?"

Wait for me, she didn't say. That only happened in fairy tales.

"Well," she said, trying to make light of it, but the words—the attempted laugh—catching in her throat, "it was nice while it lasted."

Nikos squeezed her hand. "Come on, let's get you home."

"Before I turn into a pumpkin?"

He laughed. But his amusement sounded as sad as hers. Up ahead, Joss and Declan were throwing the silver crash helmet in the air for one another to catch, each throw higher than the last. Dec hooted with laughter. He was far from happy with *her*, but it made her smile to see him enjoying himself.

At the mopeds, Nikos and his cousin handed them the crash helmets.

Shiv checked her watch. "Jesus, guys, it's *eleven-fifteen*."

"No worry," Joss said, heaving himself onto the saddle and kicking the stand away. "We rides like the winds."

At first they didn't ride fast at all, as the 50cc engines struggled up the coastal road's winding ascent. In the dark, it formed an unspooling ribbon of pale gray, yellowed by the mopeds' headlamps. To their right, the shape-shifting shadows of the hillside; to their left, the inky yawn of a sheer drop to the sea.

Shiv pressed herself against Nikos's back, arms encircling him, shifting her weight with his as they leaned into one bend and out of the next. Then, as they crested the highest point of the climb and swung into a sharp descent, the speed came.

"Woo-hoo!" Shiv yelled in Nikos's ear.

"Hold on to your hats!" he shouted back, in a *yee-haa* American accent.

So far, they'd led the way. Now, downhill, Joss's extra weight gave the other two an advantage and, as they sped past on the wrong side of the road, Declan called out, his words snatched away by the whine of the engines. Turning in the saddle, he flicked them an *L* for losers.

"Catch them!" Shiv shouted.

"Shiv—"

"Go on!" She was laughing, slapping the saddle. "We are *so* getting back first."

"This isn't a good place to—"

"Nikos, the road's *empty*. Catch them!"

He laughed along with her, shaking his head. Told her to hold on tight. Even so, the burst of acceleration almost tipped her off the back as he opened up the throttle.

"Woooo-hoooo!" she cried.

The other moped was thirty meters or so ahead, Dec's yellow T-shirt and the silver helmet bright in the beam from Nikos's headlamp. Urged on by Shiv, Nikos let rip. The engine screamed in protest and the wind buffeted them, but he was a skillful rider and the gap began to close.

"We've got them!" Nikos yelled as they entered a set of bends, narrowing the distance to no more than a bike's length.

"Go on, go on!" Shiv shouted back. "Take . . . them . . . *down!*"

Moving into the wrong lane, he opened up, the front wheel lifting off the ground for a second as they zipped past the other moped.

"Yaaaah!" Shiv hollered, letting go with one hand for a moment to send Dec's signal right back at him. *"Loooserrrs!"*

But they'd hit a steep, long straight and, with no bends to slow it down, the other moped gradually drew level again. Shiv shot a sidelong glance at Joss, his dark eyebrows raised and mouth wide in a hysterical grimace. He looked like a madman.

A *drunk* madman.

Shiv was suddenly, appallingly, aware of how boozed up Joss must've been. Nikos, too. Images flashed through her mind of them at the beach party—drinking, dancing, goofing around.

Joss cranked up the revs again, pulling ahead as both mopeds hurtled toward a serious-looking bend where a house hugged the nearside verge, its whitewashed walls and green shutters gleaming in the twin headlamps.

Declan turned to give his "cleaning windows" wave. A bye-bye-see-you-later-losers wave.

Shiv tugged at Nikos's waist, hollering in his ear to slow down, to let them go. Whether he heard her or not, or whether he was about to ease off, she would never know. Because at that moment, veering sharply into the bend—too fast, *way* too fast—Joss lost control, his rear wheel fishtailing on loose grit, the moped slewing across the road on its side in a cascade of sparks and a terrible screech of metal on asphalt.

Heading directly for the edge of the cliff.

Nikos hit the brakes, hard, just about holding a straight line, Shiv's helmeted face banging into his back. She lost sight of the others. There was only a scorched smell and a colossal *thwump* that dragged silence in its wake. Almost before Nikos brought them to a halt, they dismounted, the bike toppling over and Shiv yanking off her helmet and flinging it aside. They'd overshot the point where Joss crashed and had to sprint back up the road in the dark, Nikos punching numbers into his phone as they ran—gabbling into it in Greek.

"The ambulance is coming." He shut the phone off.

Shiv's breathing was so rapid she thought she was going to hyperventilate.

Please, Declan. Pleasepleaseplease.

Just then, a light came on at a window of the solitary house, casting a strip of illumination across the road, a finger pointing to the wreckage. And there it was. The moped had skidded into the crash barrier. It hadn't gone over the edge. It *hadn't*.

The noise started then. At least, Shiv became aware of it.

Dogs, barking furiously in a compound next to the house—leaping and snarling, scrabbling dementedly at a chain-link fence.

The other noise. The atrocious moans of someone badly hurt.

"Dec!" Shiv shouted, breathless, trying to make sense of the crumpled mess where the bike had finished up. *"Declan."*

In the light from the window across the road, she could see the barrier was buckled but intact, the moped wedged beneath it, debris strewn in its wake—metal, glass, a handlebar grip, a wing mirror, a sandal. A long wet smear of what might've been oil. Or blood.

And there—trapped by the bike, motionless—lay a dark shape that could just as easily have been animal as human. Was that its leg? The arch of a back, the pale glimmer of skin?

"Dec, I'm here. I'm here now." She sobbed the words.

Nikos was at her side as they bent over the wreckage, tentative and panicky all at once—Shiv afraid of stepping on a foot or a hand and with no idea what to do or where to start. Nikos gently eased the figure from its side onto its back, exposing the face to the light from the window.

Joss. His legs were under the moped, his arms and head a bloody mess. Worse than the sight of him was the noise he made: a bestial panting, punctuated by high-pitched whimpers that seemed to incite the dogs over the way to even greater outrage.

Shiv stepped round him to reach her brother.

He wasn't there.

Beyond Joss was just a bent rear wheel, pieces of

taillight, a sheared-off license plate—a black hole where the crash barrier had been bowed out of shape by the impact, its support posts uprooted, hanging above the drop like tooth stumps in a gaping mouth.

"Nikos, where *is* he? Where's Dec?"

But Nikos was tending to his cousin. Shiv wheeled round, peering into the lit-up strip of road and surrounding shadows for some sign her brother had been thrown clear before the moped hit the barrier. Calling his name, frantic. Stumbling back and forth, searching, listening for his cries. Nothing. Just Joss's hideous grunts and the clamor of the dogs.

A figure emerged from the house opposite—a middle-aged man, sleepy-headed, in a string vest and creased white boxers. He was carrying a flashlight, playing its powerful beam toward the scene of the crash. Behind him, three children watched from an upstairs window until a woman appeared and ushered them away.

"Please, my brother," Shiv said as the man crossed the road toward her. She gestured at the flashlight. "I have to find my brother."

Nikos and the man spoke to one another in Greek.

"My brother!"

Nikos said something else and, grabbing the man's flashlight, stood up and approached the barrier, the guy from the house taking over with Joss. Nikos was shining the flashlight along the verge, along the cliff edge, standing right by the barrier and peering over, aiming the flashlight down there.

"No, Nikos, he must've fallen off bef—"

"I saw him, Shiv."

She picked her way over to him. "*Saw* him. Where?"

Nikos leant out dangerously far over the barrier. "I saw him go over."

"No. *No.* He must've . . . Nonono."

Shiv clutched at Nikos's arm, trying to make him come away from the edge and help her look for Declan in the road. He didn't move.

"*There.*" That was all he said.

She looked where the flashlight beam had settled—a shelf of rocks at the base of the cliff, right at the foaming water's edge.

Declan lay on his side, as though asleep, his yellow T-shirt and the silver crash helmet stark against the wet black rock. The shirt was rucked up under his armpits, one arm was bent grotesquely behind him, and there was blood.

But he looked perfectly comfortable. Perfectly peaceful.

"We have to go *down* there," she said. "We have to get—"

Just then, a wave broke over the shelf—a roiling froth that shimmered in the flashlight beam, covering Declan and the rocks completely for several seconds.

When the water dispersed, her brother was gone.

Shiv was over the barrier before Nikos could stop her.

The cliff wasn't sheer just there, but the slope was plenty steep enough and—more or less in the dark but for the flicker of the flashlight overhead—she half scrambled, half slid down the scree of mud and rocks, dislodging a shower of debris as she went. The last bit, she fell altogether; a maybe four-meter drop onto the slab where Dec had landed. Shiv's hands and knees were cut and she'd done something to her shoulder. But she was down. She was there, standing up and yelling her brother's name.

Another wave cascaded over the rock, almost sweeping her off her feet.

"Declan!"

She peered into the dark, frantically scanning the surface of the sea, trying to make out something— anything—that might be her brother. Screaming at Nikos to hold the flashlight steady, to search the water with it, when she realized he was scrambling down after her. Stones and bits of earth rained down.

"Give me the flashlight," she said as he dropped heavily beside her.

Nikos was winded, struggling to his feet. "Shiv—"

"Quick, we have to *find* him. I have to get him *out*."

Shiv grabbed at the flashlight but he wouldn't let her have it. "You can't help him," he said, panting. His hands were slick with blood; his own or Joss's, she didn't know.

"He's in there!"

"Shiv, you'll *drown*. You'll be smashed to pieces. Look at it!"

She turned to the sea again as yet another wave crashed onto the slab, Nikos clutching her arm to keep her from being washed over the side. The water was black and furious all about them, rising in huge swells and thundering into the rocks and the base of the cliff like it wanted to bring the whole lot tumbling down on top of them. They were soaked through already, blasted by spray, barely able to stand up.

Nikos yelled in her ear. "Even if Dec was still alive when he—"

"No. *No.*" Wrenching her arm free, pushing him away, Shiv went to the edge of the rock, set to jump in. To find her brother. To pull him out of the water.

But Nikos grabbed her again, wrapped her in a bear hug—dragging her away, back toward the foot of the cliff where the water couldn't reach them. Holding on, no matter how hard she shouted and swore and fought. Holding on. Holding on until he no longer needed to. Until she was spent. Until she slumped, sobbing and defeated, to her knees and released Declan's name into the night with one last, almighty bellow.

SEVENTEEN

For the next few days Shiv is mostly confined to her room.

No PTU sessions, no Talk or Write. No Rec time. No visitors. Her meals are brought by an orderly who stays to watch her eat them. She is given calorie-loaded fruit drinks. Someone checks on her every hour. Once a day, Nurse Zena weighs her. They must build her strength back up, Dr. Pollard says. Mental as well as physical. The clinic has to make sure she's fit and ready if her treatment is to resume in the final week of her program.

The director stresses the word "if."

"Were you trying to starve yourself to death?" she asks Shiv, at a one-to-one (they meet every day, now). "Or just punish yourself?"

"Maybe."

"Which?"

"Maybe both." Shiv exhales. "I don't know what I was thinking. I just did it. It felt right to stop eating. It was something I could take control over."

"And now?"

Because that's the thing, of course—Dr. Pollard needs to know that Shiv still wants to be helped.

Shiv shakes her head. "I won't starve myself anymore."

One morning, they have the conversation: What next?

Dr. Pollard sets out Shiv's options. One, they can scale down her therapy—go easy on her in Talk and Write, make the images in PTU less full-on. Two, she can carry on with the daily activities at the same level as before.

"Alternatively, we can end your treatment altogether."

"*Discharge* me?"

"Just say the word and I'll arrange for your father to come and collect you."

"You'd do that?"

"At this stage, it's pointless keeping you here if you've given up on us."

Shiv imagines it: packing her case; hauling it downstairs and along the gravel path to the parking area; Dad, standing by the car chatting to Dr. Pollard; he sees Shiv and breaks off, moves toward her; white open-neck shirt, moist-eyed smile; he's ready to enfold her in his arms . . . *Just say the word.* They'd head down the drive and through the gates and the gates would swing shut behind them, a summery breeze murmuring through the half-open window.

That's it. She's going home. She just has to say the word.

Fifty-five days. For what, though?

Pointless keeping you here if you've given up on us. For "given up on us," read "given up on yourself." Can she do that? Simply leave this place and say, *Oh, well, I gave it my best shot. Sorry, Dad, but you've no idea how tough it is. Sorry, Dec.* Can she? Go home, back to her life, with one more reason to hate herself?

Shiv looks at Dr. Pollard. "What if I don't choose any of these options?"

"Is there an Option Four, you mean? Would you like there to be?"

"The images in PTU . . ." Shiv falters, unsure of what she's trying to say.

"I know how distressing they were for you."

Shiv waves the remark away. That wasn't what she meant. "If I hadn't stopped eating—you know, if you hadn't had to pull me out of treatment for a bit—would you have kept on showing me more of the same?"

The woman hesitates. "No," she says.

"What, then?"

This time the pause lasts so long Shiv wonders if she's ever going to answer. Finally, she does. "Siobhan, the images would have got worse."

Shiv nods. It makes sense. More photos and footage must exist, beyond what the clinic has used so far; if they obtained *those* from Dad's lawyer, why wouldn't they have the others as well? Of course, the treatment *would* escalate. It's the way of things here, the ethos: you get worse before you begin to get better.

If she hadn't starved herself; if they hadn't had to protect her from herself—

"I want you to show them to me," Shiv says. "I want to start PTU again and I'd like you to use the images I haven't seen yet."

Dr. Pollard studies her. "Are you absolutely sure?"

"Yeah, I'm sure. I have to see my treatment through to the end."

"Look what it did to you before."

"No. I did that to myself."

The director gives that some thought. Then, "I have to warn you, they're—"

"I don't care how bad they are."

The first is a set of stills the Greek police took on the beach where her brother washed up. The photographs taken *after* the removal of the tarpaulin covering his body.

The second is a film from the TV news, showing Declan's flower-bedecked coffin being carried from the hearse to the chapel. Dad is one of the pallbearers; Shiv and Mum—ashen-faced, tear-streaked—walk arm in arm at the head of the procession.

The third is an audio. No images, just white walls and the whine of moped engines in five-minute bursts, once every half hour for four hours. Shiv couldn't say which is worse: listening to the noise or waiting for it to start up again.

Day Fifty-Eight. Shiv is sitting with Caron on beanbags in the rec room. Docherty plays pool by himself, robotically potting balls until the last one clunks into a pocket and he racks them up again. Helen sits cross-legged on the floor in one corner, dealing hand after hand of solitaire. Lucy no longer comes in here. Marking time, Shiv supposes, until the sixty days are up.

In their own ways, the residents are withdrawing, knowing that in a couple of days they have to face whatever lies ahead without one another.

Side by side on their beanbags, Shiv and Caron talk

inconsequentially. The undercooked potatoes at dinner; the chances of sunshine tomorrow after two days of rain; the state of Caron's hair, Shiv's nails. They don't discuss PTU this morning or Talk and Write. None of the patients do now. The sheer brutality of the treatment has stunned them into silence. At mealtimes and at Recreation, they sit in a collective daze; like a team of rescue workers resting up after a long shift digging corpses from the rubble of a collapsed building.

"Two more days," Caron says.

"I know."

"It's weird, but I can't imagine being anywhere else but here."

"On that beanbag?" Shiv asks.

"Yeah, *exactly* that."

"Take it home with you when you leave, then."

"The bean bag is *purple*," she says, like she can't believe how dumb Shiv is for not realizing why that's an issue.

They do this a lot—silly conversations, mock-bickering banter. It has reached a point where they no longer need to laugh, or even smile, to show each other how amused they are. After a moment, Shiv asks, "Are you going to take up smoking again once you're out of here?"

"I hope so," Caron says. "I'll be very disappointed in myself if I don't."

Once you're out of here.

It hangs over them. It barely seems possible that their stay at the Korsakoff Clinic is almost at an end—that it wasn't just a few days ago when Shiv turned from the window that first evening to find a girl in a scarlet dress breezing into her room. Will they stay in touch after they're discharged? She doesn't ask. It's another of those topics the residents don't discuss. "Out there" has too many unknowns.

Shiv swivels sideways, rests her bare feet on Caron's lap. Caron gently massages them, starts up another bizarre line of conversation.

"You have the toes of a pianist."

"Mm." Shiv closes her eyes. "I hope she lets me keep them."

Another voice. "Shiv."

She snaps her eyes open. Mikey, standing over them. She didn't hear him come in. As though she's been caught doing something she shouldn't, Shiv swings her feet off Caron's lap and sits up, arms clasped around her knees.

"Hey, Mikey."

She can't recall the last time he appeared in the rec room.

He remains there, perfectly still—*strangely* still, like they're playing musical statues and he desperately wants to win. His eyes don't stray from Shiv's face; Caron, right next to her, might as well not be there for all the notice he pays her.

"I need to speak to you," he tells Shiv. *Not here,* he means.

"Mikey—"

"It's not about nothing or anything."

Caron lets out a snort. Mikey ignores her totally. Still looking at Shiv, he gestures at the door. "You coming, or what?"

Since she returned to the treatment, she has avoided

Mikey. Not because Dr. Pollard advised it but because Shiv has come to realize he isn't good for her. She doesn't know what he wants from the clinic, but it isn't the same thing she wants. It has taken her all this time, but she finally understands that. From the little he reveals in Talk and Write these days, Mikey seems to be pretending to participate while actually not giving a shit. Like he has a program of his own running in the background, undetected. Shiv can't figure him out. At least when he was bashing his head against a tree and cutting his hands to shreds hauling a log up and down a hill, his anger was plain to see.

"Mikey, why don't you—" Caron begins.

"It's okay," Shiv cuts in, getting up and following him out into the corridor.

"What's up?" Shiv asks, her voice whispering off the blank walls.

"Nothing's up."

"Then . . . what?"

She's aware of a hardness in her tone with him that wasn't there before. She knew it would be tough, shutting him out after she'd gone to such lengths to win his trust. She expected him to make it harder still for her. But he hasn't. When he saw the way it was between them after she resumed treatment, he appeared to accept it as the natural order of things.

She apologized; told him she had to look out for herself from now on. He just nodded and said he had to do the same.

Now here they are in an echoey corridor, the reflection of the light off the walls casting a sickly green veneer over Mikey's complexion. The jumpsuit is more gray than yellow. He looks at her as though *she* was the one wanting to speak to *him*.

She's about to ask again what he wants, when he says, "Don't tell nobody nothing."

At first she thinks he's misquoting the Salinger T-shirt. "What d'you mean?"

"Don't tell about me. The stuff we talked about—before, yeah? About Feebs."

"Tell who?"

"Anybody."

Shiv frowns. "Mikey, why would I—"

"You can go back now." He nods at the rec room door. "I'm all done."

With that, he peels away and walks off down the corridor. At the end, before he rounds the corner and disappears, she's sure he'll turn to give her a small wave.

He doesn't.

"Don't think about him," Caron tells her as they say goodnight outside their rooms.

"It was like he was trying to tell me something important."

"Shiv, you're not responsible for Mikey."

"No. Okay."

"You and Declan is all that matters."

"I know."

They hug. "See you tomorrow, yeah?" Caron says.

Tomorrow. Their last full day here. Forty-eight hours from now, this clinic, these people, will be part of her past. As though each day she lives, everyone she used to know, every place she leaves, everything that happens to her—everything she *does*—can be switched off like a light.

EIGHTEEN

When the alarm jolts Shiv from sleep, her first thought is: Wake-Up. But it can't be morning already, can it? And the light hasn't snapped on automatically like it usually does—the room is still pitch-dark.

Not yet fully awake, she fumbles on the bedside table for her watch, squinting at its luminous hands. Ten past ten? No, ten to *two*. Jesus.

The alarm continues to ring out. That isn't the Wake-Up buzzer—it's too shrill—and it's coming from outside her bedroom. In the instant she notices this, the sound changes to a much louder, intermittent two-tone wail she recognizes right away from the weekly test.

Fire alarm.

Emergency lighting comes on. A dull, greenish glow from a panel above the door—enough for Shiv to see what she's doing as she stumbles out of bed and yanks on jeans and a top. The voices start then. Shouting. Banging doors and hurried footsteps. She shoves her feet into her shoes and heads out into the corridor, half expecting to find it filled with smoke.

It isn't. What it's filled with is people—Caron, Helen, she can see Docherty and Lucy, too, and a night-duty orderly jogging toward them from the head of the stairs. He's calling to them. But it's impossible to hear a word above the fire alarm, and the additional din from all the alarms the residents have tripped by opening their bedroom doors during Shut Down. The orderly has to yell in their ears to evacuate the building.

They assemble in the yard behind Eden Hall, rows of blank windows looking down on them like so many expressionless eyes. Assistants Hensher and Sumner have joined the residents outside. Nurse Zena is here, and a security guy. The cacophony of alarms is loud even out here, overlapping like some piece of experimental music. Docherty is shirtless, Lucy and Helen still in pajamas and slippers; Caron's dressed but pretty much asleep standing up.

Sumner, her frizz of blond hair a mess, face greasy in the wash of security lighting, organizes everyone and begins a head count.

"Where's *Mikey*?" Shiv asks.

At this moment, Assistant Webb appears from round the side of the hall, out of breath, speaking into a walkie-talkie. He lowers the handset. "There's—"

"Mikey's still inside," Sumner says.

Shiv, like everyone else, is looking up at the building, as though expecting the boy's face to appear at a window, wreathed in flames and smoke.

"I'll go in," Hensher says, making for the rear door.

"No." This is Webb. "There's no fire. It was Mikey who triggered the alarm." He indicates the walkie-talkie. "I just spoke to Steve in the CCTV room."

Apparently, Mikey tripped the first alarm by leaving his bedroom, then could be seen sprinting to the end of the corridor, where he smashed the fire-alarm panel on the wall by the entrance to the stairwell. By the time everyone else started emerging from their rooms, Mikey was already downstairs and letting himself out through one of the emergency exits, setting off a third alarm.

"He's on the grounds," Webb says. "This racket is a diversion."

On cue, the alarms all cut out at once, leaving a ringing silence that makes the night seem instantly darker and colder as well as shockingly quiet.

"I've messaged Dr. P," Webb tells Sumner, then turns to Zena and instructs her to return the residents to their bedrooms. The remaining staff are to grab flashlights from the utility room and form a search party. He points. "The last time CCTV picked him up he was heading for the Walk woods."

"I know where he'll be," Shiv says. She *does* know, with absolute certainty, the one place Mikey will have gone. And what he intends to do there.

"Where?" Webb asks.

"The lake."

Before anyone can stop her, Shiv starts running.

In the luster of a half-moon, everything is made of gray plastic. Lawn, grass, shrubs, flowers, trees—nothing looks real. It might be a park in a model village, with Shiv and those in pursuit shrunk to the size of toy figures. Her breath scorches her throat. Her feet—her legs, her entire body—tingle as though with static electricity.

Only once in her life has she ever run so fast.

How much of a head start did Mikey have? Not much. But long enough to be in the water by now.

Webb catches up with her fifty meters or so before the lake. She expects him to grab her, make her stop, but he falls in alongside her, stride for stride, like this is a long-distance race and he doesn't want to hit the front too soon.

"How d'you know?" he asks, panting, the words fractured by his pounding feet.

Because of Phoebe. Because of how his sister died. Because he tried to say goodbye to me yesterday evening and I didn't listen.

She doesn't have to say anything, though. Almost as Webb asks his question, the lake sweeps fully into view over the crest of the lawn and Mikey is plain to see, silhouetted in the spill of moonlight across the surface of the water.

Webb slows as they near the gate, with its DANGER: DEEP WATER sign. "How did he get to the other side of the fence?"

Shiv doesn't bother to dilute the sarcasm. "Maybe he *climbed* it?"

The real question, though, is what Mikey's *doing.*

He's turned away from them, walking along the shore—on all fours, it looks like—loading something into a bag, then continuing on his way, feet crunching and clicking on the shingle. More shadow than figure; Shiv could believe he's a figment of her imagination. Another confabulation. For once, he isn't wearing the jumpsuit but is all in black, with a hooded top that mostly obscures his face. If he has registered them, he gives no sign.

"*Mikey,*" she shouts.

He carries on with whatever he's doing, with greater urgency.

Assistant Webb produces a bunch of keys and jingles among them for the right one. Sumner reaches them, gasping for breath. Before she can recover sufficiently to ask what's going on, Webb finds the key to the gate and inserts it. At this moment, Mikey straightens up, hoists the bag—a small black rucksack—onto his back and makes for the old wooden jetty. The rucksack looks heavy; with a lurch in her gut, Shiv knows why.

"Stones," she says.

By the time Webb has swung the gate open with a metallic shriek, Mikey's at the end of the jetty.

"No one comes near me!" he shouts, turning to show his whitewashed features in profile. He aims a finger at them as though it were a pistol.

They stop where they are, although Shiv can tell Webb is itching to go after him—can almost see him calculating the odds on reaching Mikey in time. They all know what a rucksack full of shingle and pebbles will do if he jumps into the lake.

"I'm going to him," Shiv says.

Webb puts out a hand to stop her. "I can't let you do that."

"I'm the only one he'll talk to."

"No way are you—"

"She's right," Sumner says. "Let her go."

"Are you *kidding*?"

"Clarence, if that boy goes in—"

"He said *no one*," Webb says. "That means you as well as us, Siobhan."

"So what do we do?" Shiv says. "Stand and *watch*?"

Webb looks at them in turn. Shiv doesn't wait to hear what he has to say, just pushes past him and through the gate.

"Hey," she says. Mikey doesn't turn round.

"One more step." The warning is clear enough.

Shiv is at the start of the jetty, her feet firmly on solid ground, the lake spread before her like so much spilled ink. She's holding on tight to one of the life-belt posts, the splintery wood biting into her palm.

The dead-of-night hush hangs over everything like an outcast spirit.

Shiv is shaking. She focuses on Mikey, fixing her gaze on him, sitting right at the end of the jetty with his feet dangling in the water.

"Is this what you were trying to tell me last night? Is this what you were planning all along?" No reply. She's conscious of Webb and Sumner creeping closer from the gate, watching. "Can I sit with you, Mikey? I won't do anything."

He doesn't say no; doesn't warn or threaten either.

It isn't the sea, she reminds herself. No rocks, no waves—no sudden surge to sweep her off her feet, or dash her against a cliff, or drag her down into the swirling depths. The water is perfectly calm. In the moonlight, it might not even *be* water but a second silvery-charcoal sky unfurled beneath the one above.

There. Her first step. Her second.

She has to pause a moment. Mikey sits a little straighter, a little stiffer, that's all. The *water* moves, though. Laps at the shore, slaps the posts that support the jetty, with its aged, gappy planks. She tells herself it's a gentle sound: a whispering breeze in the treetops; the trickle of a tap filling a basin. It isn't a sound to be scared of.

Shiv's breathing slows. Her heartbeat steadies.

One painstaking step at a time, testing each board like a tightrope walker—eyes on Mikey all the while—she makes her way to the end. Tentatively, she sits down beside him—not too close. Cross-legged. No way is she letting her feet hang over the edge like his.

"Don't think you'll stop me," Mikey says.

"Have I tried to stop you doing anything before?"

"I'm just saying."

"Mikey." This is Webb, closer still.

"Tell him to shut the hell up! Tell him to get *back*. *Tell* him!"

Shiv doesn't need to relay the warning to Webb—Mikey screamed it so loudly he startled the waterfowl in their nighttime roosts; a squabbling of unseen ducks, coots and geese that might be the lake itself protesting at being woken up.

She waits for their noise to subside, gives Mikey time to calm down.

"Did you hear what Sumner called him just now?"

Mikey sniffs, swallows. "What?"

"*Clarence.*" Shiv laughs. "How has he kept *that* a secret for so long?"

She can't see his face for the hood but senses him trying not to show that he finds Webb's name funny. He shifts his stone-filled rucksack into a more comfortable position. The water is up to his shins, setting up eddies with the motion of his feet.

"This is where they went," he says.

"Where who went?" She has one hand palm-down on each knee; braced, trying to stop shivering.

"Feebs. Declan."

Shiv finds her eyes drawn to the water, as though her brother and Mikey's sister might suddenly break the surface. "Not here."

"Same thing."

She imagines a vast subterranean ocean connecting all the rivers, lakes, seas of the world—an underwater afterlife for the drowned. Is this where Mikey believes he'll go when the lake takes him? To be reunited with Phoebe? She doesn't think so, given the things he's said before and the way his mind works. His sister drowned because of him; his punishment should fit the crime. That's what this is.

"We're the same, you and me," Mikey says.

Shiv wants to disagree, to say that Dec didn't drown, like Phoebe, but that's not true. At the inquest, the pathologist said the presence of water in the lungs suggested her brother was still breathing as he entered the sea. The injuries from the crash and the fall down the cliff "would almost certainly have proved to be fatal," but he was still just about alive while Shiv stood on that rock, giving him up for dead.

She has lived with that knowledge.

"We're not the same," she says, even so.

Mikey turns to look at her. His hood makes a ghostly oval of his face. "It's why you stopped eating," he says.

"And all the stuff you did before—breaking things. In here"—he raises a hand and presses his fingers against her forehead, as though giving her a blessing—"you can't ever forgive yourself."

He lowers his hand, but the impression of his fingertips on her skin remains.

I can't ever forgive myself. She told Dr. Pollard exactly that. "I can't ever forgive myself. Can't ever hate myself enough, no matter how hard I try."

"How do you measure self-hatred?" Dr. Pollard asked.

"By how much you don't want to wake up each morning. By how much you go to sleep at night wishing tomorrow wouldn't come—wishing you didn't have to live another single day with what you've done."

"Sounds to me like you have more than enough self-hatred, Siobhan."

"But that's the point. I *do* wake up. Every morning, I wake up."

Not wanting to live with what you've done—is that the same as wanting to die? For Mikey, yes. For her, though?

Gazing out the surface of the water, Shiv imagines standing up and *one-two-three* leaping into the water. The lake erupts, exploding in her eyes, nose, mouth. Cold. Stunningly, breathtakingly cold. She's tumbling into pitch-black turbulence, thrashing uselessly, a whirl of bubbles scouring her face. Up and down have no meaning; there is only water, engulfing her—simultaneously pushing her away and sucking her in, repelling her but refusing to let her go.

Is this how it was for you, Dec?

Down. Down. Down. Her lungs are ready to burst.

This is it, then. Her repentance, her atonement: offering the thousands of days she has yet to live in payment for the thousands she took from him.

She stops resisting the lake and lets herself spin wherever it takes her. Nothing to fear. It's not even water but feathers, she imagines—a sea of black down, soft and warm enough to sleep on. Shiv shuts her eyes. When she wakes she'll be afloat on her back in the pool at Kyritos.

Declan will be there, in his red swimming shorts, sitting cross-legged on the end of the springboard. Grinning. Ready to splat her with the yellow tennis ball.

He opens his mouth. *No.*

What?

No, he repeats.

Dec, I'm com—

But her brother stands, retraces his steps along the board and walks away from the poolside, bouncing the ball on the flagstones as he goes. *Thud-catch-thud-catch-thud-catch.* Even when he's lost from view, Shiv still hears it, like the thump of her heart and the thrum of her pulse in her ears. Slowing. Fading. Stop—

She opens her mouth to call him back and her lungs fill with water.

It becomes darker all of a sudden, and Shiv glances up to see a scrap of cloud crossing in front of the half-moon, looking for all the world like an X-ray of a lung. The wooden boards are hard and cold beneath her.

"I used to have this dream," she tells Mikey, "where I dive into the sea and swim out to Dec and manage to drag him onto the rocks. I'm pumping the water out of him, giving him mouth-to-mouth, thumping his chest to get his heart going." Her voice breaks. "But he's just lying there. Just . . . dead."

Mikey isn't listening.

He's staring straight ahead, at the water—placid and dark, utterly indifferent to them. Not his river, but it'll do. That's what he's thinking, for sure. Now the moment is finally here his intensity comes off him like an aura.

"What if this isn't it?" Shiv says.

Mikey gives her a sidelong look. "What?"

"What if this *isn't* your punishment?"

He goes on looking at her, his face etched in shadows, shoulders hunched beneath the weight of the rucksack. "You said you wouldn't try to stop me."

"Just suppose the price you have to pay isn't *dying* but *living*?"

"That don't even mean nothing."

"Cos that's *my* punishment. Every day for the rest of my life, I have to live with what happened—with what I did."

Beside her, the boy rises to his feet, carefully, balancing himself, adjusting the shoulder straps. He straightens up, toes at the very edge, like a diver on a board. Out of the corner of her eye, Shiv's aware of movement. Webb and Sumner, edging closer to the jetty. The security guy is with them.

Another figure too. Dr. Pollard.

Not now. Please not now. One word, one sudden move, and he'll jump and that rucksack will take him straight to the bottom.

They stop. They remain silent. Shiv exhales.

"I came to this clinic," she says, "wanting them to teach me how to do it—live with what I did to Dec." She keeps her voice even, not wanting to show any sign that he has unnerved her by standing up. Or to alert him to what's happening behind them. "I guess I wanted them to take away the guilt and the loss. The pain. The *blame*."

Mikey ignores her. Stays perfectly still.

"Without all of that," she goes on, "I could get on with my life. I could *live*."

"Don't talk to me. I don't want—"

"But I *can't* get rid of it, can I? That's the *real* punishment, Mikey: Declan is dead . . . and I'm not."

Shiv stands up too. Slips a hand into his. He tries to pull free but she holds on.

"Dec lives in here now." She touches her forehead where Mikey pressed his fingers a few minutes ago. "And here." She places a hand over her heart. "Same for you with Feebs," she says quietly. "If you kill yourself, she can't live there anymore."

Mikey is trembling. Shuddering. He might be crying, but she doesn't dare look. She stares straight ahead at the lake. Keeps his hand firmly in hers.

"Let me go." He tries to break her grip.

She tightens it. "I'm not letting go, Mikey. If you go in, we both do."

"Let *go*."

"No."

Two realities open up in Shiv's mind.

In one, Mikey propels himself off the end of the

jetty, taking her with him, the weight of the rucksack dragging them both down, hand in hand, to the depths.

In the other, he doesn't.

Which is the true reality and which the false, Shiv doesn't know yet. But she will wait right here with him until she finds out.

They fly to a neighboring island and transfer to Kyritos by boat to avoid the TV crews and photographers. To be on the safe side, Shiv wears a floppy hat and shades. Dad's lawyer meets them at the dockside and drives them to a "safe" house: his uncle's, in a village up the coast from the main town.

These tactics will only delay her encounter with the press—they'll be waiting for her on the steps of the courthouse tomorrow morning.

"Is this where you usually stay?" Shiv asks.

Dad shakes his head. "No, I stay in the town."

Of course. His isn't the face they want to splash on their front pages and news bulletins. He isn't the star witness.

The lawyer is a little man, shorter than Shiv, with an unpronounceable name and dark hair on the backs of his hands. He spends the morning briefing them about the hearing: going over the questions Shiv's likely to be asked, coaching her how to answer them. Just as important, how to *present* herself to the court.

Both defendants admit driving while intoxicated, he explains—they couldn't deny it, after their breath and blood tests the night of the accident. That a young boy died as a result adds another layer of severity to the charges. But the pair deny they were racing. If the lawyer can nail them for that, they'll go down for a *long* time.

Shiv is the prosecution's emotional trump card: a grief-stricken fifteen-year-old girl traumatized by her brother's horrific death. If she stands in that witness box and says the right things, cries in the right places—paints a vivid picture of Declan's last moments of life—the jury will be believe her over the two in the dock.

"I made them do it," Shiv tells the lawyer, not for the first time.

"That is not our case, Siobhan."

"It's the truth, though."

"Shall I tell you what is the truth?" he says. "They were the ones who rode the mopeds when they were drunk. The ones who raced with each other. It was one of them who lost control and crashed."

"But—"

"*They* killed Declan. Not you." He stares her down. Then, miming bags under his eyes, he says, "Stay up late tonight, yes? And no makeup tomorrow."

Yeah, and make sure to shave your hands, she doesn't tell him.

"He wanted Mum to testify as well," Dad says after the lawyer has gone. An extra tug at the jury's heart-strings.

Like that would happen.

Her mother is improving, but she won't be coming back to Kyritos anytime this century—and certainly not for a court case she wanted nothing to do with.

In the difficult silence that follows the lawyer's briefing, Shiv wonders if Dad has begun to have doubts too. Before she went into the clinic, his *quest for justice*—for revenge, really—was an obsession. He wanted Joss and Nikos punished. Now that the trial is here, he seems uneasy. Like someone caught up in events he initiated but which have gathered their own momentum, sweeping him along. Dad used to tell the lawyer what to do; these days, it's the other way round.

After lunch, Shiv takes a nap beneath the deliciously cool draft of a ceiling fan in a bedroom that houses a small shrine to a haloed Greek saint. She sleeps for an hour.

She sleeps a lot just lately. Nightmare-free, mostly. In between sleeps, she has been eating the food Aunt Rosh piles up before her. That's where they're staying, now, Shiv and her mother and father, while they're waiting for the house sale to go through so they can start again in a place where Declan never lived.

Going to her aunt's, rather than home, was the second surprise when Dad collected Shiv from the Korsakoff.

The first was the sight of Mum standing there with him in the car park.

That was seven weeks ago. Her mother is still an imitation of the woman she was before Kyritos, but day by day, she is evolving into a new version of herself. Like her family, Mum will never be whole again, but she is finding a way to live with what's left. When they hugged beside the car, it was as though Mum was the one who'd spent two months in a clinic and Shiv had come to take her home.

Her parents, her aunt, have barely asked Shiv about her time at the clinic.

They treat her like a shell-shocked soldier; whatever they do, they mustn't upset her with talk of the war.

So they sit in Aunt Rosh's lounge and watch TV, or a DVD, or play Scrabble, or read. She's fine with that. She doesn't need to talk about her treatment and they don't need to hear it. And so Shiv sleeps and eats and makes a start on resuming something like normal life. She's met up with Laura and Katy a couple of times (coffee shop, cinema). She's even catching up on her schoolwork, and there's talk of her being able to go back in January.

Phase Three, as Dr. Pollard called it, at Shiv's final debrief. Life without Declan.

In the months between leaving Kyritos and entering the Korsakoff Clinic, what Shiv had thought of as learning to live without her brother was nothing of the sort. Her greatest delusion—her "primary confabulation," according to Dr. Pollard—was that when she looked in the mirror of her life, all she saw was her brother, the embodiment of her everlasting guilt.

"We've tried to help you smash that mirror," Dr. Pollard told her.

"By making me look over and over at the thing you didn't want me to see."

"Yes. If you stare at something long enough and closely enough, it begins to change, to become—to *mean*—something different."

Shiv couldn't help laughing, giddy and a little reckless with the imminent prospect of being discharged. "I still think psychotherapists are full of crap," she said. "I guess I just have to sort out the good crap from the bad crap."

Dr. Pollard smiled. "I must include that phrase in our promotional material."

A glimpse, there, of the woman who'd thrown

everyone's case notes into the bin all those weeks ago. Shiv had liked her back then. After what the treatment had put her through, she wasn't sure "like" was the right word anymore. But she'd ended up trusting Dr. Pollard.

Had ended up thanking her.

Looking back, Shiv isn't sure she'd have been so ready to understand the point about the mirror if it hadn't been for Mikey. Witnessing his torment that night down at the lake—staring into *his* abyss, with him—brought Shiv face to face with the chasm that might open up in front of *her,* if she let it. The treatment had taken her to the edge so that she saw exactly what she was stepping back from. But standing at the end of the jetty with Mikey, talking him down, Shiv found that the words she spoke to him were also the ones she needed to hear herself. That the reasons he shouldn't die were indistinguishable from her own reasons for relearning how to live.

Mikey.

She doesn't suppose she'll ever see him again. Isn't sure she wants to, or that he'd want to see her. In any circumstances it would be hard to have a friendship with someone whose life you'd saved—to have that hanging over both of you. Harder still when the other person didn't want to be saved.

Turning away from the lake, still hand in hand with Shiv, retracing their steps along the jetty onto solid ground, he had looked despondent. As though he had failed.

Maybe he'll have another go when no one's there to stop him.

Or maybe, one day, he'll feel differently. Come to value his life again, find a way of living without Feebs, and be glad Shiv helped him have that chance. Maybe, years from now, she'll see Mikey on a bus or train, or in the street, or in a café or pub, and there'll be a spark of recognition in their eyes. A shared, tentative smile. The awkward beginnings of a conversation that might or might not lead somewhere.

She splashes cold water on her face after her nap and heads downstairs. Dad's in the kitchen with the lawyer's uncle; they're sipping coffee. The sight of the tiny cups and the bitter aroma rekindle a memory of dancing in the street with Nikos.

She dwells on that for a moment.

There are flowers on the table, wrapped in cellophane. Dad starts to ask if she managed to sleep but Shiv interrupts, indicating the bouquet. "What's that for?"

"I thought we could go out there." He hesitates. "If you want to."

Out there. The road where the crash happened, he means. Or the beach where Declan's body washed up. But those places have nothing to offer Shiv.

"Dad," she says, "I want to go to the villa."

The uncle drives them along the coast road in a battered blue Fiat. He pulls up in the approach to the holiday villas and Shiv gets out onto the track, standing in a slowly dispersing cloud of dust kicked up when the car braked to a halt. Dad asks the guy to wait, please. He answers in Greek and flicks on the car radio.

As they set off, Dad explains that he got the old man to park here, rather than right by the villa, in case the current occupants are in. On foot, the pair of them could recce the place more discreetly.

"Recce?" Shiv says.

"It's short for reconnoiter."

"I know what it means, I'm just wondering if we should black up our faces or wear camouflage or something."

He gives her a look. She's seen the same question in Mum's and Aunt Rosh's expressions: *Do we do "funny" yet?*

Shiv shoulders her bag and walks silently beside her father, unable to help remembering the time she sat on the front step watching Nikos's pickup bounce along this same track with two windsurfing rigs in the back. Or the time she followed Declan back to the villa in the dusk after her brother had caught them kissing.

"I still don't think this is a good idea," Dad says.

Shiv doesn't reply. They've had this argument already, in the kitchen of the safehouse. She has something she needs to do, she told him. That's all. Since she left the clinic, there's been a quiet resolve to Shiv that none of her family knows how to deal with. There'll come a time when they learn to refuse her again, but for now she gets whatever she wants.

As they near the villa, Dad diverts them onto an overgrown path.

His plan is this: they follow the path into the olive grove, where the low wall will offer a clear view of the rear of the villa, the garden and pool area. If anyone is about, they'll simply carry on as though they're out for a stroll and skirt back round to the track where the lawyer's uncle is waiting.

Shiv looks at him. "You've done this before, haven't you?"

He doesn't answer for a moment, and she thinks he's going to deny it. But he says, "Yes," his voice a little husky. "I've come up here a few times."

"To do what?"

"Just . . . I sit on the wall. And look. That's all I do, Shiv, I look." Then, with an odd laugh, "You know, I even thought about renting the place so I could come here whenever I felt like it."

"Bloody hell, Dad."

"I know, I know."

"And *I'm* the one gets sent to a clinic."

He laughs, and the look he gives her is so full of love it takes her breath away.

The villa is different from how she remembers it, the images in her head merging with those projected onto the walls of her PTU. She knows she'll never quite be able to separate the two from now on.

Bizarrely, as she gazes at the rear of the villa, she half expects to see Caron—in her scarlet dress—lazing on a lounger beside the pool, smoking a cigarette. *Ah, you* made *it,* she says, spotting Shiv. When she messaged Caron on Facebook about her plan to visit the villa, her friend replied: *r u TOTALLY mad?!?* Then another message: *dont u DARE come back with a tan!! ;-) xx*

Laura and Katy said pretty much the same thing, oddly enough.

Shiv's going down to London to stay with Caron next

weekend, meet her folks, see the sights. Her first nights away since she left the clinic.

"No goat," she says to Dad, nodding toward the olive grove.

It might be dead or just tethered somewhere else. She asks if her father recalls Dec trying to feed it an apple, but he doesn't.

Shiv steps over the wall and into the garden, catching Dad by surprise.

"Shiv, no—what if they come back?"

She keeps going and he doesn't have much choice but to follow, drawing up beside her as she comes to a stop at the poolside.

It's late October, the end of the holiday season, but the villa is in use. A pink inflatable dolphin, a raft and a stripy beach ball cluster at one end of the pool. Other signs of occupation: a game of quoits not cleared away; a cup on the table under the pergola; four pairs of flip-flops (two adult, two child-sized) by the patio door; towels flapping listlessly on the line. But the windows are shut and everywhere is perfectly quiet.

"I wonder if they know," Shiv says. *About us,* she leaves unsaid. About who rented this place back in the spring and what happened to their son.

"It's like we were never here," she says under her breath.

Beside her, Dad says, "I thought the same, first time I came back."

"When I was little, I imagined the places we stayed on holiday didn't exist except for the time we were there. I couldn't bear to think of other kids sleeping in our beds or swimming in our pool or playing where we played."

We. Her and Declan. Shiv slips a hand into her father's.

"Why did you come here, Shiv?" He's being gentle, patient, but she can tell it bothers him that the holiday makers might return.

If she didn't want to do the thing with the flowers, what *does* she want to do?

Her gaze settles on the pool. She thinks of the hours she and Declan spent in that water. Then another thought: the lake, the jetty. Funny how the lake at Eden Hall used to remind Shiv of the sea at Kyritos—and now the pool reminds her of the lake.

Dad's hand is sweaty in hers. The sun is bright and warm but Shiv's arms are covered in goose bumps.

"You coping okay with this?" Dad asks.

"Not really, no. How about you?"

"No." Then, giving her hand a squeeze, "Look, we should—"

"Yeah. Okay."

He doesn't know yet, but Shiv won't give evidence tomorrow; not the way the lawyer wants her to. Won't help them "win" the case. The two defendants *weren't* racing, she will say, her voice strong and clear. It was an accident. No more, no less. She shouldn't have gone to the party in the first place, or accepted a lift home when she knew the guys had been drinking. However much trouble it would've got her into, she should have phoned to ask her parents to collect them in the taxi.

Then she will describe how Nikos risked his life to save hers—scrambling down the cliff and onto the wave-swept rocks, pulling her back from the edge when she was about to dive into the sea after Declan. Holding on to her.

"I'd have died if it wasn't for him."

That's what she'll tell the court.

Dad will be furious. Or not. Perhaps it won't surprise him that much. In time, maybe he'll come to realize it was the right thing to do.

Dad has clung to this case as grimly as Mum once clung to Declan's room, just as Shiv once clung to the idea of her indelible guilt. As though, so long as they have something of Dec to hold on to, it prevents him from being finally, irretrievably dead.

Her brother *is* dead, though. But Shiv's love for him remains. Her memories of him remain. It is these things—weightless, formless as they are—which raise her to the surface and let her live in the light. Not absolved of guilt, not freed from grief and loss, but absorbing all of it into who she is. Atoning for Declan's death by living the life that she can, with enough joys and sorrows for both of them.

She goes to the patio and picks up a plastic spade from the beach set. It's encrusted with sand, and the buckets, she notices, are half filled with pretty colored pebbles.

"What are you doing?" Dad asks.

Shiv doesn't answer. She makes for the flower border where she spotted the ball that time. Finding a clear patch of soil, she kneels down and starts to dig—little scoops of earth that she sets aside in a heap, conscious of Dad watching her from the other side of the pool.

When the hole is deep enough, Shiv sets the spade down and opens up the bag, her hands grubby and damp with perspiration. She reaches inside.

"What's that?" Dad says. She didn't hear him approach, and the closeness of his voice makes her jump.

Unfurling the T-shirt, Shiv holds it up for him to see. *Don't ever tell anybody anything. If you do, you start missing everybody.*

Her father doesn't speak.

She folds the T-shirt again and places it in the hole. A pause. Shiv looks at the shirt for a moment, then covers it over with soil, filling the hole right up and leveling it off so that you'd never know the ground had been disturbed.

She stands up, brushes the earth from her hands. Dad doesn't say a word, or hold her hand, or pull her into a hug, or anything like that. But he stands next to her by the flower border, and when she turns away he turns with her.

A last gesture, as they step back over the wall and into the olive grove. Shiv stops and takes another item from her bag.

A yellow tennis ball.

She stands on the wall, takes aim, and gently lobs the ball into the swimming pool for one of the children to find.

ACKNOWLEDGMENTS

I am more grateful than I can adequately express to my editors—Mara Bergman at Walker Books, in London, and Wendy Lamb at Random House, in New York—for their patience, skill and diligence. Their detailed, incisive feedback on various drafts, along with that of Wendy's colleagues Dana Carey, Caroline Gertler and Janea Brachfeld, went way beyond the call of duty.

Huge thanks too to my UK and US agents—Stephanie Thwaites, at Curtis Brown, and Tina Wexler, at ICM Partners—who also provided valuable editorial input and much-needed encouragement at crucial moments. When my belief in this novel wavered, theirs never did.

Above all, heartfelt thanks to my wife, Damaris, who makes everything possible and whose own recent challenges put mine into stark perspective.

Martyn Bedford has written one novel for young adults, *Flip*, and five for adults, including *The Houdini Girl*. A former journalist, he teaches creative writing at Leeds Trinity University. Martyn lives in West Yorkshire, England, with his wife and two daughters. Learn more about him at martynbedford.com.